Do not pray for an easy life, pray for the strength to endure a difficult one.

~Bruce Lee

For Ryan Hobson:
Who got me into the game of serial killers.
Miss you, my brother.

THREE WEEKS FROM NOW

"You're a weak-assed bitch. Pathetic and weak. You're the one that needs to be locked in the cage. Weak-assed pathetic bitch—"

"*Fuck you!*"

My world flashes red. My fist goes up before I can stop myself —and I shatter the bitch in the mirror with a left cross. Glass rains down into the sink and onto the floor, glinting and sparkling in the moonlight. My left fist drips with blood, which appears black in the darkness. The familiar, mineral smell of copper taints the air, a stench I know all too well. Mirror fragments of myself reflect back at me.

"You're gonna have to get no-holes-barred bloody on this," the bitch growls at me. "And that means not spilling your own blood. That means gutting that son of a bitch who's been ruining your life from stem to stern, throat to balls. Gut him like a mackerel."

"But I'm vegan."

"Fuck that bullshit label. You're an animal, *we're* an animal. Animals kill when they're backed into a corner. Now let me the fuck out so I can do some good. Stop trapping me."

Yeah, not one of my better conversations with myself.

1

"What's it like to kill?"

The woman with bleach-blonde hair sporting a cornflower blue suit asks me this. This is three weeks before the stimulating pep talk with myself. On the local TV show *Top Talk*, we've been chatting for about five minutes now. Most of what we were discussing was just introductory stuff, reminding audiences of what happened a year ago in my town of Pickman Flats.

It made the news, so you probably heard about it.

There were some killings—six, if we're going to get technical.

Actually, I've killed seven people total, but I won't get into that now.

Now, we're just talking about the six. I'm a serial killer, you see. My name is Clare Marie Bleecker and yes, I've...extinguished a few people, one after another. You can opt-out of reading this right now and I won't blame you—it's kind of a long and bloody story.

2

Just for the record, and this is a kind of record, a kind of confession since I go to DeFeo Catholic High School. This year I'm a junior. And for the record—I don't want to kill anyone. Killing and I have broken up. We've called it quits. *Finito!*

Yeah, I'll never be normal, I know this, but I'm actively working at not being abnormal.

We can dream, right?

"Clare?"

"Yes."

"I know that's probably a difficult question to answer," September Jones, the *Top Talk* TV host, says. "I understand your hesitation. Do you need me to repeat it?"

I shake my head.

What's it like to kill? What's it like to kill? What's it like to kill?

As a confession, Father, let me tell you—for I have sinned. Give me your eyes and ears.

You've been warned.

3

A year ago, last October when I was sixteen, I killed for the second time. His name was Joe Morton and he tried to get me into his car, a shitty Mazda, under false pretenses, to kidnap me. He had a Taser, a knife, and chloroform in a rag. He planned to render me unconscious and then take me somewhere to do horrible things that scary/creepy men do to teenage girls.

Mr. Screepy didn't get the chance.

After sticking his knife in his chest and killing him, I wiped down any incriminating evidence with his chloroform-soaked rag, then stole his Taser and knife. Parting gifts.

You see, I have what I call *psycholepsy*. When I'm stressed, and feeling under attack, one part of me slips into sleep and another—I call her the Other Clare—awakens. Usually she's in a pissy mood and starts going batshit crazy. Usually, when the Other Clare goes back to sleep and I wake up again, somebody's dead.

Psychologists call it DID or dissociative personality disorder. It used to be called multiple personality disorder. But I'm more than some random, clinical acronyms. I think *psycholepsy*, like narcolepsy, falling asleep against your will, but with more psycho, best describes what I consider a unique case.

Hey, I'm special—I *am* a beautiful and unique snowflake, after all. But don't attack me or I'll go all blizzard on you. And it ain't pretty.

We cool?

4

Pickman Flats, Washington, population 19,659, makes its money in the tourist trade, mostly with its many wineries in the Walla Walla Valley. Murder is bad for business. So, after I killed Joe Morton, AKA Mr. Screepy as I called him, it kind of opened the Pandora's box for a whole bunch of evil shit lurking underneath my town.

This underground element was kidnapping teenage girls, forcing them to do undesirable things in front of a camera with creepy men, and then selling the videos to other creepy men internationally. Detective Timmons, a hard-nosed guy who investigated me for Morton's death (somebody saw a girl that matched my description in Catholic school clothes), turned out to be the ringleader. Seems Timmons wasn't making enough as an upstanding member of law enforcement and had to supplement his income with the seedy underbelly of underage porn.

Joe Morton's brother, Randall Morton, was also involved, along with three other guys...

They all died, in one form or another, attacking me.

They underestimated a five-foot-eight, 129-pound girl.

They thought I was normal.

They thought I would cower.

They thought I would submit.

They thought I would die easily.

They thought wrong.

The only killings that were attributed to me were the deaths of four men, four dangerous men, three of which invaded my home and tried to hurt my grandparents and boyfriend. Later, I killed Detective Timmons. Since each killing was deemed an act of self-defense, I walked.

Well, as I said, it wasn't really me, it was the *other* me, the Other Clare. She's the killer.

She's the bitch to talk to about it.

After that, I kind of became a local celebrity. September Jones interviewed me last year on her *Top Talk* show. It's strange how killing people can make you a hero. What's the saying about how killing one person makes you a murderer, but killing thousands makes you a conqueror?

So, I'm only Clare—going to Catholic high school, working part-time at my favorite vegan restaurant, and going through life.

Yes, I've ended some lives to stay alive, but nobody's perfect. Right?

5

"What's it like to kill," I finally answer my waiting host. "It's... (*let's not say anything to incriminate myself on television.*) It's upsetting. (*Lie, I have no empathy. I feel nothing.*) It's taken me a long time to get over it, and I don't know if I ever will. The look on their faces as they died still haunts me. (*Actually, I've forgotten most of that and moved on*). Sometimes they haunt my dreams when I close my eyes. Guess I have post-traumatic stress from the whole thing. Yeah, I'd rather not talk about killing."

"Killing?" my pearly-toothed TV host says. "I'm sorry, I said what's it like to *make* a killing. I meant with your book, *Killer Smoothies and Other Vegan Recipes to Die For.* I understand it's selling rather well. Guess I should have chosen my wording better... I didn't mean to upset you, Clare."

After the self-defense killings that shook my small town last year, I wrote a slim book that was published independently and has made a, uh, killing. Well, small killing. Yes, I realize the title is kind of in, um, bad taste, but apparently, people enjoyed it enough to buy it. So far, I've banked about $9,696 in royalties. That's ~~stalked~~ stocked away for college.

What's it like to ~~kill~~ make a killing?

Ugh, I can't believe that just happened—I'm so distracted. Get me off this show. Other than the loads of attention and admiration I secretly crave, why did I bother coming back on? We went over all of this a year ago. September Jones only wanted to call me back to try to grab more eyeballs. She received pretty good ratings last year when I was on. She always goes for some of the tawdrier topics and brings on rating-guaranteed people like religious nuts, people who've been abducted by aliens, racist types that go on ignorant rants, angry spouses that cheat on each other, conspiracy theorists talking about the end of the world, and, well, a teenage serial killer who's trying to blend in with society. Except only you and I know who I really am.

"The book has sold rather well," I say and hold up a copy because ABP: Always Be Plugging. "You can always buy it directly from the bio link on my Instagram page, @clare.bleecker. Give me a follow too." (wink)

"You started that social media page not long after the incident, do you find that sort of media a form of therapy?"

No.

"Yes." I beam with a fake smile to match my host's. "It's very therapeutic to focus on positive things and try to forget the negative. Mostly, I post a few sample recipes from my book, animal and nature pictures, inspirational quotes, and some funny memes. We all have to appeal to the better angels of our nature."

"Oh, that's one of my favorite quotes. Gandhi, wasn't it?"

"Abraham Lincoln, actually."

OK, I practiced all the stuff about my book and that last quote for a few hours in my room. When you don't have feelings and always wear a societal mask, you must be an actor. Actors need lines to be convincing. Sometimes I can improvise, but I find that I perform better when I memorize my lines by reciting them a thousand times and then make them seem spontaneous.

"Oh, well there you have it," Jones says, wrapping up this segment featuring yours truly. "Clare Bleecker from Pickman Flats, everyone. Thanks for coming onto *Top Talk* once again."

We hold there for a moment before the camera operator, an

uneasy-looking woman sporting horn-rimmed glasses and wearing a t-shirt depicting *The Handmaid's Tale*, cues us off.

Pulling the tiny microphone off my lapel, I hand it over to my blonde host. Time to get the hell out of her studio. The walls of this place, which appear much bigger on TV, are closing in on me.

6

"Clare," September says.

"Yes," I say, checking my heart rate on my Fitbit. It's right around sixty-seven. My typical low resting heart rate is around fifty-eight. As long as it doesn't creep up past 150, I'm fine. Trying to take it easy.

Typically, people with no empathy and only rationale in its place, operate on a low-vibration level. Nothing much stresses us out. In fact, a lot of times we're prone to high-risk behavior for a kind of dangerous thrill. That's exactly the kind of thing I'm trying to avoid. The idea for the Fitbit came after I saw a *Hulk* movie on Disney+. Bruce Banner used something like it to keep his ugly green monster in check. If his heart rate didn't spike too high, no massive amounts of uncontrollable destruction would ensue. Yeah, I know, it sounds completely stupid, but it kinda works. It definitely keeps me centered and aware. In addition to the creepy guys in my past, I'm my own worst enemy.

Zen and the Art of Keeping the Monster Asleep.

7

Grams Arleen and Gramps Ellis wait for me in the lobby. We head out.

"You only flubbed up once," Grams says. "And it wasn't too bad of a flub."

Thanks, Grams.

"You were great," Gramps says and kisses my forehead. "So proud of you."

They insisted on coming with me. My friends wanted to come too, but I refused. Dragging my grandparents along was enough. Of course, I care for them, as much as somebody with no feelings can. However, I tend to be a lone wolf...

My quiet time is sacred.

My thinking time.

My scheming time.

My time where I don't have to act.

My time off life's stage when I can just be the real me.

Grams wants to head to Granny's Home Cookin', appropriately enough, to celebrate. We do. Grams and Gramps load up on the all-you-can-eat buffet-style food. I grab only a few things like salad and some cooked vegetables that I'm one-hundred-percent sure are vegan.

Yes, a hardcore vegan serial killer doesn't make any sense when you really think about it, but what in life does?

8

It's about forty-five minutes from Granny's Home Cookin' in Richland back to Pickman Flats. The deal with the grandparents coming along is that I get to drive. It gives me something to do and something to focus on. For my seventeenth birthday on May 21 (yeah, Gemini duality, of course), Grams and Gramps bought me this zero emissions Nissan Leaf. Blood red, naturally. They spent some of their life savings on it. Best present ever. They bought the car—I pay for insurance and fork over a few bucks each month for the electric bill to charge it at the house.

My grandparents only have me as a grandkid, so they spoil me rotten. Growing up, I used to live in Broomfield, Colorado with my parents, but they died coming home from an Alcoholics Anonymous meeting (for my mom, the vodkatarian). A drunk driver swerved and hit them head-on. One of life's cruel ironies. That happened when I was fourteen.

But even before my parents were smashed to death by another vehicle, I've always loved walking to school. It's allowed me to have more time to myself. But driving is pretty damned cool. Every time I slip behind the wheel and crank up the contemporary indies on Sirius XMU, Channel 35, I feel like I'm in charge. In charge of my destiny. In charge of my life. Yeah, I sound like your typical teenager, but I don't take for granted the little things you probably take for granted. Right now "Queen" by Perfume Genius is on—I love the dreamy, booming chorus on this song.

These long drives give me more time to think. And to listen.

But Grams insists on talking the whole way, commenting on billboards and passing cars. She complains about a yellow car in front of us, wondering why anyone would drive a yellow car. Grams is happiest complaining, I'm pretty sure. Gramps usually dials down his hearing aid and stares out the window, literally tuning her out. Most of the time, the stuff that spills out from Grams's mouth is pretty funny. Right now, I'm kind of annoyed because I'm angry at myself for blowing that question back on *Top Talk.*

What's it like to kill?

Pretty sure that's what she asked.

What's it like to kill?

Yup, I could tell you stories.

What's it like to kill?

But to keep a long story short September Jones, killing keeps the Other Clare happy. To use a Beowulf metaphor (thanks, Advanced English class), she's kind of like that Grendel monster that comes out of its cave every now and then and decimates a few Vikings. The monster kills because the monster *needs* to kill.

For nearly a year, I've been starving that monster. And let me tell you, she's a bitch. There are some killer hunger pangs. After joining a gym close to school, I've beat the hell out of some speed bags and heavy bags—punch and kick therapy. I've also tried yoga, meditation, scrapbooking, long walks in nature, journaling, writing a really bad screenplay, and even took a stab at writing a suspense novel on my MacBook Pro.

Everything to keep the beast from waking up.

Tiptoeing around Grendel's cavern entrance.

9

A big diesel truck passes us on the curvy, two-lane highway before cutting me off and making me overcorrect. The driver raises a chubby hand and hoists a sausage-thick middle finger.

Wow, and people think *I'm* dangerous. My Fitbit actually stays fairly steady at ninety-nine. If Grams had one, it would be climbing the charts like a Pop 40 hit.

"Can you believe some people?" Grams says. "I should get their number." She fumbles with her smartphone, trying to bring up the camera app. By the time she does, the truck has vanished over the crest of a hill.

"Everyone all right?" Gramps asks.

"We were almost killed."

No, Grams, no we weren't. If working out like a fiend to try and stay sane hasn't done that for me, at least it's tightened up my reflexes. And being close to death? Naw, that's happened too often to me. This wasn't even a tease. It did nudge that Other Clare slightly though. Slightly.

"Don't ever drive like that, Clare," Grams says. "You won't live to graduate."

"No worries, Grams," I say. "I plan to live a long and fruitful life as a law-abiding citizen."

"Thank the Lord for that," Grams says. She and Gramps laugh. Their laughter is about as sweet a sound as you can hear, outside of a new Tame Impala album.

So, I'd love to tell my grandparents about who I really am—Clare, your serial killer grandchild, who must lie and hide things from you regarding her wicked deeds. But it's probably a bad idea, though. It might make my favorite two people in the world hate me.

10

Thirty minutes later, I'm pulling into the driveway of my grandparent's two-story Victorian house. Home sweet home at the Newberry residence on 237 Straw Street. My room used to belong to my mother; her name was Chloe. Since I've blocked out many memories of my mother, it's not weird at all to dwell where she once did. It's now my inner sanctum, my sanctuary, my safe space where I can dream and scheme. My *casa* within the *casa*. It feels good to have a place away from the darkness with warm light and love within, as well as the people who live there that take care of me. Pulling into the driveway, the automatic floodlights snap on, robotically welcoming us home. I really savor this moment the best I can.

I'm glad I do as it will all be taken away from me.

Soon, I will lose everything that is important in my life.

And the Other Clare will not sleep through the chaos.

My segment on the *Top Talk* show airs. At school, I am the local celebrity for a few more days and I sell some more books online, so not too bad. My on-air faux pas, which I had hoped would have been carefully edited out, wasn't as bad as I thought. Basically, I looked like a clueless, overeager seventeen-year-old. The mistake may have even helped to reinforce my average-girl persona a little longer.

Not exactly one of my best performances, but it will suffice.

In the morning, I make my famous Blood Lust smoothie—made of berries and beets—see page eleven of my book, *Killer Smoothies and Other Vegan Recipes to Die For*, to make it. ABP: Always Be Plugging. Grams and Gramps are watching the morning news in the kitchen while eating turkey bacon and oatmeal. Yeah, I tried to get them to switch to veggie bacon, but turkey was as far south as they would fly. Time to unplug the Leaf and then swing by Julie's to pick her up.

DeFeo Catholic High School, which I attend, is pretty much the most cliché private school ever. Girls wear knee-length pleated plaid skirts with navy blazers and white blouses. Boys wear khakis with white shirts and navy blazers. All students are required to wear the signature navy blue and cream tie in the school's colors. For that special, added variety, we can also wear cardigans and pullover V-neck sweaters in the autumn and winter.

Not that I'm complaining—I like fitting in and looking like everyone else. It's safer for me that way. No one knows you're a psycho if you look like everyone else. My clothes bear the hot iron every morning. I'm pretty ritualistic about my dawn routine— wake early, yoga, shower, press my clothes, breakfast. One of the benefits of being a total psycho is mundane regularity. People are always trying to dress different or be different to try and be unique. Me, I'm the wolf in the same navy-blue blazer and plaid skirts that all the sheep are wearing. There's safety among the herd.

Especially for the wolf.

12

"Do you know what this total bitch said to me after I clipped her Shih Zhu?"

Julie Gabriella Ramos, folks.

"She was being so freakin' microaggressive because I didn't trim her dog's ears the right way. She said I wasn't doing it right, and then asked if I was born in America. I'm so over the entitled, old white bitches in this town. Over it."

"Good morning to you, too."

Julie's looking a bit ruffled in her DeFeo ensemble of navy blazer, tie, and cardigan. Can't really blame her, she has to work nearly thirty hours a week plus go to school to help support her mom and her younger twin sisters.

"Can we stop by Burger Bliss for one of those kickass breakfast burritos?"

"Burger Bliss be damned—we're going to the Goats."

Julie goes into all her work woes. She clips dogs at a place called Furry O'Malley's. She's been overworked and I've been helping her with most of her homework as she's been too exhausted to do it.

"Did you read the chapters I told you to and answer the questions on theme?"

"Who the hell has time?"

As I pull up to the Dancing Goats, our regular afterschool hangout (when we have time to hang out, that is), Julie forks over a ten-spot. "How about this—you fly, I buy."

"Keep your money, *puta*, I've got this."

"You're the only *puta* around here," she says.

I blow her a kiss.

13

As I climb out of the Leaf, leaving Julie's head bobbing to The Dollyrots on satellite radio and feeling particularly good on this bright and crisp October morning, I can't help but feel like I'm being watched.

It's 7:47 in the morning and Main Street of Pickman Flats is buzzing with commuter traffic. None of the stores, save the caffeine dealer, Dancing Goats, are even open. My senses are tingling like a spider biting the back of my neck.

Heading inside, I use my peripheral vision to check my surroundings, trying to be covert so the observer won't be aware that I'm aware of him/her. There's a dude in dreadlocks and a Bob Marley shirt chaining up his rusted blue mountain bike to a light pole. Nope. A plump woman driving past in a silver Toyota Yaris patting on her morning makeup with one hand. Certainly not. A bow-legged old man wearing worn-out Adidas sweats and rocking earbuds is walking a chipper white Maltese dog. Not him. A studious girl from the local college behind her skater sticker-littered laptop is working on what looks like a report. Hells no, she's not even aware of my existence.

A sun-faded curtain moves in the top floor of a building that says FOR LEASE.

It's supposed to be empty.

Was the watcher up there?

If he/she was, were they aware I was looking for them? Was it somebody homeless squatting inside the building? Something more sinister? Taking a mental inventory of all the enemies I had last year—they're either dead or have moved on to less aggressive prey.

Inside, I pass Plum Adams. Her hair is plum-colored and she's texting somebody on her phone. Her drawing pad is open and a half-drawn sketch of somebody I don't know is laid bare. Yes, Plum is her real name. She goes to the public high school. She's always here, and I swear probably pays rent.

Sliding up to the counter, I order Julie her usual blended double-mocha frappe with whipped cream and chocolate sprinkles on top, and I add a spinach and tofu scramble wrap. (Julie will be vegan one of these days, it's my personal mission.) My usual is an almond milk latte with sugar-free vanilla. Studies have said that people who are homicidal are only supposed to drink their coffee plain and the color of midnight. Those studies are wrong, thank you very much.

As I go to pay, I'm intercepted. "I've got that!" A Visa Gold Card gets slapped on the counter.

"That's nice of you, Amity, but it's not really necessary."

My benefactor smiles. "It's completely necessary."

If you had seen this scene play out a year ago, you wouldn't have believed it. Last October, Amity Liston, along with her friends Hope Dalquist and Mercy Franks, ran what I called the God Squad. Your basic asshole, God-fearing girls who made everyone's lives at DeFeo Catholic High, who didn't look or act like them, a living hell. Not that I've gone to too many schools before DeFeo, but I suspect every house of education has girls like that roaming the halls.

Hope and Mercy died last year. Amity is flying solo these days.

The ex-members of the God Squad didn't die by me but because of me. Hope and Mercy were each in the wrong place at the right time. Amity would have died too at the vengeful gun of Detective Timmons, but I saved her life. Pretty sure that traumatic incident zapped her head like electroshock therapy. Amity's now like my number one fan in that Stephen King movie. She's always at my heels like a whipped dog. It's like if she ever loses sight of me, she'll no longer be safe. Guess you call that trauma bonding. Pretty sure she was lying in wait for me here as she knew there was a decent chance that I would show up this morning. Amity even dyed her blonde hair the same coffee color as mine and went vegan. In our matching Catholic school outfits of navy blazers, pleated skirts, and striped neckties, it's like there are two of me standing in Goats.

Pickman Flats can barely handle *one* of us.

"I made your Sleepy-Time Slayer cookies from the recipe you posted on your Instagram last night. I put in a few extra espresso beans just to be naughty." She opens her backpack. "See." She smiles. "Want one?"

"That's OK."

"Hey, selfie!" She leans in close, whips out her iPhone like a gunfighter, and shoots a photo of us leaning in close before I can say Annie Oakley. "Wow, that's a good one—it's like we're twins! I'll post it to IG Stories and tag you."

Please don't ask for a ride to school. Please, God, please.

"You heading my way?"

Why have you forsaken me, oh Lord?

"Uh, yeah."

"Great," Amity says and beams. It's like I'm looking in the mirror except in this reflection, I've overdosed on some high-caliber happy pills—the image is frightening, even to me. "Daddy has my Beemer in the shop. It's like a miracle you stopped by. I would've had to walk the *entire* three blocks to school!"

Amity is one of those girls who I call rich 'n bitch. Her dad is an investment banker for a big firm, and they live up on the hill, what locals call The View, in a big mansion. They also have a summer house in beautiful La Push, yet she always complains about having these money problems like us commoners. Hence rich 'n bitch.

Amity waves one of my Sleepy-Time Slayer cookies above her head at the barista. "You guys need to stock these—pronto. Check out Clare's cookies on her Insta!"

Wow, not only do I have a self-made doppelgänger, I also have my own marketing manager.

It's not that I don't like Amity. Well, actually, I don't. It's just that the puppy-dog Clare cosplay thing gets old as fuck. Think I liked Amity more when she used to insult me and was trying to kick Julie's ass with her holier-than-thou minions any chance she could get.

Walking out of the coffee shop, I peek back up at the dark window in the for-lease building. The curtain is still. I can't shake the feeling though. That old feeling like last year. That feeling that something totally fucking evil is looking to punch and claw its way into my heavenly peace.

"Uh, hello... Amity," Julie says with an annoyed face.

"Hey, Julie," Amity says, climbing into the back seat. "You look tired today. Want a cookie? They'll turn that tired frown upside-down pronto!"

"Thanks. No."

"Here's your drink," I say to Julie, handing her some liquid resurrection and then the tofu and spinach scramble. "And your breaky."

"I paid!" Amity beams from the back seat.

"Uh, thanks," Julie says and rolls her eyes at me. We both grin and I mouth, "I know" back at her.

I get Julie and the cosplay Clare to school on time, but I have other plans.

A little bit of excitement.

A little bit of danger.

And a change of clothes.

15

After first period, algebra with Sister Robin Malone, I grab my backpack, which is a little heavier than usual, and head for the front door.

You see, I'm on a mission.

Over at the public school, Carver High, my favorite author, Lois J. Cain, will be giving a talk and signing books. She's been writing novels for decades. Some of my favorites: *The Killer, Mr. Smith, Look Behind You and Die, A Birthday Gift of Madness,* and her latest, and greatest, *Darkness on the Edge of Summer.* Yes, they're sort of outdated, and she uses some hackneyed and derivative plot elements, but I love 'em.

In my next life, I want to live in a Lois J. Cain novel.

In my backpack, I have a copy of *Darkness on the Edge of Summer*—and she's going to sign it. She's active on Instagram and I follow her (and she follows me!), and sometimes she'll respond to a comment I write, which always makes my day.

DeFeo Catholic High School would never have a secular writer like Lois J. Cain here—and forget about her books filled with teen angst, forbidden sexuality, and intriguing murders. So, like I said, I'm on a mission—I *will* meet Lois J. freakin' Cain!

Like a movie clip on a constant loop, this scene has played in my head since last Tuesday:

INT. CARVER HIGH LIBRARY — DAY

LOIS J. CAIN, a graying African American woman, age sixty-seven, signs a stack of books to some adoring STUDENTS. She's a stately-looking woman wearing a maroon blazer and paisley scarf. She looks tired though, and overworked.

CLARE BLEECKER, appearing like all the other students except way-cooler looking, holding her copy of DARKNESS ON THE EDGE OF SUMMER, finally gets a chance to meet her favorite author.

LOIS: (reading Clare's t-shirt) Type O Negative —- *Bloody Kisses*. Don't know what that is -- maybe I'm too scared to know.

CLARE: They're a super-vintage band that's a little on the dark side. You'd like them.

The author's demeanor changes with Clare, she smiles easier. This stunning girl in the Type O Negative shirt is clearly a breath of fresh air. A one-in-a-million goddess in low-top Converse sneakers.

LOIS: Looks like you have a book there for me to sign.

CLARE: (star-struck) Huh? Oh, yeah.

Clare surrenders the book she's white knuckling.

LOIS: Did you get a chance to read it?

CLARE: Only twice.

LOIS: Impressive, it's only been out a couple of weeks.

CLARE: I'm a fast reader. And thorough... I write too.

LOIS: Wait, are you Clare Marie Bleecker on Instagram?

CLARE: Oh my God, you recognize me?

LOIS: Are you kidding? Every morning before I write I'm sitting down with my breakfast, usually a smoothie from your recipes, and I check out what you've posted. It always makes my day.

CLARE: I-I am so happy... I think I just peed a little.

LOIS: So, you say you're a writer, Clare?

CLARE: Yes, I wrote this novel. It's about this girl -- she's a teenager like me. But unlike me, she harbors a dark secret...a secret she cannot show the world. Because if she did, people would want to hunt her down and kill her. They wouldn't like her. But this girl is kind and sweet, she's misunderstood. And there's this secret society in her town that --
LOIS: Say no more! Don't spoil it. (in sotto) Do you have a copy?

Clare pulls out a flash drive.

CLARE: Happen to have one right here. I think you'll like the metaphor of the girl -- it's like she's society but the side of society that nobody likes to see, but they know it's there. You know, like each person has an obsession and in their own way is crazy. They don't want to admit it, though, and they hide it from others so they'll find acceptance. But in the end, they're never truly happy because they can't share who they really are with anyone. They must live in secret like a sin too monstrous to mention.

LOIS: Wow, you're a very bright young girl.

CLARE: Yeah, well, I tested above Mensa level IQ...and many people say I have an old soul.
LOIS: (revering the hard drive like it is the

Holy Grail) If this is one-tenth as brilliant
as what you told me, I will send it to my
agent. She's itching to sign a new, young
writer with a distinct point of view. She could
probably get you an advance at a major
publisher in the six figures easily.

CLARE: Oh, that's nice about the money. I write
to stay sane.

LOIS: (winks at her) Don't we both, sister,
don't we both.

The author hands Clare back her book. Clare
can't wait to read it.

CLARE'S POV

*"To my darling Clare: The most brilliant young
mind I think I've ever met in the years I've
been meeting young people. Thank you for
granting me the opportunity of meeting you. We
should vacation next summer. Thinking Cabo with
swaying palm trees, icy drinks on hot, sandy
beaches, and plenty of well-tanned cabana boys.
Wanna come along? Your friend forever, Lois."*

Clare's on cloud nine -- this is the greatest
day of her life!

Except, when she turns, there's a SHADOWY
FIGURE like a six-foot-tall raven with glowing
red eyes. The thing grabs her book in a thin,
clawed hand and the novel immediately goes up
in a burst of flames.

Wait, *that's* not part of it.

17

Sister Prudence Head, like a black and white juggernaut, is marching down the hall from the other direction. She's probably the oldest nun on the face of the planet. She's from back in the day when you could basically cane students into submission. Certain regimental practices like that have lapsed in Catholic schools like DeFeo over the decades, but somebody forgot to tell Sister Prudence Head. Pretty sure she thinks that it's from God's mouth to her ears, and His red right hand to hers.

The story around school goes that Sister Prude was transferred here this year from a school somewhere in northern Idaho. Last year, apparently, she threw a kid down the stairs, and he broke an arm. The boy claimed that the sister pushed him down the stairs, but she claims he fell when he was trying to run away from her. Why was he trying to run? I know—because she's creepy and intimidating as fuck.

Anyway, she's now here. Guess she's been transferred to so many Catholic schools that they don't know what to do with her, so Pickman Flats was the next stop. Lucky us. Sister Prudence is basically Nurse Ratched in a habit. She's like a bad habit. Except you don't break this bad habit, she breaks you.

Sister Prudence is thundering in my direction.

Think I'll duck into the girls' restroom.

Guilty move on my part, but hey, I go to Catholic school. We're all guilty of something.

If it had been any other nun, I would have lied right to her face and told her I had a splitting headache and needed to go home. (And say one hundred Hail Marys later for lying to a sister.) That won't fly with *this* ancient, twisted sister. If she doesn't give me the third degree with her lipless face made of granite and narrow flinty eyes judging every move I make, she'll send me to the nurse's station, and I can kiss meeting Lois J. Cain goodbye.

In the nurse's station, I will have to act sick and lie on an uncomfortable cot that smells a little like Listerine antiseptic and vomit—that's worse than a jail cell.

So, into the girls' restroom I go—and duck into a stall. There's not much time and I'm cutting it close. Probably should have skipped my first class, but I heard a rumor from Amity that Sister Malone was going to pull a pop quiz in algebra—and she did. Missing even one of those quizzes could seriously affect my perfect GPA and that's not happening.

Pulling out my jeans and Type O Negative *Bloody Kisses* t-shirt (must blend in with the public high school kids), I start changing while squatting on top of the toilet, my backpack hanging on the stall door's hook.

I don't know if Sister Prudence saw me duck in here or not. The traffic in the halls was thinning out and despite being all dressed alike, I tend to stick out like a sore thumb. Sister Prudence Head has been riding my ass like a dark angel of death since I started this year. Haven't given her any reason to, but I can tell she's taken an instant dislike to me. None of my superficial charms that win over the other sisters even faze the stone face behind her habit. You know that scary movie starring Bonnie Aarons about the demonic nun? Sister Prudence reminds me of that but at least you can shut off a movie—this is a real-life horror!

"Looks like you're up to your knees in shit again."

Bob, go away.

Leaning against the wall, the dead mailman leers at me. His face is bloated and discolored from drowning two years ago. Bob Rextor, the late postman, was my first kill—only because he tried to chloroform and assault me under Lowell Street Bridge on my fifteenth summer. The Other Clare saved my purity, but ol' Bob smashed his face on a rock as he was going down, my BE KIND TO ALL LIVING THINGS t-shirt wrapped around his neck (irony much?), and he drowned face first in the creek. Bob, the dead mailman, always shows up at the worst times. But is there ever a good time to talk to a dead mailman that you murdered?

"What, nun got your tongue?" Bob laughs, exposing his green and black teeth. May I recommend some extra-whitening toothpaste, Bob, for that fresh and clean smile? And maybe some deodorant, like a few sticks, you stink like a dead cat. Yeah, he's only a figment of my abnormal mind, but he's real to me, okay?

My black Type O Negative shirt is halfway over my head. Sister Prudence is prowling around outside the stalls seeking tardy girls—or me. Why do I now feel like I'm the final girl in a slasher film? Am I not the slasher here?

"She's going to find you and you're going to burn," Mailman Bob says. "She'll burn you like a witch in her holy fire."

Normally, I'd tell Bob to deliver himself to some obscure zip code but I'm not giving myself away in here.

"Is there anyone in here that I should be aware of?" Sister Prudence's question echoes through the girls' tile and brick restroom like the voice of God—permeating everything.

Just a sinner crouching on top of a toilet seat. No big.

"If I have to look in each and every stall to find you," the sister says, "there will be grave and serious consequences."

19

Quietly, I slip on the rest of my street rags and bundle up my school clothes and dump them in my backpack. They're going to be wrinkled but that's the least of my problems right now. Throwing on some sunglasses, the best plan I can think of is bolting out the door and running out of the school. Maybe Sister Prudence Head will think that some vagrant girl slipped into DeFeo and is squatting in the lavatory.

Yeah, and maybe I'm the Ambassador of Peace for Zimbabwe.

"It's about time you take a few lumps, Clare," Bob says. "You've gotten away with too much. You've racked up seven deaths in two years. That's gotta be some kind of record."

All I can do is stare daggers at Bob. If I had a dagger, I would slip it into his bloated, rotten belly—if he were actually here. Don't ask why, please, thanks.

"You are the biggest sinner in this school. The biggest sinner in this town. Your sins should not go unpunished. You have to be held accountable, just like insufficient postage."

BAM! One of the stall doors gets kicked open by the six-foot-tall raven.

BAM! Another one.

BAM! Getting so close.

BAM! The stall right next to mine.

All I can do is fix the biggest smile on my face and claim temporary insanity.

"Temporary insanity, are you kidding? You are permanently out to lunch. Gone, girl. Wacko!"

The black habit swishes under the stall door. Her gleaming black shoes look like they were probably fashionable in an Eastern-Bloc country about sixty-five years ago. My reflection in them, of me crouching on the toilet, stares back.

This is it. The moment of truth.

"Sister Prudence?" a voice from outside the bathroom asks.

"What do you want, Sister O'Brien?"

"Please come quick."

"Can't you see I'm busy?"

"Larry Pearson cut his hand wide open in the woodshop and he's bleeding out all over the place."

The ugly, black, shiny shoes don't move. They stay fixed in place. It's as if they know I'm there, like two hunting hounds pointing right at me. *There's the witch! There's the witch!,* they seem to say with their silent barks.

"Very well."

And then, in a swoosh of black fabric, they're gone, the clomping steps echoing away and out into the hall. Still, I don't move. Call me paranoid, but if I wanted to play mind games with somebody, I would make them think I was walking off and then bust them when they were emerging from their hiding place.

One minute seems like ten. Nothing.

Mailman Bob appears disappointed. "You think you've won this round, little miss, think again. Those chickens will come home to roost."

"Suck your chickens, Bob, I'm vegan."

Jumping off the toilet, I grab my bag, move past the imaginary, dead postal worker, and out of the stall.

Going out in the hall is still risky. Who knows what's going on out there? Pulling the fire alarm is an option but the school would do a headcount and my absence would definitely be noticed.

Flipping open the window (thank goodness this restroom is on the first floor), I throw out my bag and then climb out myself, edging my way under the frosted glass.

Carver High is on the other side of town. Hopefully, I can make it in time.

Lois J. Cain and I have a date with destiny.

20

Lois is giving a talk to the students in the Carver High School gymnasium. Thanks to the nun from hell, I'm late so I have to slip in and try not to let anyone see me. There's a teacher who looks like a Russian powerlifter in a salt and pepper blazer standing with his arms folded and appearing like a security guard for the CIA.

Slipping past him, I take a seat on the bleachers next to a couple of girls who are giggling and peeking at their Facebook pages on their phones. In fact, most of the kids here at Carver seem pretty checked out as Lois talks about her books. I bet few have actually read them. More probably saw the movie adaptations of *The Killer, Mr. Smith*; and *Look Behind You and Die*. Both were pretty bad. They kind of took the book title and left the story, turning them into these low-grade slasher movies. They bombed at the box office and quickly died on home video and streaming.

Always stick to the book!

Still, it irritates me that half the students in this filled-to-capacity gymnasium aren't paying attention to such an amazing author and woman. To think, I had to almost get flushed by Sister

Prudence Head and then race across town—risking about fifty speeding tickets—to get here.

Guess you can take a teen to an amazing speaker, but you can't make them listen.

Lois wears her paisley scarf and maroon blazer jacket like I imagined she would. Who am I fooling, that's her trademark outfit. I'm pretty shocked to see Plum Adams in the crowd. Figured she would be drawing at the Goats. She's still drawing, looks like a sketch of the author. May have to get that from her later.

"My point is—do what you love," the author says. She's standing at a wooden podium in the middle of the gymnasium. A folding table stacked with her books sits next to her. "Find that one thing that really grabs you and makes you cry out and go absolutely crazy for it. That's what the meaning of life is—allowing yourself to go absolutely crazy for what you love."

Hey, Lois, I'm there, girlfriend, I'm there.

"When I was your ages, growing up in Augusta, Georgia, I picked up this raggedy, old paperback called *The Killer Inside Me* by Jim Thompson that was sitting abandoned on a city bus seat. It wasn't the kind of thing I usually liked to read, but there was this image of a beautiful woman wearing a yellow dress and laying in a pool of blood on the tattered cover. I *had* to know what *that* was about." This gets a few laughs. "After I read it, I had a love affair with crime stories. Albeit, very dark crime stories." This gets a few more laughs. "And that's when I knew I wanted to be an author. I started writing suspenseful short stories. Most were rejected when I submitted them. And that's OK. Rejection is a big part of life. Keep holding onto your crazy. Keep it burning like a great big cast-iron stove inside of you. Keep poking the coals when they're only embers. Keep the crazy fire burning even when nobody can or wants to see the beautiful light inside you. If you keep those fires burning, eventually someone will be drawn to your light. Yeah, it's obsession. But it's obsession that gets you through those dark days and lonely nights."

Don't I know it, Ms. Cain, don't I know it. Obsession and I were joined at birth.

"Eventually," Lois continues, "somebody will spot the smoke and feel the warmth, fueled by your obsession. Pretty soon, I started getting my suspense stories published in certain women's and men's magazines by the time I entered my second year of college. But I had to submit them under 'L.J. Cain' as nobody was taking women genre writers seriously at that time, especially a Black woman. In college, I was the editor of the newspaper and I continued to write. I put myself through school mostly with short story sales. After college, I had this idea about a group of church camp kids who suspected that their counselor was a serial killer, and then I wrote *The Killer, Mr. Smith*. Now, don't blame that bad movie on my book. I didn't have any input." More laughs. "Never blame a book for its movie."

All this talk of keeping the crazy fires burning is really connecting with me. There's a motherfucking inferno burning in me, and I've been trying to quell those fires as much as possible. Trying to turn a homicidal trash fire into a blazing matchhead. It's hard. The struggle is real!

"OK, that's about all I have to say. Keep that obsession of yours burning, keep that dream alive." She smiles. "Before I sign some books, I'd love to field some questions."

21

The big Russian bodybuilder-looking guy in the salt and pepper blazer raises his thick hand. He doesn't seem to have a neck. Lois calls on him.

"Uh, hi," the man says in the mousiest voice I have ever heard coming out of such a big man. "I'm Mike Gregory, English teacher. And my question is—why do we need all these movies and books and Netflix shows about serial killers and criminals doing bad things to people? I mean, really? There's so much death and suffering in reality—just watch the news—why do we need it in popular, escapist entertainment, too?"

Are you fucking kidding me, fire-plug dude? Yeah, I've been responsible, more or less, for the deaths of eight people. Lois J. Cain's books and horror movies have basically prevented me from killing more.

They save lives!

Lois smiles and then gives a chuckle. "Ah, I have *never* answered that question before." This gets some laughs. "We read and watch these things because it's a safe way to cheat death. We can't control the death in our life. We can't control what eventually happens to us in the end. A few of us in this room, statistically speaking, are going to have our lives shortened before we've lived our lives to their fullest. It's the same for people who either bungee jump, skydive, or eat Tide Pods. When we experience fiction that pits us at the edge of death, we survive. We cheat death for one more day. And that's important. Say you read a suspense book or watch a horror movie each week. That's fifty-two 'deaths' you've survived in a year. There's something powerful in that, something cathartic that's in the very nature of our souls—survival information. Think about that!"

22

Lois answers a few more questions, mostly inane stuff and even bullshit about the lame movies—did she meet the actors and what were they like. Infuriating and embarrassing. Then it's time for her to sign books. About one-tenth of the gym heads over to get a book signed, and the rest kind of shuffle around, staring at their phones like an electronic zombie horde.

My bulging backpack stuffed with her books will make her day. She's going to be so happy to see such an avid fan.

The line isn't super long, but impatience is eating me up inside—hurry the hell up!

Finally, it's my turn.

It's gonna be like the movie in my head.

Lois gives a slight smile. She doesn't say anything about my *Bloody Kisses* t-shirt.

Uh, this isn't going quite as planned. Time to improvise.

Opening my backpack, I dump all my books on the table.

My favorite author leans back in her chair with her eyes wide and seems stunningly overwhelmed.

"It's probably no surprise that I've read *everything* that you've written," I say, beaming, "some two or three times. And I even do some of my own writing."

"Writing's tough," she says, sighing and acting bored with half-lidded eyes. "Don't expect immediate results. Trust the process, even though it's a long, arduous one."

Then she gazes at my mess of books on the table. "Oh, so as to not hold up the line, I'm only signing one book. And one that you buy from the selection here." She pats the stack of gleaming new books.

"I already bought *Darkness on the Edge of Summer*. Read it twice. Your best one yet!"

"Well, I can't have you holding up the line, so I'll sign your *Darkness* copy."

Shrug. "Guess that's fine. Make it to Clare." Hopefully, my name would spark something. Anything. "That's C-L-A-R-E."

"Ah, the masculine version of Claire. It means 'clear and bright.'"

"That's right." Waiting. "Do you recognize me? We've shared comments online. On Instagram. Clare Dot Bleecker. That's me."

She sighs again. That bored expression returns. "I correspond with many people on Instagram."

"Oh. Yes. Guess you probably do." Hmmm. "You mentioned you were going to try one of my recipes. The Smart Bomb trail mix from my book, *Killer Smoothies and Other Vegan Recipes to Die For*."

Lois narrows her eyes. "I seem to remember a recipe for a trail mix that gave me diarrhea for about three days. I got so dehydrated, I had to go to the emergency room."

"Oh."

My favorite author slides my signed book back at me like it bit her.

"Enjoy." She looks away. "Next."

"Uh, thanks."

OK.

She's much friendlier to the girl behind me, Plum Adams, complimenting her bright hair.

Whatever.

Peering into the book, I'm hoping for a nice inscription, something like, "To the Greatest Girl Ever—Clare. Your buddy, Lois."

All it says is: "To Clare" and her swirly signature. So generic. So disappointing. If I had a heart to break, it would have burst into a million little bits.

Oh well.

Never meet your heroes, as the saying goes. Lois J. Cain seems so much more gregarious and engaging online. In person, though, she's kind of rude and standoffish. Pretty disenchanting. Kind of takes the sting out of the enthusiasm I had for her. Maybe she's just tired.

Maybe.

23

Time to head out. My phone buzzes. I forgot that I had turned the ringer off. There's a ton of missed calls and texts.

One is from my boyfriend, Truman Quirk. Last year, I strangled his stepfather, Detective Timmons, to death with one of my school neckties. Since his stepfather killed another girl, Hope Dalquist, and tried to kill me and Amity Liston as well, Truman kind of gave me a pass. That was nice of him.

His text: Where RU? Sister Prude came into class looking 4U. Doesnt seem happy. She ever? Hit me back when U get...

Texting back, I tell him I had to step out, keeping my Lois J. Cain mission to myself.

There's also a couple of missed calls from Grams, and a text: Worried about you. The school called. Said you're not there. Are you somewhere dead in a ditch? CALL ME.

Oh great.

I text back that I had an errand to run. And before she predictably asks what errand, I say I'll explain later. If Sister Prude is on the hunt for me, I'm not going back to school. Just going to say that I had an explosive case of stomach virus and went home.

"I seem to remember a recipe for a trail mix that gave me diar-rhea for about three days. I got so dehydrated, I had to go to the emergency room."

My Smart Bomb trail mix does *not* give you the shits, Lois J. Cain.

24

"Pick it up! Pick it up, you fat-assed freak!"

That's what I hear as I'm heading to my Leaf in the parking lot.

At first, I think the voice is directed at me. I am a bit of a freak after all, not fat though. But upon further inspection, there's a boy with his arms folded—a big boy, at least 225 pounds, a moose in a black t-shirt. Wow, they sure grow 'em big over here at Carver High School. Moosey is with a couple of other boys and they're all sneering and laughing at somebody on the ground. I can't see, though, too many cars in the way. Yes, I know people are freaking out as to my whereabouts, but the curiosity is strong with this one.

Getting closer, Moosey and his friends have a kid on the ground, can't tell if it's a boy or a girl. They're heavy-set in a powder blue shirt and short-cropped hair, trying to get their asthma inhaler. The other boys keep kicking it around to each other like it's a hockey puck to keep it away from the owner. The kid on their hands and knees is red-faced, tears running down their cheeks, and gasping for breath.

"Do you use the girls' bathroom or the boys'?" Moosey asks his victim. "D'you squat to piss or stand up, new kid?"

My Fitbit chugs along at a steady clip—heart rate normal at seventy-two BPM. Let's keep it that way.

But this kind of shit pisses me off.

Don't go there. Let the Other Clare sleep.

Instantly, I have a flash to about a year and a half ago when the God Squad bullied Julie in the girls' bathroom for also being different. The Other Clare wasn't having it and almost broke Amity Liston's arm.

OK, I'll just try to talk to them.

Serial killer to boy(s).

No, girl to dipshit(s). Definitely their pronouns.

"Excuse me," I say, smiling, displaying all the superficial charms in a sociopath's bag of tricks. "What's the sitch here?"

Moosey turns to me. He cracks a grin.

"You its mom or something?"

"Some*body*," I correct.

"Whatever. Make tracks."

"Yeah, I can't do that. This, uh, kid looks like they really need that respirator."

"It'll get it," Moosey says. "When it tells us if it's got a dick or a slash."

"Do you really need to know that badly?"

"Thought I told you to make tracks, Mother Teresa."

Remember the Fitbit, remember the Fitbit.

My heart rate's increasing. This kind of bully macho bullshit really triggers me. Stay back. Stay out of striking distance. Stay back.

"Just let them up already."

Moosey thunders up to me, puffing out his chest.

"So now you're going to try and intimidate a girl who's half your size?"

"Try?" His breath smells like beef jerky. *Vomit.*

"Your mom must be so proud of what a strong boy you are who's not afraid to show it off to someone smaller."

Keep it cool, Clare. Back down and walk away.

"Do you even go to this fucking school?"

"If I didn't, would you still be acting like a raging hormone?"

"You've got a pretty smart mouth, stupid bitch."

"Don't let my intelligence intimidate *you*."

Moosey goes to grab me. I anticipated that, and instead of engaging, which might set off my more dangerous half, I side-step him. I could've easily parried and smashed him in the ganglia of nerves in his neck and dropped him like a colossal sack of shit. Classic move I've practiced a thousand times on the gym's heavy bag.

"We don't want to get into this," I say, steady but with an acrid taste to the words. "We really, really don't."

"Oh, you think you could kick my ass, Wonder Bitch?"

His friends laugh. They sound like a couple of antique pickup truck ignitions trying to turn over.

"So, is it Stupid Bitch or Wonder Bitch?" I ask. "I'm confused."

"Both," beef jerky breath says.

"If that's your best display at wit, Moosey, I'm grateful that I go to a private school."

Moose tries for me again (as I knew he would), and again I side-step him.

Problem is, the glare of the morning sun blinds me for a millisecond, but it's a millisecond enough for him to drop a blow.

He clocks me in the stomach.

Right below the solar plexus.

Trying to take another step, I am now gasping for breath like the kid on the ground. At least for that kid, the other two boys forgot about they/them enough so they/them could grab the inhaler and take a huge hit of whatever-makes-they/them-breath again.

Good solid punch. My knees wobble and I try to stay up, but I drop to one knee. And I try to suck in as much crisp October air as I can.

All three boys sound like ignition-challenged antique trucks now with their laughs.

Glancing down at my Fitbit, it's in the red. 149 beats.

People like me, as I've said, vibrate on a usually low frequency. It's hard to get us agitated. But like everyone else, we have triggers. Big bullies are my triggers. Always have been. They simply piss me off. You don't have to have much of a heart to feel a kind of deep-seated primordial rage. *Red, red, red.* My psycholepsy swallows me up, consumes me like a hungry shark.

Oh, Fitbit, I've failed you.

And then, just like that, the Other Clare awakens.

25

After all my yoga, meditation, working out, eating right, reading Lois J. Cain, writing, relaxing walks in the woods, and so on.

It's all gone out the proverbial window. Down with a swirl in the porcelain throne.

The bitch is awake.

And she's never in a good mood.

"Shouldn't have done that," my other half says.

"Oh, look who got her wind back."

The Other Clare (TOC) isn't looking at him. She's looking at the shadow on the ground, gauging his movements and proximity, feigning pain. Moosey makes the lethal mistake of leaning over to talk down to the girl he slugged in the stomach.

Never lean down. Why?

An uppercut rocks his fleshy jaw.

Blood squirts out of his mouth. Guess the Moose bit his tongue.

He's bleeding from the mouth like a B-movie vampire.

"Before we continue," the Other Clare says. "Who's the toughest motherfucking fuck here? Moosey here or one of you wastes of sperm? Bet the best part of you ran down the crack of your mama's ass."

Apparently, TOC scared the other boys as they have backed up a step. The victim in the powder blue t-shirt stays on the ground. Watching.

Moosey gives a big-hearted charge.

His second mistake.

Flashback time:

INT. DOJO — DAY

Instructor GEM, AKA iGem, teaches a fourteen-year-old Clare and a group of students Krav Maga, an Israeli Special Forces fighting technique. iGem is a lithe woman with well-toned muscles and ginger-colored hair. She wears a tight, black t-shirt with KRAV MAGA in gold letters.

iGEM: When you're a little fish, bigger fish are gonna want a piece of you. It's the law of the sea. It's the law of the land. What do you do?

A STUDENT, new to the class, raises a hand.
STUDENT: Fight?

iGEM: Do you think I'm here to train you to fight?

STUDENT: Isn't that what Krav Maga is?

iGEM: No, it is not. Krav Maga isn't fighting, it's staying alive. And why engage an opponent if you don't have to?

STUDENT: So, we just run then?

iGEM: If you have the opportunity to run, do so. Krav Maga is when that option is no longer an option. And it's the best chance, at that point, of preserving your life. Clare, out on the mat.

Clare comes forward.

iGEM: Brutus. On the mat.

BRUTUS, well-named, is a big biker-looking dude with a beard and a belly that his KRAV MAGA shirt can barely cover.

iGEM: Brutus, you're the big fish. Clare, you're the small fish. What do you do?
Clare tries to run, but the wall's right there, so she has to fight.

Brutus has ridiculously thick hands and python-round forearms. If he grabs her, she's done -- he'd twist her like a pretzel. Brutus tries. Clare moves, ducks his arms, then sidekicks the back of his knee, folding it down. Then she

simulates various devastating blows to his head
and throat region.

iGEM: Ah, my favorite student doesn't disap-
point. When Clare came here a few years ago,
she was weak and awkward. Right, some of you
remember? Now she's as deadly as a trap-door
spider to an unsuspecting cricket.

The students laugh in agreement.

iGEM: Brutus is a full-head taller than Clare.
You see how she brought him down to her level?
That's how the little fish makes a meal of the
big fish. You've got to be smarter than the big
fish. Smarter and faster. And ruthless. Or you
die. You understand?

All the students do and acknowledge it with a
hearty HOO-AH.

Back to our regularly scheduled program. Big fish and little fish. Big Moosey and Little Clare. Except this is supercharged Clare. The Other Clare—TOC. The Clare that you don't want to bite because she bites back.

Moosey comes charging like a bull during mating season.

Normal Clare might run.

Other Clare doesn't run.

She meets aggression with more aggression.

She's great at parties.

Moosey grabs the Type O Negative t-shirt. The Other Clare traps his hand against her chest with her right, pinning Moosey's wrist, and rolls her left elbow over his extended arm. She pulls on the crook of his elbow and brings the guy to his knees. She jab punches him in the throat with her left. Not enough to crush the esophagus—only enough to cut off his wind. The way Moosey cut off that kid on the ground's wind. The way Moosey cut off Boring Clare's wind.

The Fitbit flashes—warning against an overload. Too late.

The Grendel beast in the cave has awoken...and it's hungry for moose.

Moosey, on his knees, tries to suck in breath like a fish that's been thrown out of a stream.

A big fish.

Moosey's friends watch from a safe distance, their eyes the size of saucers.

Time to finish Moosey off. The beast just got a taste. Time for the full-meal deal.

"Step away from him!"

Who said that?

"Step away now!"

The Other Clare saw everything but the police officer behind her. And the flashing lights.

And him standing in front of his cruiser, his hand on his holster.

28

The gleaming name tag on his dark blues reads: ALVARADO. He has his brown hand on his gun, but he has kind, dark eyes. He may not shoot unless he's provoked.

"Step away from him now! Back up!"

The Other Clare is hungry for moose meat. But she's not stupid.

Better to go away with an empty stomach than one punched full of lead.

"Let me see your hands," the officer says.

The phone in Clare's jeans buzzes. It's been buzzing. Wouldn't those on the other end of the line love to know what's going on now? Out of the frying pan and into the parking lot brawl.

There's that feeling again. Of being watched. Not by the cop. Not by the others. Another set of eyes. The gaze of evil. Too many cars in the parking lot. Too much happening.

Breathe, breathe, breathe.

Breathe the way Instructor Gem taught you. The way it's saved your life in the past. The way it can save your life now.

Breathe, breathe, breathe.

Officer Alvarado seems like he could be a nice guy, but he also seems like a guy who's not going to take much shit from a crazy-looking girl in a Type O Negative *Bloody Kisses* t-shirt either. He smells of spearmint, probably from the gum he's chewing incessantly.

"You OK, kid?" the officer asks.

Moosey sucks in a breath. His voice is hoarse. "Y-yes."

"Get up, slowly," Alvarado says. "Back away from him, girl."

The Other Clare does. Moosey gets up, slowly.

"What's going on here?"

Nobody says anything.

"Huh?" the cop asks. "Who started this? I was driving by and..."

"They did," says the kid on the ground, holding the inhaler. They/them points to the three boys. "They were attacking me. They took away my inhaler. She told them to stop. Then they attacked her. She was just fighting back."

"She tried to kill me," Moosey says.

"You outweigh her two to one," Officer Alvarado says. "You really think she could kill you?"

"She's crazy. Look at her."

"Who are you, girl?"

"Name's Clare."

"Clare? Clare what? Let me see some ID. Everyone show me some ID."

I hand the cop my driver's license and school ID card.

"You don't even go to this school, Clare. What are you doing here?"

"I came to see my favorite author. Afterwards, these limp-dick wonders were attacking that kid."

"Well, I only saw you hitting big boy here."

"That's exactly what happened, officer," the kid says. "She's not lying."

"Can we just drop it?" Moosey says.

"What?"

"Can we just drop whatever, officer?" the big boy says. "I don't wanna, you know, press charges or anything."

"You attacked me, asshole," I say.

"Hey, language," Alvarado says.

"I just want to go back to class," Moosey says.

"You don't want to file a report because a girl half your size beat you up, is that right?" the officer says.

"I don't want to talk about it," Moosey says.

"Do you have a way to get back to school?" the officer asks me.

"My car is right there—the Nissan Leaf."

"Well, Clare Bleecker from DeFeo Catholic School, I suggest you get back into your Leaf and drift back to where you came from."

"Hey," the they/them kid says, ambling up. "Thanks for helping me. My name's Tracy."

They shake my hand.

"All part of my service, Tracy."

"No," Officer Alvarado says. "If something like this happens, you call the police, Clare. You don't take matters into your own hands. You got me? You're not a vigilante."

Says who?

"Got it," I say.

29

Pickman Flats has exactly two bookstores left in town. Grams told me there used to be a half dozen years ago, but they met the fate that most brick-and-mortar retailers encountered when people started shopping online. The two survivors hanging on by a thread are Bookish Things and Firelight Books. Bookish Things is more of an upscale, snooty seller in the center of town that's designed for the wine tourists. They sell all the bestsellers plus knickknacks like refrigerator magnets, t-shirts, and shopping bags with PICKMAN FLATS stenciled on them so tourists can return home and make their friends envious of their weekend winery visits.

If you're looking for the real literary treasures, though, Firelight Books has the best shelves around. It's in a more run-down part of town. Sun-faded books clutter the windows in no discernible order and there's usually an overfed cat or two sleeping on them. As you make your way in, the walkway is cluttered with dusty boxes of books the owner has purchased from locals dropping off their unwanted tomes. Joyce Sanders, the owner, is a crazy cat and book lady who can often be found hunched over a stack of tomes behind the counter.

If anyone has a copy of that novel Lois mentioned, it's here.

Usually, I love to lose myself in this place, the smell of stale paper and acetic dust burning my nostrils, along with the aroma of a cat box somewhere on the premises. But I don't have time to lose myself today. People, it seems, are freaking out as to my whereabouts. But the more they want to find me, the less I want to be found. Think I'll just call in "sick" for the rest of the day, and crash in my room.

If I can find that book.

"Do you have a copy of *The Killer Inside Me?*"

Joyce gazes up from whatever she was doing on the computer. Looking at cat videos or organizing her massive inventory? Thinking the former. She flaunts tattered, gray dreadlocks and I can smell the spicy chai in her teacup all the way from where I'm standing. She's wearing a faded purple shirt that advertises Alice Walker's most famous book.

"Oh, that's one of those retro John D. McDonald books."

"Somebody named Jim Thompson, actually."

"If I do..." The bookseller disappears from behind the piles of books and somewhere in the labyrinth of book stacks. It feels like that last scene in that Indiana Jones movie where the Lost Ark gets tucked away in a massive warehouse, lost again forever.

A round, calico cat saunters up to me across the counter. Her tail is crooked in a C shape. The cat responds to my pets, then bites my finger and quickly licks it.

"Lizzie Borden usually doesn't like too many customers," Joyce says, a paperback with yellowed pages in her hand. "You must be an animal person."

Lizzie has that air about her like she just doesn't give a damn. It seems we're sisters.

"Guess they like me OK."

The shop owner plops the book on the counter. "Let's call it seven-fifty plus tax."

The cover of the book, published by Black Lizard/Vintage Crime, features a black and white photo of a man with flinty eyes. The killer, obviously. Killers are always portrayed that way—dark and creepy. But we don't all look like that. We don't want to look like killers, that's for sure, we want to look like everyone else. There's a cover blurb by Stanley Kubrick, who co-wrote and directed one of my favorite movies, *The Shining*. "Probably the most chilling and believable first-person story of a criminally warped mind I have ever encountered." Guess you never met me, Stanley.

"That's an unusual choice of book," the book hustler says. "For you?"

"Yes."

"Girls your age are usually hunting for books by John Green, J.K. Rowling, Stephanie Meyers, or Suzanne Collins."

It's funny, I'm a semi-regular shopper here and Joyce never seems to remember who I am.

"Guess I'm of the more unusual variety," I say.

Joyce smiles and hands me my change. "Good for you."

30

Leaving the store with my Killer book in hand, I think about what she said. And my response—*guess I'm of the more unusual variety.*

Once, I read in a book about sociopaths that they make up only about four percent of the population. So, for a town like Pickman Flats, with a population shy of twenty thousand, that's roughly 786 people who might qualify as having antisocial personality disorder.

You see, I'm hardly alone.

Another study stated that less than one percent of annual homicides, around 15,000 to 16,000, are committed by serial killers. That's like one hundred and fifty murders. So, even though four percent of the people in the country have ASP, it doesn't mean they're all serial killers, not by a long shot. Last October, there were seven deaths in our little town. All were because of me. I was only on the hook for four and they were all in self-defense.

As I walk to the car, I get that sensation that I'm being watched again. This is the third time now after Dancing Goats this morning and the Carver High School parking lot later.

Is somebody following me?

A few cars drone past the street outside of the bookstore, but nobody is paying any attention. I don't see anybody sitting inside any cars either.

Then I spot someone.

Behind a weather-beaten, six-foot paneled fence separating the bookstore parking lot from another building, there's a narrow alley between the properties. The shadow of somebody moving behind that fence is clear in the late morning light.

Time to figure out who the watcher is once and for all.

31

Strolling to the car, I act like I'm going to climb in, except I sprint to the fence and rush around the corner.

Someone *is* hiding behind it.

He was staring at me between the wooden slats. He tries to run but he trips over his BMX bike. It's a twelve-year-old kid. He looks scared.

Dropping my book, I grab him by his red hoodie and spin him around. He's wearing a black ball cap that says FBI in bold, white letters.

"Who are you and why are you spying on me?"

The kid, who has beige skin and dark eyes, looks back at me terrified. He's trying to form words but he's either too scared or can't.

The kid still doesn't speak. He only makes these forced guttural sounds. Does the FBI normally make a practice of hiring young and inarticulate boys?

"Leave him alone."

An Asian woman wearing cream-colored slacks and a matching blazer is standing there with her hands on her hips. Oh, she's also wearing a gold badge on her belt and carrying a Glock pistol.

And she doesn't look happy to see me.

32

"Is he with you?" I ask the cop.

"No, that's Tony. He's a local boy. He's in the special ed program at the middle school." She motions to the kid. "It's OK, Tony, you can go. She won't hurt you."

Tony picks up his bike and his ball cap, gives me a final puzzled look, and then rides off.

"He should be in school. And so should you."

"Well, I was heading that way."

The woman with the badge picks up the Thompson book off the ground and reads the title. "You drop this?"

"Yes."

"Kind of a weird book, isn't it?"

What can I say? I shrug.

"I'm Sergeant Jaqui Zang. Officer Alvarado reported this morning's altercation in the Carver High School parking lot. When I heard your name, I got curious. And now you're in another...altercation. Trouble seems to follow you everywhere now, doesn't it, Ms. Bleecker?"

"How'd you find me?"

"You're the only one in town who drives a coulis red Nissan Leaf. Luckily, it's a small town."

"Oh."

"Firelight Books is also on record as being one of your semi-regular haunts."

"Record?"

"I'm Sergeant Timmons's replacement. I transferred down from Seattle. Naturally, since you strangled the detective to death, I dug up everything he had on you. He kept extensive notes."

"Yeah, he kinda had a thing for teenage girls."

She shakes her head. "Detective Timmons was a bad apple in the department. But he didn't spoil the whole box."

"Well, now that we've met, I should probably get back to school."

"Somehow I doubt that's where you were planning to go."

"It's not a crime to miss a couple of classes."

"No, and for the most part, you have an almost perfect attendance record and GPA."

"You've been checking that too?"

"I'm a detective, it's what I do."

Detective Timmons was a hard ass; he always leered at me, but I could usually catch him doing it and embarrass him, which always worked to my advantage. This detective doesn't miss a beat. She seems to see everything—and she's no-nonsense.

"You seem like a really good detective. Bet nobody gets away with much when you're on the case."

Zang cracks a slight grin. "That cutesy routine might disarm the little boys at school, Ms. Bleecker, but it does squat here. I keep my eyes on spoiled, white, rich girls who might have gotten away with murder."

My superficial charm affects her about as well as bullets affect Superman.

"Not rich."

"Say again?"

"My grandparents and I aren't rich. We're just your average, middle-class family."

"Suppose that's what you'd like everyone to think, isn't it?"

"What are you getting at?"

"There was a lot of strange stuff going on last year. The fire at the 333 Oak Street house destroyed lots of the evidence and one person died there. Then you single-handedly killed three men who entered your grandparents' home. You got away with a little more than a scratch."

"Actually, I was shot and nearly bled to death. Wanna see the scar?"

"Saw the investigation photos already, thanks." She takes a step closer. "Then you published a book called *Killer Smoothies and Other Vegan Recipes to Die For*, almost making a joke of the whole thing. I have a feeling there's a lot more going on behind those icy blue eyes and that easy smile than you would like people to know. What kinds of secrets are you hiding?"

"Well, I'm just your average, red-blooded American girl in Small Town USA."

Zang looks down at the book about a serial killer in her hand. "Somehow I doubt that." She hands it to me.

"Does this mean I can go?"

"For now." She stares at me with dark, relentless eyes. "But keep watching your six, Ms. Bleecker, because I'll be right behind you."

"Were you watching me earlier today? At the Goats?"

"What are you talking about?"

It wasn't her. *Who* was it then?

"Nothing. Gotta bounce. Have a lovely rest of the day, Detective Zang."

As I'm about to round the fence to my car—

"Female Body Inspector," Zang says.

"Huh?"

"That's what F-B-I stands for on Tony's hat. I suspect he was doing just that."

Oh yeah, that's a relief. (sarcasm font)

33

After my failure of a day seeing my favorite author, I go home, talk to Grams and Gramps, read a couple of chapters of my new book, and then put on my work clothes. I told my grandparents I wasn't feeling well and so I left school and went to the drug store for some anti-nausea medication. Then I told them I sat in my car in the parking lot and fell asleep.

All the lies I must tell to save them.

They would never accept me leaving school for any reason other than being sick, and neither would DeFeo. Sister Prudence Head has a raging God boner she wants to stick into me and break off, but I'm not going to give her that opportunity. Grams wrote me a note to excuse me and even brought me some tomato soup and a grilled vegan cheese sandwich. Julie texted me what assignments I missed.

What happened today wasn't exactly *Ferris Bueller's Day Off,* but it was rather exciting.

The lies are the sugar to make the medicine of deception go down.

For someone like me, lying is something I must do all the time. The truth is so elusive, I'm not even sure what it is anymore. The more you care about a person, the more it seems you must lie to protect them from the truth.

The truth about me.

The truth about Clare.

And so, lying becomes the soup du jour. You have to pepper it, spice it up, and make it tasty—it goes down smoother that way. It's regretful that I've had to lie to the people who've taken care of me the most, like my grandparents—who are far better to me than my mother or father ever were. My lies to them are the sweetest as they mean the most to me. How messed up is that?

Yep, lies are all part of the disguise. The disguise to make Clare seem normal.

There's that creepy Kevin Spacey movie where he says that the greatest trick that the devil ever played was to make people believe he didn't exist. So on point. My greatest trick is for people to believe that the emptiness and darkness in me doesn't exist, "the devil," for all intents and purposes.

Truman texts me and I tell him to stop by work.

He's another recipient of my lies. But he's a bit different. My grandparents believe my lies because they *want* to believe them. It makes things easier. Truman is a guy who's always trying to figure things out. After I killed his stepfather, he and his mother have been trying to pick up the pieces. Detective Timmons was the ringleader for an underage pornography and human trafficking ring for over a year while living with them. Whatever minuscule positive vibe that Truman had about his stepfather was shattered. Like me, I suspect the late detective was a terrific liar who could put a tasty, bullshit soufflé together like a gourmet chef at a French bistro.

My relationship with Truman has been strained, for lack of a better word, for the year that we've been together. He's needed physical and emotional comfort from me. Providing either is hard. Sure, I'm a warm body he can hug and hold, and I know how to say all the right things, but that's about the best he can hope to get from me. For being in a romantic relationship, there isn't much romance. It has been helpful for me though to understand people's emotions. Truman has helped me to better understand that, otherwise I'd be blank. He's the poster where I've learned all the cartoon cues of pantomime.

Being a sociopath isn't all it's cracked up to be.

It's a lot of work to appear "normal" like you.

Feel lucky you're not me.

It's a full-time job.

34

After school, I work at the Garden Spot, or what I call the G-Spot ('cause I'm kind of demented and deviously clever that way), from four to nine-thirty most weekdays. Going to school, going to work, going home and doing homework, and then back to school the next morning is a bit of a slog, but it's kept me out of trouble for the past year. It's kept the beast at bay until today.

See what happens when I break my careful routine?

Thanks, Lois J. Cain.

Thanks a book load.

Not long after the mass murder incident that rocked the town —and hell, briefly nationwide—I started working at my favorite (and only) vegan restaurant in town. Skye Duncan, the owner, always liked seeing me and thought I'd be good for business. She's actually the one who put me up to self-publishing my book. We sell copies here at the counter, signed, by moi, of course. Come pick up yours while they're still in stock. ABP: Always Be Plugging.

You'd think that being a Level 5 vegan and working in a vegan restaurant would be the greatest thing ever, right? Like the cliché kid working in the proverbial candy store. Well, for the most part, it's pretty boring. As you may have guessed, we don't get many customers. Mostly students from the local Palouse College, which is only a block away, and curious and health-minded folks from out of town who are staying at the four-star Cayuse Hotel, two blocks down. Skye had to cut back on personnel and I'm one of the few who uh, pardon the pun, made the cut. So, it seems, I'm always here. One perk is that I can often do my homework while getting paid. When that's not happening, I can sneak-a-read behind the counter.

That's what I'm doing now, reading *The Killer Inside Me*. It's a Wednesday, which is the slowest day of the week. We pick up on weekends. Other times, I'm polishing up my social and mental skills with most of the college students. As I've said before, I rock an above-Mensa IQ and I've been told by many of my elders that I have an "old soul." Picking the brains of college students is one of my favorite things. They're not locals, so I can be anyone I want to be. For fun, I often put on name tags (we have a drawer full of them from former employees) so I can be Alexa from Spokane, or KaDee from Twin Falls, Idaho, or Saige from Ferndale, California. Sometimes I imitate those girls, who quit or were terminated from here for one reason or another.

Sometimes I make up an entirely new persona. Last year, I was one of the supporting characters in Ira Levin's *Death Trap* at our local theater. This year, I don't have time to play around, so to speak. The fall play is another suspense thriller, *The 39 Steps*. And I'd love to be in it, but instead, I make the G-Spot my stage, and me the one-woman show.

Now you're probably thinking I'm some kind of a demented, attention-seeking asshole, and you would be right. But who's perfect? Ever take a serious evaluation of your strengths and weaknesses in the mirror in the morning? It's rather reflective. Wow, I'm the Pun Nun today.

Then there's the time I saved a girl from death.

No, shit. Shocker, right?

Saved. A. Person. From. Death.

Eight people died because of me in the last two years.
One person is alive because of me.
Atone, much?

35

Here's how the death-defying act went down. This girl came into the Spot last March. She was a transfer student from another school in Bellevue. Can't remember which one. Her name was Meghan Greene, and she had a death wish. You see, Meghan wanted to study liberal arts at a prodigious school like Palouse College. She was also in love. Her fiancé back home, Nick, worked for a law firm as an up-and-comer. Nick and Meghan met at the University of Washington. Then she wanted to check out Palouse. She had a free scholarship there. Well, on paper, it seemed doable to Meghan, but it didn't work. It went down like a movie scene:

INT. GARDEN SPOT — NIGHT

MEGHAN GREENE, a studious-looking blonde with a morose way about her, commiserates at the counter of the restaurant sipping a cup of chai. CLARE BLEECKER, sixteen, chats with Meghan. Clare's wearing the wrong name tag; it states her name is "Trixy."

MEGHAN: I don't know what to do. Last weekend I

drove up there and it's like Nick can barely make the time for me. He's acting all weird around me and my best friend Tiffany. Later, back at Nick's place, after we had sex...he was far away and distracted with that too... I checked his phone when he stepped into the shower. His passcode is my birthday.

TRIXY: (chewing gum and affecting an East Coast waitress in a cheap diner) That's rather deceitful, sugar. Don't you think? Hacking into someone's phone when they don't know you're hacking into their phone. That's kind of some NSA shit —-

MEGHAN: Did you just freakin' call me "sugar"? (beat, wiping away a budding tear) I had to know what the *hell* was going on. It's *also* deceitful to keep distancing yourself from your fiancée. To no longer call and barely text and then keep using the excuse that you're "over-worked." And deep in your heart and soul, you know that something is up. A *lie*. A *total* lie. Yeah, that's unethical too.

TRIXY: Yeah, I guess see your point, sug-Meghan. I was, you know, playing devil's advo-cate for all intensive purposes.

MEGHAN: Intents and purposes.

TRIXY: Huh?

MEGHAN: It's "all intents and purposes" not "intensive purposes." I should know, my ex-fiancé is a junior lawyer.

TRIXY: Wait, what? You said ex. Why'd you
say ex?

MEGHAN: While you were across the counter
playing devil's advocate and smacking your gum,
sugar, I was trying to explain what the shit is
going on. Can I finish now, Trix?

Trixy nods, now not quite as into her Juicy
Fruit gum as before.

MEGHAN: So, I got into his phone and there were
all these texts and Facebook messages from
Tiff. Hundreds of them.

TRIXY: What'd they say?

MEGHAN: The worst possible things you can
imagine that your former best friend and ex-
fiancé could message each other. I could practically picture each and every sexual position
they did. All their dinners together, nights
together.

TRIXY: That son of a rotten bastard.

MEGHAN: Trouble is, I didn't have to picture
it. He did. That creepy bastard even set up his
phone to record him and Tiffany having sex. And
I found other videos with other girls. One
right in the office bathroom of the law firm he
works at with some dumb-looking secretary.
TRIXY: Tell me you confronted him about all
this after he got out of the shower.

MEGHAN: No, I didn't. He's a junior lawyer,

after all, he knows how to debate. He knows how to make me feel stupid and tongue-tied. We've had arguments where he was clearly wrong, and at fault, and he was able to flip the script and make *ME* look like the incompetent and guilty one. Nick's a gaslight master. He's going to be an invincible defense lawyer someday.

TRIXY: So, what'd you do?

MEGHAN: Nothing. Just acted like I was asleep and put my face in the pillow. If I saw Nick's face after he stepped out of the shower, knowing what I knew, I would have lost my shit. He quickly dressed, gave me a kiss on the cheek, and said he had a late-night deposition with a client. Except I saw the text from Tiffany inviting him over. There was a picture of hand-cuffs, a feather duster, and other assorted...toys. (starts crying) He was never that way with me. I thought I knew him. What kind of deceptive monster was I going to marry, huh? Is there anyone with a shred of decency out there?

TRIXY: (sighs, spits out her gum, and takes off her fraudulent name tag) Hey, my name is Clare. Sorry for the Trixy act. Sometimes I do that just to kill time.

MEGHAN: What...is wrong with you?

CLARE: Too many things to count, believe you me. But I'll be honest with you right now -- as honest as I've ever been with anyone. It will

be all right, Meghan. Just forget him. Let go.
Keep going to school. You'll meet a cute guy.
Lots of them come in here. Believe me. Pickman
Flats is a nice place to reinvent yourself. I
was like you a couple of years ago when I moved
here from Colorado.

MEGHAN: How old are you?

CLARE: (reluctant) Sixteen.

MEGHAN: Are you kidding? I thought you were,
like twenty, or something. Are you lying? I
just don't know what to believe anymore.

CLARE: People say I have an old soul. What can
I do? Re-invent yourself. The best revenge is
forgetting him and being the best version of
you that you can.

MEGHAN: (drying her eyes with an eco-friendly
recycled napkin) You're right... You're right.
Makes so much sense. You're wise beyond your
years, Trix-Clare. Thank you. What can I do for
you in return?

CLARE: (puts her hand on the book display) Buy
one of my books!

Meghan is aghast.

CLARE: Just kidding. I was trying to get you to
smile. Nothing. You've helped me. Being a few
years younger than you, I don't have as much
life experience. It's helpful. Kind of have a

boyfriend I'm not sure what to do with. I care for him, but...

MEGHAN: My advice. Dive in headfirst. Even though Nick turned out to be a bastard, I dove in...and I'd do it again with the right person. I can't be in love only partway. It's either diving into the deep end or it's sunning on the deck. But I can't dip my toe in the pool part-way. It just doesn't work for me. Or for anyone.

CLARE: You're wise beyond your years, too, Meg. Can I call you Meg?

MEG: At this point (wiping her eyes) call me anything you fucking want. (looks around) Where's your bathroom?

CLARE: (points) Down that hall. Don't worry about your tab. On me. Us girls have to watch each other's backs, right? (wink)

Meghan nods, rises, and without another word, heads for the bathroom, clutching her bag with both hands in front of her. It's like she's being led there by unseen strings pulling her along.

Clare picks up the cup and wipes down the counter. Soon, there's the CRASH of breaking glass coming from the bathroom area. She leaps over the counter like a gazelle and heads to the bathroom.

The door is locked -- blood seeps from
under it.

CLARE: Meghan?

No answer.

Clare hits the locked door with her shoulder.
There's more sounds, erratic, coming from
behind the door. What's going on? Clare moves
back and kicks the door. One, two, three -- it
cracks open a few inches. Meghan's body
blocks it.

Clare bench presses the door open. The disarray
in the restroom tells the story: the shattered
mirror; the long, missing piece of glass; the
pool of blood forming under Meghan; her forearm
where she slashed it lengthwise, in a desperate
suicide attempt, blood spilling out.

CLARE: What the hell did you do?

Meghan tries to answer but she's too weak and
pale from the blood loss. Clare needs to call
911, but she left her phone back on the bar.
It's after closing, there's nobody to yell to
for help. Clare goes for the paper towels.
Nope, this is an eco-friendly place, no towels
in sight. She rips off her apron and wraps it
around the bleeding wrist, holding Meghan,
telling her to not slip away. Giving her words
of reassurance. What's she going to do with
this dying girl in her arms?

36

You see, if I had been some kind of sick psychopath, I would have toyed with Meghan's emotions, and then convinced her to go take some pills or hang herself for my own personal thrill. But no, that didn't happen. In fact, Meghan Greene is alive and well because of me, thank you very much.

After dragging her out of the bathroom and into the dining area (yeah, quite a bit of spilled blood on the tiles for a vegan restaurant), I called an ambulance and they arrived in time.

Meghan and I follow each other on Instagram. She has a tattoo of ivy covering the scar on her arm and she now lives happily with a local artist and art instructor in Bellingham. He worships the ground she walks on. Meghan found the love that she deserved. Wish I knew what that felt like. Guess it's like being a vampire and never knowing what the warmth of the sun feels like on your skin, only the chill of a moonless night. Yeah, you caught me waxing poetic, what of it?

My point is, though I may have killed, I don't actively kill. In fact, I try to save lives. Shit, I'm a freakin' vegan who's trying to reduce the unjust killing of animals on a global scale. Cut me some slack. Skye, the G-Spot manager, was happy with me doing the right thing. I think she was a little surprised considering my age that I didn't freak out and go into shock. Nope, a psychopath saved her. Quick, clear, and logical thinking—pure rationalizing. Though I lack most emotion and empathy, I have rationale in spades. It helps you cut through the emotional murk that I see other people have when they're paralyzed in fear.

The perks of being a serial killer.

Someday I might write that book.

Speaking of love, my boyfriend Truman Quirk steps through the door. He's looking long, lean, and handsome per usual in his long scarf and dark, woolen trench coat. He reminds me a little bit of Benedict Cumberbatch in *Sherlock*. He can be handsome, and at other times, with his narrow face and aquiline nose, not so much. Guess I like that kind of duality in him. He shuffles up to the counter in his creaky Doc Martens. He takes off his coat, wearing a black Radiohead t-shirt with a gray thermal shirt underneath.

He drops a blue bag with Stereophile Records written on it on the counter. They're an old music store in town that still sells vinyl. They're also a head shop. The store bag smells like weed and patchouli.

"What's in the bag?"

Truman smiles and pulls out some vintage albums—Queen, Pink Floyd, David Bowie, and Joy Division.

"Oh, old music. Gramps would approve. Haven't you ever heard of Spotify?"

Truman shakes his head. "You don't get the warm and full sound with digital like with analog. Digital is cold. And this 'old music,' as you call it, was a huge influence on Radiohead." He holds up a colorful album, *Queen Live Killers*, and opens the two-disc set. "Plus, you don't get these great photos and artwork on Spotify. This shit here is vintage and tactile."

"I'd love to hear that 'warm and full sound' on your turntable," I say with a wink. "The usual?"

Truman nods. "That, uh, kinda sexual innuendo is... surprising to hear."

I pour his usual drink. "Why is it surprising?"

"You've been like a ghost," he says.

"The ghost with the most, babe."

He gets a complimentary fair-trade, eco-friendly coffee. Truman dumps about five packets of sugar in it. Not much of a sugar user myself. Makes me break out and feel all bloaty, as well as, uh, stimulate my moods to the dark side a little bit too much. Really have to watch caffeine and sugar, and tense situations in general. They bring out the beast like a bad Jekyll and Hyde movie.

"Where have you been all day?" he asks.

"It's been a long one. But I don't want to talk about it right now. Later?"

He reaches out and holds my hand and I let him. Public displays of affection aren't really my thing, well, affection isn't my thing in general, but I'm trying to be a supportive girlfriend.

"You know," he says. "I was saying you're like a ghost in a different way. You barely acknowledge us as a couple. Never mind a romantic one. And when I gaze into your eyes, it's like you're not present. You're not, you know, there. Not There Clare."

"And you're trying to flatter me how?"

He shrugs and drinks his coffee. The restaurant is pretty slow, and the manager isn't here, so I can stand around and talk. These moments, I cherish.

"Yeah, I know that may come off as kind of rude. You're not a vapid airhead like lots of the girls who go to DeFeo."

"Well, gee, I certainly have that going for me."

"It's just... Sometimes I feel lonely... You know, even when we're together. Just feels like you're placating me. Just giving me charity because you feel sorry for me or something. It feels like, well, I'm some kind of pet project."

"Is that what it really feels like?"

Hey, doing the best I can here, Tru. Don't date a psychopath if you want a warm and cuddly stuffed animal.

"Heh, I'm sorry. That just came out wrong. Low blood sugar." He glugs his coffee like a drunken uncle on free beer night.

"Sugar kicking in—feel better?"

He shrugs. "It's like I'm always saying 'sorry' even when I haven't done anything wrong." He sighs. "Guess I get envious of other couples at our school. Holding hands and kissing when the nuns aren't looking. Cuddling up when school's out."

"So, you're looking for sex and I'm not putting out, is that right?"

"No, nothing like that. Geez. I want to feel wanted, that's all."

"You are wanted, love. Wanted by me. It's just after the incident and stuff, I'm still a little freaked out."

"You're freaked out? My girlfriend strangled my police detective stepfather with a necktie like something out of a Hitchcock movie."

"Excuse me, your homicidal detective stepfather was trying to add extra ventilation holes into me with his gun. And Amity. Sorry if I had to protect myself from the police."

"Now *you're* saying sorry," he says with a sigh.

This time, I grab *his* hand and hold it as warmly as I can. His big brown eyes seem to melt like chocolate bars. "Tell you what, I'll do better. Better about letting you in on stuff. Better at keeping in touch. Better at—" motions to holding his hand "—this. Just give me a little more time."

"I love you, Clare."

He leans over and surprises me with a long kiss. From him walking in here and starting off like a Basic Bitch with demands, this is better. I do miss his closeness sometimes.

"It's mutual," I say.

He gives me a puzzled stare because I didn't repeat the "I love you" part.

"A little more time." Wink. "Now get out of here, I have work to do. They don't pay me to stand around and make out with my scandalously handsome boyfriend."

His smile beams from ear to ear. He climbs off the stool, grabbing his store bag and coat. "Text me later?"

"Yep—I'll even initiate it this time. Gonna turn over a new leaf. October's the right month to do that, right?"

I'd love to tell my boyfriend about who I really am, Clare your serial killer girlfriend who your psycho stepdad detective was right about from the beginning when he was investigating me. But it's probably a bad idea. It might make me depressingly single.

He smiles again, throwing on his coat and scarf. "You're the most ridiculously beautiful and beautifully ridiculous person I've ever known."

"I know you are but what am I?"

Like a raven, my dark-cloaked, vinyl-collecting boyfriend is out the door and into the autumn chill as the night approaches. Lost in the darkness.

If I knew then what I know now, I would have kissed him longer. And harder.

Sorry, Truman.

You're too good for me.

Like, literally.

And I wish I could be that "warm and fuller" analog sound to you rather than the cold digital one. But I wouldn't be me, I'd be a game show host.

37

Ten minutes before I turned over the sign to read CLOSED, *she* came through the door.

"You still open?"

"Absolutely."

"Your town seems to roll up its sidewalks at seven sharp," she says, scanning the place.

"Yeah, small-town life and all," I say. "What can I get you?"

"Dessert and coffee?"

At this point of the night, there was only one customer in the place—a Palouse College student who has her nursing school books and papers spread out all over a table, studying them intently. We don't even exist to her.

"Sweet things are my specialty," I say with a cheesy smile and pat the stool where Truman sat hours earlier and bared his soul.

For the second time in a day, Lois J. Cain, my favorite author ever, sits in front of me.

"I'm not much for the whole vegan thing," she says. "Probably should be—butter and bacon aren't exactly good for the arteries."

"Better be careful," I say with a wink. "I'll convert you faster than you can say Joaquin Phoenix."

"Joaquin Phoenix?"

"Uh, the only famous vegan I could think of in the moment. Guess there's Alicia Silverstone, Moby, and Billy Eilish, too."

"Well, I'd definitely kill to be rich and famous like them."

Would you, Lois, would you kill indeed? The figure of speech "I would kill to..." has always amused me.

"So, for desserts, all I have left tonight is one vegan crème brûlée. But it's bomb."

"Sold!"

Lois is acting different than she did earlier, which was reserved and a little short with people. It was like I had met Mr. Hyde, and now I was introduced to the Dr. Jekyll counterpart. Not saying she's bipolar or anything like that. Maybe she was just having a bad day or doesn't do well with crowds of mostly bored teenagers in a high school gymnasium. That's fine; I'll roll with her now good-natured self.

So, as I pull out the cold brûlée and then light the torch, cooking the sugar on top, browning it to a nice, even coat, she says—

"Wait a minute, I know you, don't I?"

Time to be the coy one now, she's on my home turf this time. "Maybe. Where do you think you know me from?"

"From earlier today at the signing. You're Clare from Instagram, right?"

"If we sold cigars, I'd give you one as you're a winner."

I serve the author her dessert and coffee. She takes a bite. "Wow, that's good. I'd have never thought it was vegan."

"Yeah, it's the organic, full-fat coconut milk and natural cane sugar that really tantalizes the taste buds."

"Hey, I know that book." She points to *The Killer Inside Me.* "You're not very far into it. Got that recently?"

"What you said today intrigued me, but it's also raised some concerns."

"Like what?"

"Well, I know I'm only a few chapters in it," I say, choosing my words carefully so as not to offend my favorite author, "but this

Lou Ford character, for lack of a better word, is a complete bastard."

Lois almost spits out her brûlée and coffee in laughter. She chokes. It would be horrible to accidentally kill my favorite author with vegan crème brûlée.

"You think so?" she says when she can finally talk.

"Not only is he a racist and a womanizer who beats women, but he's, well, not nice."

"But you're going to keep reading?"

"Of course, it's kind of hard to put down once you get started."

The nursing student rises and leaves. Now it's only Lois and me in the restaurant—just the way I like it.

Lois finishes her dessert and wipes her mouth, introspective, then she speaks. "It's not that he's a likable character. That's not always important. He's a son of a bitch of the worst kind. He's the anti-antihero. He's a train wreck with a badge. But he's *our* train wreck, the audience's. Characters don't necessarily have to be likable, but they do have to be interesting."

"Really?"

"Did you ever see the movie *The Shining*?"

Weird, the second time today that movie has come up. Some kind of kismet, right?

"Yeah, like sixteen times. Love watching that one, especially around Christmas. Makes me homesick for Colorado."

Think I freaked her out based on her open-mouthed expression.

"Uh, Christmas movie. OK. Well, anyway, do you like Nicholson's character in that?"

"He's fun to watch."

"Right, but he's a total son of a bitch. We know he's going to snap from the opening scene and we're waiting for it to happen. Lisbeth Slander from *Dragon Tattoo* is the same way. Or De Niro in *Raging Bull*."

"Never saw that one."

"He's a boxer who's brutal in the ring and who's brutal to anyone who loves or cares for him. He's a bull in a China shop, metaphorically speaking. The one opponent he cannot defeat is himself. We don't like him, but we *watch* him because he's full of flaws which makes him fascinating. And you mentioned Joaquin Phoenix, right? *Joker* made a billion dollars at the box office!"

Is this why Truman puts up with me? Is this why everyone does? Am I a train wreck in Catholic school clothes? Am I a daughter of a bitch? Am I an anti-antihero? Am I interesting but not loveable? Am I a madman with an axe in a snowy mountain lodge, a prickly computer hacker, a bullish boxer, or a troubled loner in clown make-up? Am I fascinating that way?

This is why I love Lois J. Cain. Her books, *her*, she makes me think.

"Looks like I lost you," my favorite author says.

"No," I say, shaking my head. "Only thinking. Sometimes my brain carries me away."

Lois smiles. "Hey, I'm a writer. I know the feeling. I'm never all there. I'm always thinking about stories. Things. How I can use them in my next work. Drives my family—as well as my ex-husband—crazy."

"Yeah, I get accused of the same thing. I do a little writing too."

"What do you write?"

"Well, it's kind of YA, like what you write. It's about this seventeen-year-old girl, her name's Cecile, Cecile Kurtner, and she's a serial killer. But it's not like Cecile actively goes out and kills. In fact, when she was younger, age eight, a serial killer murdered her den mother and other Firefly girls, then kicked her in the head with a logging boot. He was interrupted before he killed her. She developed some mental problems after that. She had an alcoholic mom and a dad who wouldn't stand up for her. After they died, Cecile was alone. A creepy guy attacked her when she was fifteen, and she killed him. Cecile has this other personality that flares up in tense situations and it kinda takes over. But the cool thing is, Cecile's kind of like what you like to call an anti-hero. She sorta cleans up this town she lives in when the police cannot."

"That sounds pretty ambitious. What's it called?"

"*She's Not There.*"

"Ah, a title from the old sixties pop song by The Zombies?"

"Uh, no. She really isn't there. Like your empty crème brûlée dish."

"Where'd you get your inspiration?"

That's when I tell my favorite author what happened to me last year. Yes, I realize I'm playing a dangerous game by basically outing my most vicious secrets through fiction. But as they always say, write what you know, right?

"I remember seeing a clip on TV about that. That was you?"

"In the flesh."

Lois thinks a moment. "Tell you what, give me a copy of your book. It might be something my agent wants to check out. She's always looking to sign fresh, young writers with some real talent for telling a story. You can email it to me."

"No need," I say and pull out a flash drive file from my bag. "Always have a copy handy."

Lois narrows her eyes. "Wait, did you have that to hand to me earlier? That seems like an awfully big coincidence."

"Guilty as charged."

OK, she didn't ask me to go to Cabo with her like in my cinematic fantasy, but this was as close to fulfilling a dream as it gets.

"So," I ask her, "are you writing some more books, or are you eventually going to retire?"

Lois laughs. "Authors don't retire, they die slumped over their manuscript-in-progress."

"That sounds...pretty ambitious, I guess."

"Well, Clare," my favorite author says. "It's time to head back to the hotel and pack. I have an early flight out in the morning. My book won't promote itself, you know. I have to make appearances. Part of my contractual obligation. Not that I mind meeting young people. Especially sharp pencils like you." She smiles. "But I was a little off today, wasn't I? I feel like I was a tad crabby and short with people."

"Oh," I lie. "Not at all."

She shrugs. "I didn't get much sleep last night, which tends to make me a bit of a badger in the morning."

"You were great," I say. "It was an absolute pleasure meeting you, Lois. You've been a huge inspiration to me since I was twelve. Always felt like I had a friend in your books when I was lonely."

"That's sweet to say, Clare. Is your contact information on the manuscript's title page?"

"Naturally."

"Great."

As I walk Lois to the entrance, I can't help but feel like I'm being watched again. It's hard to see outside in the night from the bright, reflected windows in here. We're like fish in a bowl that anyone could be observing. Could it be Detective Jaqui Zang who harassed me earlier? Kind of hope so, because the alternative, whoever it is, could be a tad unsettling.

Lois disappears into the night, bunching down in her coat against the cold.

Snapping the bolt on the front door, I turn the OPEN sign over to CLOSED.

Had I known what terrible events would befall Lois J. Cain, I would have given her another crème brûlée

38

As I pull into the driveway of my grandparent's house, the automatic floodlights snap on. So much for the stealthy entry. But I do love their welcoming glow. Beach House's "Levitation" is on Sirius XMU, Channel 35—*love* that song.

Climbing out of the Leaf, music emanates through the night air. Not my music, though. It's coming from behind the garage—Gramps's shop. He never works this late. He's usually watching TV with Grams or in bed by now. Maybe he left his radio on?

Walking around the garage to his shop in back, the music grows louder. It's Jim Morrison from The Doors singing "Moonlight Drive."

The shop door sits slightly ajar, so I slip in with the intent of scaring him.

His back is to me as he's hunched over something on his workbench. The shop is warm and cozy—maybe a little too warm as he has the pot-belly stove lit. In the middle of the night, I've burned many blood-stained articles of clothing in it. It's been a lifesaver.

The place reeks of alcohol. It nearly singes my nostrils. Why?

He had an addiction with alcohol once that eventually carried over to my mother. After she died, he quit cold turkey with the

Wild Turkey bourbon. I certainly hope he's not drinking again for some reason.

Sneaking up on him, I notice he's working on a wooden box, sanding it down. Wait, it's not just any box—it's a cedar hope chest. Hopefully not *my* hope chest. I keep all of my trophies in the false bottom I made. Trophies like mailman Bob Rextor's class ring. *Holy shit!* He's the last person on Earth who I would want to know my secrets. My heart beats fast in my chest, going nuts. And I'm sure my Fitbit is climbing.

"Working late?" I know, it's the most obvious thing I can ask.

He turns, grinning when he sees me. "Hey, babe. What'd you say?"

Normally I wouldn't let anyone call me a pet name as annoying as "babe," but with Gramps, it's kind of endearing.

I motion to the hope chest he's sanding. His blue flannel shirt and Levi's are covered in wood dust. He wears work goggles over his glasses. He seems tired—more tired than usual.

"Oh, yeah. I ran into Faye Maitland at Williamson's Market the other day. She wanted me to restore her old hope chest for her granddaughter as a Christmas present."

Sigh of relief. "Oh, that's great."

He nods. "She asked me what I would charge to do it, but I told her it's my pleasure."

"Gramps, you can't do that. If you're good at something, don't give it away for free." Heath Ledger's Joker said that in the movie and it's true.

"Naw, happy to make her happy. Just the process is the reward."

"Uh, OK." Now, about that alcohol smell. He notices noticing.

"Yeah, it's a little strong, isn't it?" He wanders over to the bathroom sink and pulls out his gold wedding ring from a dish. "It was a little grimy, so I was soaking it in rubbing alcohol."

I sigh again.

"You thought I was dipping into the Wild Turkey again, didn't you?"

"Uh, well, yeah, maybe."

He laughs. As he does, the next song that comes on is George Thorogood's rendition of "One Bourbon, One Scotch, and One Beer."

"Not everything is as it appears, babe. Same goes with people."

OK, random. What does he mean by that? Do I ask? Or blow it off with humor?

"Uh, totally random, Gramps."

He chuckles. "Yeah, I guess so." He yawns. "What do you say we call it a night? We've both been working hard."

I catch my reflection in the bathroom mirror. *Gah!* I look tired and about ten years older. "I'm good with that." Even though I have more work to do tonight before my head hits the pillow.

He snaps off the radio, killing Donovan singing about the Hurdy Gurdy Man, and then pats the naked wood of the chest.

"That hope chest of yours is looking a little ratty. I could finish it next, if you want."

Hell no! "You know, it belonged to Grams and then mom. It's vintage—and I love its layers of history. It'd be a sin to strip all of that away."

He chuckles. "Whatever floats your boat."

We head out of his shop, and he goes to snap off the light, but stumbles. I catch him before he falls. "Are you all right?" I help him back up.

"Never get old. Your body betrays you and it turns against you."

Though I'm not totally sure, I thought I caught a whiff of alcohol on his breath. And it wasn't rubbing alcohol.

"I want you to live forever," I say.

"God, I hope not."

He snaps off the light this time without incident and we head out, walking toward the house.

Yes, so much to do tonight before my head hits the pillow.

39

Lois J. Cain's mysterious disappearance wasn't made known to me until second period, Advanced English, with Sister Molly Walsh.

Being the principal's guard dog, Sister Prudence Head came into the room to fetch me. Even though her ancient face is pinched and pursed like a petrified prune, I swear I could see a sadistic crack of a smile when I was called out of my seat.

Pretty sure I'll be approached about yesterday. Sister Prudence will walk me down to Sister Aileen and we'll all have a little chat in the principal's office. Well, I'm ready. I have my excuses all sorted out and a note from Grams corroborating my lies. Relax, they're little white lies—nothing that will hurt anyone, especially me. If you don't game the system once in a while, the system games you.

This reminds me of last year when I was hauled into Sister Aileen's office and interviewed by Detective Timmons about the murder of Joe Morton. OK, I was guilty of that.

But whatever I was being dragged away from class for, there was one thing I was sure of—I didn't do it. The Other Clare, except for the brief exchange in the Carver High parking lot with Moosey and his minions, has laid dormant like a hibernating grizzly. Sister

Prudence seems to be enjoying this a bit too much. I swear that she has a skip in her step with those ugly, Eastern Bloc shoes. Well, I'll tell you this, one thing that's not going to happen is letting this overbearing nun get the better of me... I'll have nun of it. ;-)

Except, plot twist, Sister Prudence Head walks me toward the wooden front doors of the school.

"What's going on?" I ask. "Where are you taking me?"

The nun remains mum. She escorts me outside.

Detective Jaqui Zang and Officer Alvarado wait in front of a police car. Sister Aileen's with them. Zang and Alvarado seem as eager to see me as a couple of sharks with hunger pangs might be near a crowded summer beach. Alvarado chews his spearmint gum and smiles—I'm not sure if it's the flavor of the gum or me that's making him so happy.

"What's this all about?" I ask.

"They just want to take you to the police station to answer a few questions," Sister Aileen answers me, a merciful look in her eyes. She never has a look of mercy, so that means this situation is pretty serious. The eyes of a nun don't lie.

What does this mean? Do they have evidence of the murders I committed in the last couple of years? Did somebody find something? Did somebody say something?

"We meet again," the detective says and looks pleased with herself. She's wearing a similar cream-colored suit as she did yesterday. She must either really like that one or she bought a few on a going-out-of-business clearance rack. Either way, it's not really her color. I think about telling Zang, but I decide it's probably not the best timing.

"You have the right to remain silent," Officer Alvarado says.

"Am I being arrested?" I ask. "On what charge?"

"You're not being arrested, Clare," Zang says. "But, by law, we must read you your Miranda rights."

"As I was saying," Alvarado says, clearing his throat. "You have the right to remain silent. Anything you say can and will be used against you in a court of law. You have the right to have a lawyer. If you cannot afford a lawyer, one will be appointed to you. Do you understand your rights?"

I don't take my eyes off Zang. "Why would I need a lawyer? I haven't done anything wrong."

"Do you understand the rights as I have read them to you?" the officer says.

Officer Alvarado has boyish features, and the fit of his uniform is a little too large, as if he hasn't grown into it yet. He looks like a little kid playing dress-up cops and robbers. I think about telling him that, but again, that's probably not in my best interest.

"Yes, I understand," I say. "As much as I don't understand what's going on."

"Please step up to the vehicle," Zang says. "Place your hands flat on the hood of the cruiser and place your feet slightly wider than shoulder-width apart."

Then she frisks me for weapons. *Oh, joy.* It's probably good that I keep all my weapons stashed back home in my hope chest in the false-bottomed drawer. She's careful where she places her hands so she doesn't end up as part of a sexual assault suit for attacking a minor. She's good.

Zang grabs one arm, places it behind me, slips a cuff around it, and then repeats the action with the other arm. The steel bites into my bony wrists. The detective pulls down on the cuffs and it hurts. With her unflattering suit, she's really getting into this. Guess you have to get your kicks where you can in a small town when you're not still in Seattle.

"Thought I wasn't under arrest," I say. "Why are you cuffing me?"

"OK, we're done," the detective finally says. "Officer."

Alvarado opens the rear door and escorts me inside. Climbing in the backseat, which is awkward with your hands cuffed behind you, he pushes my head down and in I go. Then he shuts the door in my face. Wow, passive-aggressive much?

Through the rear window, I peek up at the front of the school, which has a Spanish Missionary Revival motif. Many of my fellow DeFeo students are gawking out the classroom windows at me. Some are smiling and pointing at me, others seem worried.

Julie and Truman are two of the latter.

They're the last friendly faces I see before Zang, Alvarado, and I zoom off to the police station.

Well, Clare, it seems that the hunters have separated the wolf from the sheep.

The gig is up.

What are you going to do for the mighty hunters now, Wolfie, howl for 'em?

40

"Lois J. Cain is missing—and *I'm* a suspect?"

Yes, I'm just as mystified as you are. Why would I want to hurt my favorite author? And if I did want to kidnap somebody, let alone a famous person, what the hell would I do with them? Hide them away in my closet in my grandparent's house?

"You were one of the last people to speak to her," Zang says, sitting across the desk from me in the white and sterile interrogation room at the police station. On one wall, there's a perfect reflection of us—a two-way mirror. No doubt other law enforcers are observing us on the other side of the glass. There's a portable TV on a rolling stand with a DVR player. We're in a cinderblock room painted bright white. It's as sterile as the detective's outfit.

"And who were these other people Lois spoke to? Did you ask *them*?"

Zang pulls out her notebook. "Yep. Joanna Grant, who was the night clerk at the Cayuse Hotel last night spoke to her. And Ms. Grant had a lot of interesting things to say."

"What, like where she hid my favorite author?"

"No, what Joanna revealed is that you and Lois had a buddy-buddy chat last night at the Garden Spot Café. Lois had dinner at the hotel, and then did her nightly walk. Apparently, she ended up at your place for coffee and dessert."

"The restaurant. Yes."

"She told Joanna all this. Said she was surprised how much she liked the vegan crème brûlée and how nice you were."

"Did this night clerk mention me by name?"

"No, but we checked with the restaurant, and you were the only one working that shift." Zang leans in closer. "So, what did you and Lois have to talk about?"

"Why was I dragged down here? To the police station? Like I'm some kind of criminal? Couldn't you have asked me these questions at school? Don't you think it's a little humiliating hand-cuffing me in front of all my fellow students?"

"Well, frankly, you're a loose cannon, Ms. Bleecker. A flight risk. You have been flighty lately."

Wow, really?

"Did you not sneak out of school to see Lois J. Cain? Did you not bludgeon Max Williams in the parking lot?"

"Max is his name? Oh, I just figured it was Moosey."

"Did you not accost a second individual, twelve-year-old Tony Gonzalez, outside of Firelight Books? Holding a copy of a book that the author recommended, by the way? A book about a serial killer?"

"No harm in that."

"And both instances of assault were stopped by a police officer. Who knows how far you would have gone."

I raise my hand. "Not sure this is the right time to bring this up, but I believe I'm entitled to a phone call. Possibly a lawyer."

"Do you need a lawyer, Ms. Bleecker?"

"Only that I'm a minor and I feel like I'm being harassed by local law enforcement."

"The court-appointed lawyer is on her way—she was detained with another case. And you'll get your call."

"Appreciate it."

"Nothing shakes you, Ms. Bleecker, does it."

"Of course, I'm just your ordinary, small-town girl."

"Or that's what you'd like to have people think. I've dragged girls in here your age for crimes far less serious—and they're usually a ball of tears and snot by now. But not you. You're just sitting there, calm, cool, and collected, firing back snarky remarks at me."

"I don't cry, it makes my mascara run."

Zang is not amused.

"Well, I've never been the overly emotional type," I say. "Unless I watch a movie where the dog dies, and then I'm like Multnomah Falls."

The detective nods, folds her hands, and looks at them. Studying her body language, she's got something on me, something big. Sarcasm and snarkiness are my usual defense weapons. But if I want to convince her that I have nothing to hide, I'd better start acting like an actual human girl with feelings, and not my usual dark cesspool of emptiness.

Here goes: "I-I'm scared. None of this makes any sense. I'm a vegan. I don't hurt anything, not even the ants that sometimes swarm in the kitchen sink. I escort them all outside. Why would I hurt somebody like Ms. Cain? Why would I hurt *anyone*?"

Not an Oscar performance, probably not even an Academy nomination, but I thought it was pretty convincing and as "from the heart" as possible for somebody like me.

Zang smirks. "You're not convincing, Ms. Bleecker. Why would you hurt anyone? Were you not responsible for the deaths of a handful of people last year?"

"All in self-defense. Those men would have murdered my grandparents, my boyfriend, and me. And Timmons would have killed Amity and me later. You know what he did to Hope Dalquist? And Teresa Wainwright?"

"Why were those men so bent on killing you? What makes a sixteen-year-old so dangerous they have to send three armed men into a house?"

Shrug. "Overkill?"

"Death and tragedy seem to follow you wherever you go.

Instead of being remorseful about it, you go on TV, and even write a book. You poke fun at killing."

"Seriously, I'm not poking fun. It was a clever way to market healthier ways of living."

"Why does this conversation seem like déjà vu, Ms. Bleecker? Oh, that's right, we had it yesterday—and I'm already tired of it." The detective sergeant leans across the table. "And speaking of healthier ways of living, what did you do *after* you closed up the Garden Spot Café last night?"

"Well, what I do every night—drove home, finished what homework I had, pressed my school uniform for the next morning while catching some Netflix or YouTube, and then I went to bed, reading myself to sleep."

"And your grandparents can corroborate this?"

"Of course they can, I have to check in with them all the time or they worry, especially Grams."

"So, you're telling me that you didn't go out last night. After you arrived home?"

"Nope, sorry."

Zang gives me a big toothy grin. "And what if we have video footage that reveals the opposite of what you just told me?"

Oh shit, she's got me. Yes, I did go out last night. Caught in a lie.

My vegan goose is cooked.

41

"Let me show you something that's very enlightening then."

Zang rises to the TV and hits the button of the DVR player. On the screen, images roll of Lois J. Cain. Disturbing images. Somebody cut all this close-circuit television footage together. And it's like watching the most chilling horror movie of your life. The time stamp reads 12:13 a.m.

Lois holds her bags and has a worried expression on her face. She leaves her suite in a rush and grabs the elevator. She keeps looking around like somebody is going to sneak up from behind and grab her. As Lois stumbles into the elevator and heads down from the ninth floor, the elevator bings and stops on the sixth. The doors slide open. Nobody steps in. Lois looks petrified. She holds the door and peeks out into the hallway. It's eerie to see her so scared. Then she quickly hits the DOORS SHUT button and goes down the rest of the way. She ignores the desk clerk in front, who is busy doing something else and doesn't see her leave.

Lois goes out the front entrance. She looks around, waiting. A silver minivan pulls up. The timestamp reads 12:15 a.m. The electric door on the side of the van slides open and Lois climbs inside, then the door slides closed, and the driver takes off.

What's not as chilling is Lois leaving in the middle of the night.

What's not as chilling is Lois looking scared like somebody is after her.

What *is* chilling is that the girl picking Lois up in the mini-van looks like me.

Exactly like me.

42

"That could be anybody," I say. "There are lots of tall, skinny girls with dark hair who look like me."

"Oh? And are they readers of Lois J. Cain?"

"She's a New York Times bestselling author—I certainly hope so."

"You're not convincing, Ms. Bleecker," Zang says, "and the show isn't over yet."

"What about the sixth floor?" I say. "When the doors opened?"

Zang shakes her head. "Security cameras didn't show anything."

"You mean the door just opened by itself?"

"Looks that way. Or somebody pressed the button, decided not to take the elevator, and left. But that's not the point." Zang hits the button on the player. "*This* is."

On the screen is somebody who resembles me—dressed in dark clothes, monochromatic high-top sneakers, and wearing a black ball cap— and is skulking around Main Street. The hair is tied up and put under the hat, but despite the dark, baggy clothes, you can tell it's a slender female about my size. And she walks a lot like me. Of course, I know it is me. Because where the footage is timestamped at 11:17 p.m., I was on the prowl. If Zang links this footage to Lois's kidnapping, I'm sunk. Pretty sure.

"Again," I say. "That could be anybody."

Zang watches my face carefully. She's good and I'm pretty sure she has her own, built-in polygraph test and bullshit detector. I could fluster Detective Timmons with my feminine charms, but this investigator is unflappable.

"So where were you again at, say, 11:17 last night?"

I'm going to have to choose my next words well.

They still hang people in Washington State.

Look what happened to Westley Allan Dodd.

Taut rope, meet neck, *snap!*

Zang stares at me like I imagine an eager hangman would.

43

OK, since this manuscript is my confessional, as I said, forgive me father for I have sinned—a lot— and I can reveal everything here. Yes, I am innocent of one crime but not innocent of another. No, I did not kidnap Lois J. Cain, but, yes, I am guilty. But there were cameras where I did my deed. So how much can I reveal to Detective Zang without incriminating myself in a different crime?

It's like Zang said, death and tragedy do follow wherever I go. No, I didn't murder anyone last night, so don't worry. But I could have. I really could have if I wasn't trying to be careful. The fact that I've been making a concerted effort to keep the Other Clare on the down-low has been a year-long struggle. It's like trying to keep a Bengal tiger caged with balsa wood bars. The tiger sees the bars and may acknowledge them as such, but eventually, that big jungle cat will take a swipe at what imprisons it and test it out. When those balsa wood bars splinter like toothpicks, the beast not only comes out, but she comes out pissed for being locked away so long on a lie.

Well, that she-tiger in the ball cap was out on the prowl last night.

And she fed.

Let's back up to a year ago. Back to when Wade Braden

crossed the line with me. Wade is one of the most popular guys in school. He's on all the sports teams—cross country, basketball, as well as being in extracurricular organizations like debate club, et cetera. Wade is also too handsome for his own good. He's had everything easy in life having semi-wealthy parents who are pillars in the Pickman Flats community. He has the perfect smile, the perfect body, and always knows the right thing to say.

But like me, Wade has a dark side.

A year ago, he tried to assault me sexually.

And before his attempt on me, he attacked Julie.

It happened at a party that I didn't attend. In fact, Julie and I don't usually attend the parties that all the popular kids like Amity Liston and her dearly departed friends, Hope Dalquist and Mercy Franks, did. So, the one week I was down with a twenty-four-hour virus (yes, vegans get sick too, just less so), Julie went to this party, coaxed to attend by Wade.

Pretty sure it was a group effort on the part of Mercy, Wade, and Hope. Amity wasn't there that night either. Lucky for her. One of the God Squad must have slipped something into her drink. There was a date rape drug going around called Sleeping Beauty. It numbs you to pain and consciousness like an anesthetized tooth. In a back bedroom at Wade's house, a drugged Julie was fondled, groped, and then nearly raped by Wade. Mercy recorded the whole thing on her tablet. Well, Wade tried to finish what he started with Julie, but he had had too much to drink. Doesn't matter, what he did was enough.

Later, Wade and Mercy tried the same thing on me up in the belfry of DeFeo Catholic High.

What they didn't count on was the Other Clare.

She lives for that shit. She's my Shadow Avenger.

Mercy fell to her death (the Other Clare didn't push her, Mercy backed up and leaned against a crumbling stone structure). Later, I blackmailed Wade to go along with my story to clear me—which is ridiculous as I was the intended victim. After that, I Taser-zapped his balls and told him I'd get revenge. And if he ever tried anything like that on me, Julie, or *any* girl at DeFeo again, it would be sooner rather than later.

The tablet was destroyed but not before I copied the footage onto a flash drive.

Julie has never seen the footage. And, thankfully, she does not recall anything that happened that night after Sleeping Beauty's narcotic embrace. For that, I thank God almighty. If Julie had to recall that horrible event repeatedly, Wade would not be alive today. There's nothing I can do with the footage. Can't expose Wade with it by putting it online because it would expose Julie—and I cannot even take it to the police because it would likely implicate me too. This I'm not one hundred percent sure about, but I have held onto the footage for a year, which could make me an accessory. "The law is some tricky shit," as Geena Davis said in *Thelma and Louise.*

So, I've held onto the footage and have kept tabs on Wade.

And he's been keeping tabs on me keeping tabs.

He's leery of me and always makes a wide berth whenever I stalk down the hall.

Lately, though, I think Wade's forgotten.

But I have a memory like an African elephant—I don't forget!

This year, a new girl transferred to our school, Laurie Meeks. She's a kind of corn-fed, plain Jane girl from a tiny town called Colfax, where agriculture is all the rage. Wade's been the kind of guy to have his pick of the litter of cute and cuddly girls. Lately, he's kind of gotten a rep at school based on revelations of his past exploits. Most of the cute and cuddly girls now avoid him like anthrax. It didn't help that the major support system that had enabled him, the God Squad—Amity, Hope, and Mercy—are no more. Hope and Mercy are in the ground (except, with help from their influential parents, they've had streets and parks re-named after them, ugh). And Amity, as you know, is fully employed in Clare cosplay. She once had a thing for Wade last year, hell we all kind of did, but like I said, he's sweet poison now. That's because a rumor started around school (spread anonymously by me) that he's a rapist.

But new girls like Laurie Meeks don't know that. Nobody really cozied up to Laurie when she first came to class. Yeah, at school, I've kind of thought of myself as the Champion of Misfits. Of course, I elected myself to that role as I'm the ultimate misfit with a vengeance. To tell you the truth, though, nothing really struck me as interesting about Laurie. She's a good Christian girl and all that, her family seems well-balanced, but she's about as boring as tap water. When you gaze into her hazel eyes, there's really nothing there. It's not like the emotional void that dwells behind my eyes, only vacancy. Like the lights are on but nobody's home. Honestly, I tried to strike up conversations with Laurie to get a sense of her, but they were awkward, stilted, and deadly dull. So, I kind of wrote her off. Let's face it, I have my own problems.

But I grew interested in Laurie when Wade did.

First, I noticed Wade moving up a few seats in class when Laurie sat in the middle row and Wade hung out close to the back, then I caught them chatting in the hallways. One morning, they were holding pinkies as they were strolling toward school. They quickly dropped the lover act when crossing the Lord's Prayer seal on the front steps and inside because Sister Prudence Head, pit bull for Principal Aileen, has a no PDA policy that she polices with an iron hand like a Nazi SS officer.

"*Sister Head ain't gettin' no head*," I've heard a few boys chant behind her back. *Quietly* behind her back.

So, naturally, any interest Wade Braden has in a girl at this point interests me. Casually, I employed Amity and Julie as spies to keep tabs on Wade in classes I don't have with him, and other times outside of school. Though I don't think I've had to twist their arms too hard, each of them had a thing for Wade at one time, so a new girl entranced with him is always of interest.

Then it came to my attention that Wade has been taking Laurie out on some dates—to the movies and a few times to dinner. Later, I got word from Jeremy Herrera, one of Wade's best buddies who's always flirting with me (and I use that to my advantage), that Wade was planning to introduce Laurie to Lamb Hollow.

The infamous hollow lies at the edge of town in the woods. It has a reputation of many girls losing their virginities there in parked cars since the time automobiles arrived in Pickman Flats.

Since my grandparent's house runs along the train tracks and the woods, Lamb's Hollow is fairly close.

It's a bit of a walk, and I couldn't take the Leaf. First, I didn't want anyone to see my red car there, which is easy to spot. And second, it's parked in the driveway. If I took the car, the motion-detector floodlights would snap on and alert my grandparents. Their room is right above the carport and Grams, being a worry-wart, and who often has to get up in the middle of the night to relieve herself because she has a bladder the size of a garbanzo bean, is a light sleeper. She'd notice.

So how did I get spotted on camera?

Well, I was so enamored with Lois J. Cain, that I forgot my phone and book back at the G-Spot. Since I have an extra key, I thought I would pop in and grab them.

Serial killers historically mess up—sometimes the smallest and stupidest things. A hardware store receipt led to the apprehension of Ed "The Plainfield Butcher" Gein. A parking ticket nailed David "Son of Sam" Berkowitz. A minor traffic accident led police to Aileen "Damsel of Death" Wuornos. Not that I'm like them, but when you're trying to be careful, you slip up over the dumbest stuff. Now here I am, sitting in an interrogation room, feeling the hangman's noose tightening around my neck.

But at least I saved Laurie Meeks from Wade.

Give me some credit for that.

44

And it all happened like a scene in a movie.

EXT. LAMB HOLLOW — NIGHT

Clare, dressed in black, weaves her way through
the trees, many dropping their October leaves.
A light autumn rain patters down, and her
pleather hiking boots make sucking sounds in
the deep mud. It's a cold night and her breath
vapors as she makes her way to -- a BMW 745
that sits in the clearing.

Clare crouches and sidles up to Wade's Beemer.
All the windows are obscured by a thin layer of
fog. The car shakes a little. She pulls something out of her coat. Long, dark, and slender.
A weapon? She peeks in the driver's side
window.

CLARE'S POV — Wade and Laurie making out. Wade
is all over her like a cheap suit, sucking at

her mouth, tonguing her lips. Laurie isn't used
to this kind of aggressive affection. She's
trying to hold him off. One of Wade's hands
vanishes inside her unbuttoned blouse.

LAURIE: That's enough.

WADE: It's OK, baby.

Wade ignores her and keeps at it. Laurie pushes
his eager hand away.

LAURIE: That's far enough. Stop.

WADE: You're so hot. I love you.

LAURIE: I love you too. But can't we slow down?

WADE: It's been three weeks.

LAURIE: I know... I'm just not...ready... Can't
we wait?

WADE: It's not gonna get any better than right
now, baby. Our love is like a wildfire.

Clare rolls her eyes at the tawdry line.

Really?

LAURIE: Maybe we should get going. Shelley is
going to worry.

WADE: You told your mom you were staying at
Shelley's so we could be out all night.
Tonight's the night. Let's consecrate our love.

CLARE: (mutters) Holy hell, Wade is a slice of pizza, extra cheese.

LAURIE: Did you hear that?

WADE: What?

LAURIE: Sounded like a voice.

WADE: It's the furious beating of my heart. And it wants you. Now. I've never loved a girl like I've loved you.

LAURIE: You've brought a lot of girls here?
WADE: No, only you, baby. You're special. You're my queen of the night.

CLARE: More like the sacrificial lamb.
Wade gets more aggressive, pushing his hand back under her blouse with one hand. And unzipping the fly of his jeans with the other.

LAURIE: What are you doing?

WADE: You're getting me so hot.

LAURIE: I don't want to do this. I want to wait.

WADE: Just touch it. That's all. And then watch me play with it.

CLARE: Oh, hell no.

Clare reaches up and pounds on the window with

the metal cylinder. Then she blasts the Maglite on them.

CLARE: (lowering her voice a few octaves)
What's going on in there?

Wade and Laurie fumble inside the car.

WADE: Who the hell are you, man?

Clare keeps the light blinding them so they can't see her face.

CLARE: You're trespassing. Y'all need to move this vehicle outta here -- pronto!

WADE: Are you a cop?

CLARE: Security. (she quickly flashes her ball cap, making sure her face is hidden). Now get on out of here and make it easy for yourselves.
WADE: It's not what it looks like... We were just talking.

CLARE: Get this vehicle out of here, son, and take the lady home.

WADE: Who are you?

CLARE: Security.

By this time, the back door of the Beemer opens and Jeremy Herrera steps out. He has lipstick all over his face, his shirt is unbuttoned, and a couple of fresh hickies bruise his neck. A girl in the backseat buttons up her blouse.

JEREMY: Yo, what's going on? Who the hell are you, lady?

Jeremy has a Beretta 9mm in his hand. Where did that come from? He raises the pistol. Clare tosses the Maglite and smashes his hand. The flashlight and the pistol plop into the mud.

JEREMY: That wasn't cool.

CLARE: (to self) This could have gone...better.

Jeremy, a wrestler, immediately tackles her at the waist from behind and they go down. At 190 pounds, he outweighs Clare by sixty.

JEREMY: Do I know you?

CLARE: No.

Her face goes into the thick mud, covering it. Jeremy's putting a chokehold on her. If he applies pressure, she's going to go out like a light. She only has a few seconds.

She punches him in the nuts. And then again. Again.

Jeremy groans and releases his grip around her neck, grabbing his groin.

By this time, Wade has opened the front door and is stepping out of the car, one foot planting in the mud. Clare front kicks the door on him -- it folds on his shin and the window crashes in his face. Wade screams in pain.

Clare runs and retrieves the Maglite from the mud. Time to beat a hasty retreat. Then somebody jumps on her back. It's Laurie.
She's trying to scratch at Clare's eyes.

CLARE: Seriously?

Clare drops to one knee and Laurie flops over Clare's head like a sack of potatoes, crashing into the mud. Instinctively, Clare goes for a throat punch to seal the deal and then stops inches from doing it.

In the murky darkness, Laurie gives her a wide-eyed stare.

LAURIE: What are you waiting for? Do it, freak! DO IT!

Clare picks up the Beretta and tosses it into the shrubs, then lopes off into the woods. Not quite the mission she expected.

45

"Do I need to ask again?" Zang does anyway. "Where were you again at 11:17 last night?"

My response is quick and truthful. Mostly. The detective is impatient. Why I didn't take my car. Truth. Why I went back to the G-Spot and was caught on camera. Truth. And what I did after that. Lie.

"You went to visit your boyfriend, Truman Quirk?"

"That's right."

"OK, back up. First, why were you dressed like that? In dark clothes, gloves, and a hat that says 'security' on it."

"It was raining, those are my normal clothes, and I didn't want my hair to get wet."

"Security?"

Shrug. "First hat I could find."

"And you went to see your boyfriend." Zang studies me like a poker player, trying to gauge if I have any tells that will indicate that I'm lying. Moving my eyes. Change in breathing. Shuffling my feet. Moving my hands. Nope, I'm as still as Mona Lisa. "Why?"

"Well, to tell you the God's honest truth, I missed him." I

shrug, acting needy and insecure. "He came into the café earlier in the day and we didn't leave things on the best note. Maybe I subconsciously left my phone at the restaurant to have an excuse to go and get it. And to, you know, see him afterwards. Stranger things have happened."

"And you went into his house?"

"No, to his window. Sometimes I knock on it and we talk."

"How Romeo and Juliet."

"Well, I really kind of see us as Holmes and Watson. Cumberbatch and Martin, of course, *not* Ferrell and Reilly."

"Holmes and Watson are both men."

"One can dream."

Zang rolls her eyes. "I'm not going there... What did you do? What did you talk about?"

Letting out a tired sigh, I tell the detective I only wanted to tell him that I loved him. Really loved him.

"And after you got your phone, you didn't call or text him?"

"You can't text matters of the heart. You can't text a kiss. We needed face time. Tactile sensuality."

"How romantic. How long were you there?"

"Probably about forty-five minutes."

"And then what did you do after?"

"Went back home and crashed."

Zang looks at me for several moments. "And I suppose he can corroborate all this, your boyfriend?"

Well, that's the tricky part. If he doesn't, I'm in deep shit. Deeper than I already am.

All I can do is nod.

I really wish I could make that phone call.

Zang slides my phone across the table as if reading my mind (hope not).

"You have one phone call. Who's it going to be?"

"My grandparents."

"You have five minutes." Zang rises and starts to head out of the interrogation room. "You wait right here."

Yeah, I'll wait right here. Where else would I go?

Why do I feel like Dorothy in *The Wizard of Oz* when the Wicked Witch of the West hands her an hourglass and gives her only minutes before her doom?

46

"Oh, man, I wish I had some popcorn. This is getting good."

"Shut up."

The dead postal laughs in that annoying way he does, which sounds like a dying hyena.

"Lying to the police," Mailman Bob says. "You've really dug yourself into an early grave. You're not as smart as you think. You're a seventeen-year-old girl. Zang's twice your age and she's been around the block a few more times. Suspicion is her business —and business is good when you're around. It's only a matter of time before you're caught. You've gotten away with my death. You've gotten away with other people's deaths. But you won't get away forever. The rope is only so long before your sweet little neck is going to be hanging from the end of it."

"Wow, brilliant metaphor. Bravo."

"You think so, huh?" Bob says proudly, winking one of his bloodshot eyes at me. "Yeah, it was pretty good."

"It was forced and cliché—just like its author."

Bob bares his yellow teeth at me. "Do you know it's going around school that somebody attacked Wade? It's only a matter of time before the police connect you with that. That 'security' hat is what's going to link you."

"Tell me something I don't know, dick head," I say, dialing. "Now shut up, I have a phone call to make."

As the phone is ringing, I want to tell Bob that I don't have the hat with 'Security' on it anymore. After making sure Laurie wasn't assaulted by Wade, I went home and removed everything I was wearing. My boots left some serious footprints in the mud out there, and if there are any clothing fibers at the scene, it could all come back to me. So, I incinerated all my clothes with some lighter fluid in Gramps's pot-belly stove in his workshop. And then I climbed the wisteria trellis up the side of the house in my underwear in the chilly October rain to my second-floor bedroom window. Bet the neighbors would have loved seeing that. There's still video footage of me wearing that hat, but maybe I can do something about that too. Maybe.

"Grandma, hey, guess what? I'm in jail!"

Two minutes of holding the phone away from my ear. I can still hear Grams.

"Can you put Gramps on? Please."

Waiting. Shouting in the background. Muffled voices. Fumbling with the phone.

"You're in jail?" he comes on the line and asks.

"Gramps, I don't have long to talk, so please listen. I'm being held at the police station. They think I kidnapped Lois J. Cain—which is stupid. This Detective Zang is really harassing me. Pretty sure it's because Timmons attacked me last year and I had to defend myself. Now they're coming after me with some trumped-up charges. Can you guys come down? Or maybe only you should, Gramps, you're the calm one. Yes, I'm supposed to have a lawyer, but she hasn't shown up yet. See you soon. Love you too."

Mailman Bob laughs. "Aw, that last part was sweet. Imagine how disappointed your grandparents are going to be when they find out who you really are. What you've done. Who you've killed."

"It's my mission in life to protect them from that."

"You couldn't protect a swizzle stick in a cup of coffee."

"Leave me alone, ass face."

Zang marches back into the interrogation room. "Excuse me?"

47

"Nothing," I say.

Detective Zang regards me like somebody who might stare at a butterfly in a killing jar.

"How's Gramps?" she says.

"Well, I assume you've been recording me since I walked in here, so you probably know."

Zang nods.

"And for your information, these aren't 'trumped-up charges' for some kind of revenge. This is a serious investigation with you as a key suspect."

"It's ridiculous that I'm a suspect. What's my motive? I've seen enough movies to know that when somebody doesn't have a motive, it's a little unlikely they did the crime. What am I going to do, steal a van, kidnap her, hide her in my grandparents' garage, and force her to write me books like in that Kathy Bates movie?"

"Motive can be important, that's true. But some people are beyond motive. Some people are just plain batshit crazy and want to watch the world burn."

"So you're saying I'm batshit crazy?"

Zang regards me again like I'm a rare species of bloodsucking leech. "You tell me, Ms. Bleecker."

I tell her nothing.

Silence for an eternity.

"You're free to go. For now."

"Really?"

Zang mocks me. "*Really*. After you mentioned your boyfriend, Truman Quirk, Officer Alvarado hauled him down here too. I spoke with him. He verified your story."

Truman, I just fell in love with you—truly, madly, deeply, like a normal girl. Are we too young to elope and get married?

"But don't get too comfortable on the outside, Clare. I'll be watching you like a hound watches a fox."

"Fox hunting is a disgusting 'sport' and should be banned." I give her the V symbol with my index and middle finger. "Go vegan."

"Something tells me that that vegan BS is just a front to make you seem compassionate and caring, to hide the cold and calculating predator within."

"You said I could leave, right?"

"For now."

48

Zang leads me out of the interrogation room. Truman's waiting in the hallway. He gets the biggest bear hug of his life, or at least, my life. Then I hold him close and whisper,

"Thank you."

"We have a lot to talk about later."

"I know."

Then I give him a big, long kiss right in front of Zang.

The detective rolls her eyes. "Save the sappy teen romance BS for a John Hughes movie."

"Clare?"

Gramps has his cute, worried expression. His black sweatshirt says in gold letters KEEP CALM AND HUG GRANDPA.

So, I do just that.

Then Gramps turns to Detective Zang and wags a finger at her. "My granddaughter is a good girl. And she's also a minor. You pull these kind of Gestapo police state tactics on her again, and I'll get a lawyer better than Johnny Cochran to come down on you like a ton of bricks."

Zang is taken aback. It's good to see. "We were just following up every lead we have in the disappearance of a prominent author, sir." She offers a card to Gramps. "I'm Detective Jacqui Zang, by the way."

Gramps ignores the card and puffs out his chest. "Clare has had some terrible things happen in her life. Worse than most people could bear in a single lifetime. My special girl here has lived with a lot of pain—too much. Please, detective, stop adding to it."

"Noted," the detective says, making her business card vanish and turning away, suddenly distracted with some paperwork.

The man I love most in the world gets a big, ear-to-ear smile from me. "Have I told you today that I love you?"

"Let's get you home," he says, his blue eyes sparkling and his cheeks flushing apple red. "Arleen is making your favorite soup."

"I don't deserve you."

Gramps shakes his head. "No, but we still love you anyway." He peers at Truman. "Need a ride, son?"

Truman looks at me blankly. "Thanks, I'm good."

"Suit yourself."

Gramps has always had some rival male energy when my boyfriend is around. It annoys Truman and makes him anxious, but I think it's pretty cute seeing Gramps get his awkward male hackles up. He truly loves me, this I know. And the way he put that snotty Jacqui Zang in her place—I wanna marry a man like this someday. If there are any men out there like him, that is. Doubt it.

"See you later," Truman says to me, giving me a hangdog look that I suppose is to make me feel guilty that I'm leaving with Gramps instead of him.

"Text me," I say and then blow a kiss.

I would love to tell Gramps who I really am, what makes me tick, how many people I've killed, but I'm afraid he would be disappointed in me and wouldn't care for me like I'm the only daughter he's ever had. It's strange how we have to live a lie to protect those we love. Protect their ideals of us. Gramps protects me from lies, and I protect him from the truth.

If you can find a better, more reciprocal relationship than that, let me know.

49

"It's about time that you learned how to drive a stick," Gramps says, opening the door to his restored, silver '67 Chevy Camaro AKA The Silver Stallion. He ushers me into the driver's seat.

"But I already know how to drive."

He climbs in on the passenger side. "Not a stick. Everyone should know how to drive a stick. You cheat yourself in life if you don't know how to drive a manual transmission."

It takes me five times to let the clutch out easy and not bring the Chevy to a screeching halt in the police station parking lot.

What I *don't* have to do is see Detective Zang watching me from the window. Her death stare weighs about fifty-seven pounds.

Once we're off in the Camaro, I drive slowly. Stopping at a few traffic lights and stop signs causes me to kill the engine a few more times. Gramps just coaxes me along patiently. He never once asks me what happened at the police station. Bless him for that. He's focusing on me driving his "Silver Stallion" like it's the most important thing on the planet right now.

We pull into the driveway, and I kill the Chevy's engine, purposely this time.

"We'll go get your car later after school is out," Gramps says, patting me on the knee.

"Best idea ever."

Gramps disappears into his workshop behind the garage. His home away from home.

As I trod into the house, the scent of my favorite soup, smoky corn chowder, fills the kitchen. Grams turns and has a concerned look on her face. She really wants to say something. and she looks like she's going to burst. Instead, she gives me a big hug. She smells like cooking spices and old lady perfume. Then I hear her sniffling.

"What, Grams?"

"I was so worried."

She gets another hug from me. Probably, I've given more hugs today than the last three years combined.

"There's nothing to worry about," I say, giving her a wet kiss on the cheek. "Nothing at all."

As I sit down at the table and she pours me a big bowl of soup with some Ezekiel bread toast slathered in melted vegan butter and garlic salt, she asks me about everything that happened.

Between slurps of hot chowder, I tell her what I told Zang. Then I realize why Gramps didn't ask me. He'll hear it from Grams later tonight, probably a few times. As Grams gets older, she tends to forget what she previously said and repeats herself. Guess it works for Gramps because he tends to forget what he's been told just as often. They're the perfect couple.

Gramps places her soft hands on my hand that's not shoveling in food like an escapee from Overeater's Anonymous.

"Are you and Truman getting pretty serious?" she says. "Serious enough to sneak out on us in the middle of the night? Serious enough to risk life and limb?"

"It was a onetime thing," I say between bites of garlic toast, trying to make it seem less important with a casual shrug. "Like I said, I totally forgot my book and phone. After that, I swung by and talked to Truman. I really, really missed him."

"But why didn't you just tell us and take your car? This town isn't like it used to be. So many weirdos and murderers running around. Not like it was forty years ago."

If you only knew, Grams.

"Well, I figured you both were asleep, and I didn't want to wake you." Another casual shrug for emphasis. "It's no big deal, really."

Grams nods and sighs.

"There's something...that I've wanted to talk to you about since you started living here," she says, obviously choosing her words carefully. "It's something that your mom should have told you about. But poor Chloe didn't get the chance." Grams shakes her head, and her eyes tear up. "Rest my little girl's sweet soul." She sighs. "And now that you're a mature young lady, like your mom once was, and now that you're starting to see boys more seriously..."

No, not the—

"You know what happens, Clare, between a man and a woman when they're in love and they go to bed together, right?"

Haul me into a police station. Accuse me of kidnapping my favorite author. Hell, arrest me and wrongfully incarcerate me for a crime I didn't commit. But please, please, please don't let my only grandmother give me The Talk. The Sex Talk. To me. Please, God, I pray to you, our Father who art in heaven. Just no.

Grams smiles and nods her head as if getting some vocal confirmation that only she can hear to go ahead. "I know the birds and the bees talk is a little corny and old-fashioned in this day and age, but I guess I'm just a little bit corny and an old-fashioned kind of gal."

Please don't say it.

"If you snuck out to be with Truman to have an unprotected... encounter," she continues, "you need to use protection. We can get you some. For the record, I'm not condoning this kind of unsanctified behavior. I believe you should abstain from sex until marriage like I did with your grandfather. But I don't live your life and I know kids these days do as they please anyway. I'd rather you be safe than sorry." She sighs as if the next few words are taking away copious amounts of energy from her very soul. "If you need some protection, I will go to the drugstore and buy some condoms for you. You're too young to start being a mother. Don't make the same mistake that your mom did."

Wait, I'm a mistake?

"And as much as I would love to be a great-grandmother some-day," Grams continues, "I can wait ten years. And don't get me started about diseases—people can die from syphilis."

"Uh, Grams? News flash—Truman and I are *not* having sex. I *am* waiting until I'm older and it's with somebody I truly care about. Somebody who I'll ensure doesn't have a raging case of syphilis. And no, I don't need any condoms, not now, not *ever*. Thank you."

Grams only stares at me.

So, I smile. "Great soup, by the way."

She smiles. "Oh, and have you been fooling around with the piano?"

They have a baby grand in the living room. Grams plays it from time to time. My mom played it, too. I took piano lessons for a few years. But I just didn't have the love for it. I shake my head. "Nope, sorry. Why?"

"Well, I was dusting it. Then decided to dig out some old sheet music and play. One of the treble wires is missing."

"Maybe Gramps was messing with it."

"He wasn't."

A treble wire is a thin wire. Hmmm.

"I don't know."

50

Tonight, I lucked out and wasn't scheduled to work at the G-Spot. I feel like holing up in my room tonight and being alone. Except I've had to text Amity and Julie non-stop since I got home. They got the same official story Zang got. Truman doesn't text me, so I text him and tell him we'll talk this weekend about stuff. It's a relief that he's cool with that.

After a long day, I press my uniform for the morning. It's going to be all eyes on Clare so the best thing I can do is look sharp (like I always do) and act like nothing happened. Julie and Truman will keep quiet about what happened, but I'm pretty sure Amity won't. She's a fountain of gossip that spills everywhere to save herself from bursting at the seams. Who knows, maybe my street cred will go up with my fellow students, who are all quiet rebels at best. But I guarantee I won't score any points with the sisters, especially Sister Prudence Head. Pretty sure she'll use today's incident of being dragged out of class by the police as an excuse to put her raven's talons in me even more. She'll never relent.

Bad habits die hard. Particularly nun's habits.

Hitting the pillow, sleep is playing hard to get. Grabbing Thompson's *The Killer Inside Me*, I read about half of a chapter, which might help me get sleepy, but I can't focus. The words blur together.

No rest for the wicked indeed.

Then, I recall that time back in Colorado when I was eight. A memory that's kind of hazy. It's back when I was with the Firefly Girls of America in my red, blue, and yellow outfit selling Firefly Cookies door to door and going on nature hikes. What happened during that fateful day was, without hyperbole or even the remotest bit of exaggeration, one of the defining points of my life.

It runs often like a looped video clip:

EXT. WOODS — DAY — FLASHBACK

CLARE, age eight, along with her Firefly Girls
colleagues, EMMYLOU HOLBROOK, DEZSEA LARSON,
and MELISSA KITTERAGE, all roughly the same age
as Clare, hike through the woods along with
their den mother, MRS. HARRIS, thirty-two.
The girls stop at a clearing on a hilly green
meadow to pick some colorful purple and yellow
wildflowers along the way. It's a rather tran-
quil scene, the August sun beaming down.
Clare, in her own world, strays off from the
group, following a Monarch butterfly that flut-
ters from one flower to the next. She watches
the beautiful insect with intense fascination.

A MAN in his late thirties ambles out from the
woods, wearing a flannel shirt and a five-day's
growth beard. He wears a troubled look on his
face. He's sketchier than Da Vinci's notebook.
He strolls up to the den mother. At first, she
looks a little nervous. This stranger looks a
bit problematic.

MAN: Hey, can you help me? I've been hiking

around here for the last hour looking for the
lake. Feeling a little bit like Hansel without
Gretel.

MRS. HARRIS: (points) It's back that way about
a mile and a half. Can't miss it. Just follow
the signs.

MAN: Oh, hey, thanks. (gazes over at the girls,
smiles) I remember being that age once. The
world was so new. Untainted... Pure...
Beautiful...

MRS. HARRIS: (smiles politely) Um, yes. Well,
the world is what you make it.

MAN: Yes it is. Very wise. Well said. (Strolls
past den mother) Thanks for all the help.

MRS. HARRIS: Happy to do it.

The den mother takes her attention off the
flannel-shirt man for a millisecond to check on
the girls, Dezsea, Melissa, and Emmylou.
Where's Clare?

The man produces an extendable law enforcement
baton from his dirty jeans, flicks it open.
Smacks Mrs. Harris in the temple. She drops
like a sack of laundry.

He pulls out a pair of handcuffs and cuffs Mrs.
Harris. She's dazed, mumbling something inco-
herent. Her pepper spray tumbles out of her
backpack. The man grins at the useless weapon.
He then strolls across the meadow after the

girls, who are oblivious to what's happening.
He whistles "Ring Around the Rosie."

Alone on the other side of the hilly meadow,
Clare now has the butterfly perching on the end
of her finger. She studies it.

CLARE: You're such a pretty girl. So beautiful
and strong. Wings of yellow fire. Pretty,
pretty girl.

Distant SCREAMS from over the hill shake Clare
from her world. The butterfly flitters off.
Clare runs back toward the group. Then she sees
something so horrifying, she drops down into
the grass.

From her vantage point, she can only watch
helplessly at the horrible scene and listen to
the agonizing sounds. The girls are screaming
and crying.

CLARE'S POV —The Man is torturing Mrs. Harris
with a lock-blade knife and her pepper spray
while the girls, each bound to one another,
watch in horror.

Clare cannot move. She's petrified in fear. And
if she tries to run away, she'll be captured
and tortured for sure. She starts to cry, but
at the same time, watches in the same fascination that she expressed watching the butterfly.
The August sun beaming down.

51

That first memory is clear. The second part of that memory is a bit more jarring, like the crappy DVD of a Redbox movie you rented when it's scratched and playing erratically:

EXT. MEADOW — DAY

Clare observes the Man Wearing Orange
Sunglasses ravaging the corpse of her den
mother. The other three Firefly girls tied up,
weeping, frightened.

Clare wants to run but she can't. She's
scared...and curious. SCREAMS from the girls as
the MWOS ends their lives. Clare watches.
Indifferent. Like watching the butterfly
before.

THE MAN WEARING ORANGE SUNGLASSES
Finishes his work. He doesn't even try to hide
the bodies or what he did. He wants somebody to
find them. He rummages through the den mother's

purse. Takes what little cash she has. Not so
much a robbery, just to take something. And the
wedding ring on her dead finger. Trophy.
He hears movement in the meadow. Looks up. The
wind sweeps the grass like wild strands of
green hair. Is there more fauna among the
flora?

Stuffing the money and ring in his pocket, he
heads through the meadow toward ––
CLARE who doesn't move. If she does, The Man
Wearing Orange Sunglasses will see her. If she
doesn't, he'll walk right on top of her.
The Man Wearing Orange Sunglasses stalks
closer.

Clare decides to run for it. Rises. Takes off.
Gets seventeen feet and then trips over a rock.
Falls face-first into the grass.

The Man Wearing Orange Sunglasses is upon her.
His shadow looms over her. He smiles.

MWOS: Looks like I missed one. Do you want to
see God?

CLARE: LEAVE ME ALONE.

MWOS: Oh, I will. Later.

The Man Wearing Orange Sunglasses fumbles in
his pants pockets for another zip tie. Doesn't
find one. Damn.

Clare fixates on a gaudy tattoo on the man's
right forearm. It's a skull with a dagger

through it and a scroll with a Latin phrase on it that she doesn't understand -- *MEMENTO MORI.* ("*Remember, you will die.*")

Clare, knowing the fate that's about to over-come her, doesn't scream or cry. She sits, quiet, studying the man's fascinating tattoo. Her mind goes into another place.

The Man Wearing Orange Sunglasses grabs his knife and goes to slit Clare's throat when -- SCREAMING from the trail.

TWO BACKPACKERS, a man and a woman in their mid-thirties, stumble upon the four corpses. The woman screams.

The Man Wearing Orange Sunglasses takes one last look at Clare —- no time to kill her. He kicks her in the forehead with one of his logging boots, as hard as he can.

CLARE falls back into the soft green grass. Her red beret tumbling off her head. Her ears ring-ing. The sun fading. All goes black.

THE MAN WITH ORANGE SUNGLASSES swipes up the beret. Inside, written in Sharpie, is Clare's FULL NAME. The man, red beret in hand, escapes across the meadow, away from the screaming backpackers. He's too far away for the witnesses to identify except for the color of his shirt. He gets away.

THE BACKPACKER MAN runs up to where Clare is. The woman is still screaming and crying. He

discovers Clare's unconscious body and kneels
down. A big boot print on her forehead.
The Backpacker checks her pulse. Low and slow
but still alive. He drops his backpack and
pulls out a satellite phone, starts dialing.

A MEDIVAC HELICOPTER lands in the field.

PARAMEDICS put Clare onto a stretcher and carry
her to the helicopter.

INSIDE THE HELICOPTER they work on her, giving
her oxygen, trying to save her life, rushing
her to a hospital.

CLARE'S POV —Through eye slits. Hazy and dream-
like. The paramedics seem like aliens with long
arms reaching over her. Like aliens in their
spaceship have abducted her. They work over her
with concerned faces. Scrutinizing her.

52

The story ends happily though. A few months after The Man with Orange Sunglasses did that to my Firefly friends and me, he was cornered in Greely, Colorado at a biker bar by some under-cover cops. They tried to take him down, but he fled. They shot the suspect multiple times, and he died. That's the way life ends for some people, shot and killed, face down in the cold, dark street like John Dillinger. Life gives them exactly what they gave life— emptiness, coldness, and cruelty.

The suspect's name was Garry Lee Harding.

Even though the event still lingers in my mind, especially when I close my eyes for the night, at least Harding's death gave me some closure.

Will I die the same way as Garry Lee Harding someday? Shot and killed, face down on a cold, dark street? Does that happen to all killers in the end, figuratively or literally? History suggests it does, and I'm a bit of a history buff, especially criminal history, so I know.

When my time inevitably comes, I either hope that my grand-parents will have lived to a ripe old age and have passed on, or that they can somehow find a way to forgive me and live with my actions. Yeah, I can be empty and cold, but I've never gone out and killed anyone just to kill. Cruelty is not my style. Everyone I've ever killed provoked me. They expected to swat a defenseless fly and instead they found a spider full of piss and venom. It's an easy mistake. My hope, though, is that those I care about, Julie and Truman, and especially my grandparents, don't have to bear the burden of the mistakes that others made against me—and then me making them into bigger, molehill-into-mountain mistakes.

And then there's poor Lois J. Cain.

Who would kidnap her and why?

Sure, like most famous authors, she's had her share of stalkers, but most of them turned out to be harmless. Stalkers, for the most part, are harmless... until they aren't. Could it be somebody who was at the Carver High School event?

One thing's for sure, I'm not going to get any proper sleep until this is resolved. Detective Zang certainly isn't going to give me any rest either. Guess instead of watching *Mindhunter* on Netflix, I'm going to have to become a detective. For reals.

Since sleep tonight is nothing but a dwindling hope, I get online and look up Lois's past stalkers. Many were just casual ones at book-signing events. Some even showed up outside the gates of her house in Montpelier, Rhode Island.

And then there was Tommy Keller—the King Kong of stalkers who went a little ape.

He was a preacher's son who was brought up in the Pentecostal churches of Jasper, Alabama. He was subject to all kinds of physical and emotional abuse during his life. He did petty crimes and spent time in and out of various boys' homes. Keller eventually made his home in the Pacific Northwest—Ravensdale, Washington—a tiny mountain town. Apparently, Keller had a friend who lived in Ravensdale that he served time with at a boys' home and was looking for a fresh start. Funny how the best intentions often transform into the worst of actions. Keller's no exception. In fact, Tommy Keller is a cautionary tale. A boogeyman story you tell around the fire at night to scare your fellow campers.

Three years ago, during her last book tour in Seattle, Lois reported that somebody was inside her room at the Roosevelt

Hotel. She caught a man standing over her bed, who looked like a hotel employee, recording footage of her sleeping with his phone (he must've used some kind of Infra-red photo app because it was dark). Tommy Keller—a literal Peeping Tom.

When Lois awoke, she later told police that she was petrified, afraid that Keller would assault her in bed. But her midnight caller fled. She later identified Tommy Keller from a police line-up. Keller, who dressed as an employee of the hotel and had stolen a key to Lois's room, was only charged with trespassing and invasion of privacy. He got three years. Three years. He went up for parole on May 21. My birthday. Weird coincidence.

Tommy Keller seems like the boogeyman I'm searching for. Looking up Keller's information, he seems to still live in Washington state. That makes sense since he can't leave the state due to his parole.

Ah, there's a Thomas A. Keller, age forty-nine, who lives in Ravensdale, Washington.

About a four-hour drive from Pickman Flats.

It seems for Tommy "King Kong of Stalkers" Keller, you *can* go home again.

The other Thomas Kellers I locate are either too old, have the wrong middle initial, or live across the country. How likely is it that King Kong hopped in his car and drove here? Pretty likely, actually.

Detective Zang is pretty sharp. No doubt she's probably looking into this angle too.

The picture of Tommy Keller I find is a little old. He has a beard and glasses in the photo, but he could be clean-shaven and wearing contacts now. Who knows? And the Cayuse Hotel connection is also a possibility—it seems like Keller's modus operandi. Maybe Keller knew about the cameras? Maybe he got Lois's contact info, threatened her with some kind of extortion or something, and told her to meet his accomplice (who oddly looked like me) down at the entrance. Maybe the King Kong of stalkers threatened to do something to her or somebody she cares about if she didn't meet him.

Who was the girl? Keller's daughter? Girlfriend? Somebody else Keller kidnapped and forced to do his dirty work?

All this information is finally making me drowsy. Time to crash for a few hours before school.

And I slept like a baby.

53

Morning: coffee, Julie, Amity (ugh), and then school. We serial killers love our routine, even if it's the most boring one you can possibly imagine. It keeps us sane (heh).

"What do you think of Plum's hair?" Julie asks me.

"It definitely suits her. Her name's Plum after all."

"I wanna do something like that."

"Color your hair?"

Julie nods. "Something wild and crazy. I'm tired of the same ol' same ol'."

"There's a strict policy against piercings, hair coloring, and street clothes at DeFeo."

Julie shrugs. "Maybe I won't go there anymore."

I stop the car. "All right, what are you *really* talking about here?"

"Oh, so I have your undivided attention now?"

"And what's that supposed to mean?"

She shakes her head. "I'm just tired. And bored. And so fucking lonely."

"Oh, gee, thanks."

"You know what I mean. You have Truman. I don't have anyone."

"Is that what this is about? You wanting a boyfriend?"

"Who says it has to be a boy?"

Well, I always suspected my best friend had a thing for girls. Now maybe it's more than suspicion. "Uh, OK. Anyone in particular, male *or* female, that you have in mind?"

Julie looks off into the distance. "We're going to be late for school."

I smile. "Nice deflection. I'm onto you, bitch."

Julie laughs. "You wish. Bitch."

"No, *you* wish."

We have a laugh, and head to DeFeo. As we do, I think about possibilities for Julie. I'm no matchmaker, and I can't think of anyone who might be into her. Something to think about, I guess. Maybe Truman has some ideas. No, I can't be distracted with that right now. I'll have to be sharp when I get to school. Wade and Jeremy will be there, and I need to observe.

Wade is tooling around the hallowed hallways on crutches. Guess he hurt his leg doing something he shouldn't have been doing.

"Wade and Jeremy got jumped by a bunch of Carver guys," Amity tells me as I stroll into the building. "Guess Wade and Jeremy beat their asses, but Wade hurt his leg kicking one of them."

"Oh really?" I blurt out, trying not to laugh.

"You think that's funny?"

Actually, yes. It's funny these bros who pump up each other down in the weight room every morning before class must invent a bravado bullshit story. They can't admit that some skinny girl with a bad attitude and zero tolerance for date rape kicked the testosterone-laden shit out of them. OK, I didn't really beat them up that bad. Jeremy Herrera had me in a pretty good hold. He could have definitely snapped me in two like a dry twig. But I fight dirty —and all is fair in love and war, as they say. And good thing for the dirt, the mud, all over my face or they might have recognized me. Hell, maybe they did. Maybe Wade knows. Maybe that's why he's going around school floating that lie like a hot-air balloon. It's like when Hope and Mercy died, he's now the big hero at school. Everyone is patting Wade on the back and telling him congratulations for showing those secular, public school Carver boys that when you're educated by dour nuns, you're not a person to be messed with. Although, I notice Laurie Greene is staying pretty mum about it. Jeremy's girlfriend, Angela Grimes, who was in the car and a little out of it, didn't see anything, so she's going along with it. Laurie's silence is incriminating. Wonder if she'll crack?

After lunch, I go up to Wade when he's not surrounded by false admirers. Yeah, it's pretty risky, but hey, I'm a serial killer— and we live for risky behavior! Yes, I'm trying to get better, but nobody's perfect. On Wade's notebook is a colorful *Duck Dodgers in the 24½th Century* sticker. Heh, more like, *Fuck Dodgers in the 21st Century!*

"Heard about your skirmish," I tell him, walking up behind Goldilocks and giving him a friendly punch in the back of one well-toned arm. "Pretty badass protecting your lady love like that. Downright white knight of you, Prince Valiant."

Wade recoils when he sees me, and so I flash the widest Cheshire Cat grin I can.

"Y-yeah," he says. "Those Carver guys... they had it coming. They must've thought Jeremy and I were a couple of pussies."

"Did they mess up your leg pretty good?"

"It's just a little tender. It'll heal."

Wade seems like he wants to sink into the brick wall behind him.

"So, any idea who did this heinous deed to one of our DeFeo own?"

He shrugs. "Just some Carver pricks. I've seen them hanging around the Dancing Goats."

Must admit, Wade's pretty good at the lying. Almost as good as me. He looks at me directly, not looking away or up, like many liars do, his voice doesn't waver. He's told this lie so many times in the last two days he's beginning to believe it himself. Bravo, liar, liar, proverbial pants on freakin' fire.

"Maybe we should form a posse and go after them," I say. "We can let those Carver High pricks know we're *not* a bunch of pussies over here at DeFeo. We do have the Lord on our side—it could be like the second Crusades."

Wade gives a fake laugh. "Wow, that's kind of beautiful. Deranged and weird, but beautiful."

I toss back my dark hair like a supermodel at a Cosmo photo shoot. "You've just named two of my main traits. Glad you noticed."

"Wait, I said deranged, weird, and beautiful."

"Pick two."

Wade is speechless.

Jeremy walks up and claps his bud on the shoulder. "Hey, bruh, Laurie's looking for you." Then Jeremy gives me a bizarre look. "Uh, hey, Clare."

"Mr. Herrera. It's good to see you're unscathed from the attack." I grin. "At least from what I'm seeing here. Maybe they, you know, hit you in some place you can't see."

If Jeremy could have crossed his legs right then and there he would. He gives a slight wince, no doubt remembering my balled-up fist nut-punching him repeatedly like a deleted scene in Tchaikovsky's *The Nutcracker*.

Jeremy tries to restore his wounded manhood. "Yeah, well, they're lucky I'm not a good shot or those bastards would've been breathing from the holes in their chests."

"And are you of legal age to own a firearm?"

Jeremy stops smiling. "It's my dad's."

"Your dad lets you pack that piece around like a gangsta?"

Jeremy shrugs. "Sure."

And then I flash another Cheshire Cat grin.

"Don't do anything I wouldn't do, Fuck Dodgers and Space Cadet."

They each get a punch in the shoulder from me.

A little harder than playful.

54

Fap, fap, fap.

Love the sound of my fists punching something hard.

Fap, fap, fap.

It's like a brutal kind of sonata played with my fists on the heavy bag.

Fap, fap, fap. Fap, fap, fap. Fap, fap, fap.

So, I don't always get to work out, but when I do—I go full-blown psycho. If I'm lucky, I get three workouts in a week. Hey, I'm a full-time student with a part-time job, I have zero time, right? Matthew McConaughey once said you should sweat at least one hour a day. If you've seen him in *Magic Mike*, you know that he knows what he's talking about.

My gym, called Iron Works, is kind of a run-down rat hole on the second floor of what used to be a stodgy old lodge hall, freemasons or somebody, from the last century. It's ugly and grim in here —worn mats on the floor, and lamps hang from the rafters barely illuminating the place in dreary pools of light. Old equipment that's been secured with silver duct tape on the worn seats. Some rusty and dusty free weights are racked in the corner. Some ratty mats that were probably used for high school wrestlers about the time Nixon was president. But the Iron Works is my gym. The monthly charge is super cheap. Most people in Pickman Flats go to Body Dimensions, a chic workout center with big-screen televisions yammering ESPN or angry cable news, a trendy juice bar, and floor-to-ceiling mirrors everywhere. People there spend more time gawking at themselves and their phones than working out.

Don't get me wrong, I'm not a gym rat who nests in this sweat and grime factory 24/7. I like coming in, getting what I need to get done, and getting out. No socializing, just hitting the weights—or something else.

Sometimes I'll hit the machines and do some resistance training. Sometimes I'll work the free weights or hit the stair climber, which is about ten years old and falling apart. But when I'm really feeling down and dirty, I hit the heavy bag, followed by the speed bag. And sometimes I do some drills that iGem taught me back in the day, some punch-kick combos. Talk about getting your cardio. When I get going, I rock that heavy bag. It weighs almost as much as me, but I can get it swinging. Watch out for my back kick!

Tonight, I'm thinking about everyone I'd love to drill with a few punches—the Detective Zangs, Officer Alvarados, Wade Bradens, Jeremy Herreras, and the Tommy Kellers of the world. Let me tell you, it's therapeutic. And considering my psyche triggers can turn on the Other Clare in a flash, this kind of punch-and-kick therapy helps me manage that. You sometimes gotta let the beast down in the basement come up and play. And when she does, it's like letting the proverbial fox loose in a hen house.

Fap, fap, fap. Fap, fap, fap. Fap, fap, fap.

And what's more—every workout, no matter how subtle or brutal, must have the perfect playlist cranking in my AirPods. Here's mine if you ever need an hour or more to sweat. You might know I'm heavily into '90s bands. Blame that on Truman Quirk—my boyfriend's been a bad influence. (kiss)

- Clare Playlist #3 (Find it on Spotify)
- Shitlist – L7
- Christian Woman – Type O Negative
- Pot Kettle Black – Tilly and the Wall

- Quiet – Smashing Pumpkins
- Blue Monday – Orgy
- Desire – U2
- Boys Wanna Be Her – Peaches
- Fast & Frightening – L7
- Chemical Beats – the Chemical Brothers
- Death Comes Ripping – Ms. Fits
- Gutless – Hole
- Shadowplay – The Killers
- Brackish – Kittie
- Emotional Haircut – LCD Soundsystem
- Bamboo Banga – M.I.A.
- Stigmata – Ministry
- Psycho Therapy – The Ramones
- Atomic – Sleeper
- Temple of Love – The Sisters of Mercy
- I Don't Wanna Be Me – Type O Negative
- Blur the Technicolor – White Zombie
- Stupid in the Dark – Xiu Xiu
- Bad Reputation – The Dollyrots
- We Bite – Ms. Fits
- Youth of America – Birdbrain
- Violet – Hole
- Bring the Noize – M.I.A.
- Run for Cover – The Killers
- Living in America – The Sounds
- Kick Out the Jams – MC5
- Sugarhigh – Coyote Shivers
- This is the Day – The Cranberries
- Butterfly – Crazy Town
- Through the Never – Metallica
- Make It Count – Junkie XL
- Smells Like Teen Spirit – Nirvana
- I'm Not Your Girl – Estrons
- The Driver – Night Runner
- Down with the Sickness – Disturbed

- Fake – Five Finger Death Punch
- A Love Unreal – Black Label Society
- Hey Boy Hey Girl – The Chemical Brothers
- Jekyll and Hyde – Five Finger Death Punch
- Rebel Girl – Bikini Kill
- Plump – Hole

As I'm abusing the bag, thinking of the Tommy Kellers of the world, I'm trying to figure out if Keller did or did not kidnap Lois J. Cain. If he did, what's his plan for her? What is somebody like that capable of?

OK, this is going to sound a little insensitive, but here goes.

In addition to losing my favorite author, I'm also completely bummed that my one shot at the big time has gone, too. She got a flash drive with my *She's Not There* novel manuscript, after all. She was going to forward it on to her agent. There's a snowball's chance in hell her bigshot agent in some New York City ivory tower would ever consider publishing the amateur scribblings of a Catholic high school girl trying to write suspense novels. But, on the other hand, I'm a teen writing about teens. Lois J. Cain is one of the few adults who can still write with a teen's voice. She remembers what it was like. Most adult authors who write teen characters are painfully annoying. It's like they're cribbing their dialogue from other adults who think they know how teens talk and think. Hey, I'm the real deal here. And now that chance is gone—gone with Lois. So much for dreams of better things and a better life.

Fap, fap, fap. Fap, fap, fap. Fap, fap, fap.
The heavy bag receives no mercy.

55

Cue an inconvenient flashback with a lesson:

INT. DOJO - DAY

iGem: You let your anger control you.

iGem watches as young Clare lands some punches
in a focus mitt.

CLARE: Fighting is about anger.

iGem: Fighting *can* be about anger. Successful
fighting is about the absence of anger.

CLARE: Huh?

iGem: Anger blinds you. When you're blind in a
fight, you're done. Even if you win, your anger
has still won over you. And most times, your
anger will allow you to get hit with something
you were too blind to see.

CLARE: But everyone has anger.

iGem: Yes. Everyone does. Especially everyone like you.

CLARE: There's nobody like me.

iGem: You are unique. And I'm still trying to figure you out. We've been training for two years since your therapist recommended you come and train.

QUICK FLASHBACK PART DEUX:

INT. THERAPIST OFFICE - DAY

Clare and her middle-aged therapist, JOAN WEAVER.

JOAN: (tears off note) My two kids, well my one boy in particular, study with this sensei. She's really helped him. Andy is so much calmer and better in school. More focused. I think the exercise will help you, Clare.

Clare studies at the piece of paper.

CLARE: Sounds boring.

JOAN: Sometimes the things that are exciting to us may seem boring at first. Give it a try.
CLARE: Maybe.

BACK TO SCENE

Clare tries to hit the focus mitts but iGem

keeps moving them. Clare gets more pissed, red-faced, until she starts lashing out. iGem quickly taps her face.

iGEM: You left a blind spot. See how easy that was for me?

Clare huffs.

CLARE: I hate this.

iGEM: No, you *hate* the anger.

CLARE: What?

iGEM: Make an enemy of anger. Don't let it consume you.

CLARE: How?

iGEM: Anger has triggers. Recognize those triggers and avoid them.

CLARE: Triggers?

iGEM: Yes. And breathe. Breathing is key. Anger's like a bad house guest, don't invite it in. Now, breathe.

56

It's another slow night at the G-Spot and I'm contemplating closing up the place early when this guy comes in out of the rain. He's wearing a black slicker and hat, and he appears like a killer out of a slasher movie. He only needs a hook for a hand to complete the random cosplay.

The rain has been thumping down with Biblical proportions all day. The streets outside are slick and shiny with the town's lights mirroring off them. It's like another town on top of another, but the lines are vague. In a way, it encapsulates Pickman Flats perfectly—smooth and shiny to the public and a little darkness and vagueness on the other side.

"You're the only sign in town that still says open."

"And I was just about to close."

"Coffee," he says, smiling at me. "Grant me the mercy of coffee."

"It's about two hours old," I say. "But I can do a pour over if you give me a nice tip."

The man smiles. "I'm not too much of a fancy guy. The old stuff is fine."

"I'll make it to go."

"That's mighty kind of you."

He saunters in, dripping the sky all over the floor as he ambles up to the bar. Guess I'll be doing some mopping. Damn it, I want to get home and see if I can learn anything more about Tommy Keller. All night I've been searching with my phone, but I'll search with my laptop at home so I can work undistracted from the usual pain-in-the-ass customer who needs something. Oh, I'm sorry, did that sound bitchy?

"So, we've got a blonde roast, a French roast, and the nuttier, bolder Sumatra roast."

"Just plain ol' coffee. Like I said, I'm not fancy."

Definitely a guy who knows what he wants. I pour him a French roast in the tallest to-go cup I have and then slide it over to him.

"Cream and sugar?"

"Just black as the night."

"Wow, crazy."

"Huh?"

"Well, I've read some studies where psychopaths generally like their coffee black. Of course, I've also read where geniuses and entrepreneurs like it that way, too, so which are you?"

"Like I said, I'm a guy who's not too particular and fussy about his pleasures." He pulls out a wad of bills that would choke a giraffe. "How much do I owe you?"

"Eh, I was just going to dump it all out in a couple of minutes anyway," I say with a shrug. "Let's call this first cup free."

"That's mighty generous of you." He plops down a twenty-dollar bill. "Here's that tip you wanted."

As much as I want the money, I slide it back over to him. "Can't really accept that—I was only half-joking anyway."

"Well, I'm not taking it back." He looks around. "Put it in the business fund—place is a little dead tonight."

"Not just tonight."

"Not much call for vegan food in Pickman Flats?"

"Well, only for the college students mostly, and a few tourists who are out to 'try something new' and the occasional coffee seeker when the Dancing Goats and Starbucks are closed."

He combs back his graying hair with his fingers. His blue eyes dart around the place. "What is 'vegan' anyway? Hear about it all the time. Kind of like a trendy health thing, isn't it?"

"Well, it's simply just not eating or utilizing any animal products. If you're a true vegan, you're doing it to stop the exploitation of animals like, say, through factory farming. Do you know that millions of animals are killed and raped every year just for people's plates—"

"Oh, I really don't need a sermon," he interrupts, "just curious. I'm a ham and eggs guy myself. Pretty much all I eat. Unless I can have a tenderloin steak with a shot of rye whiskey. Now that's what I call living."

Challenge accepted. "So, you've never had vegan food before?"

He shakes his head. "Never," he says with a smile. "But never say never." He laughs at his joke.

"Try this tiramisu—made it myself."

"Naw."

"On the house."

He studies the wedge of cake like it's a bomb that might go off. "Well, twist my arm."

He forks a bite into his mouth. At first, he grimaces, then he starts choking and then clutching his stomach. "Do you have a bathroom?"

Really?

"That way," I point.

He jumps off his stool and runs three quick steps in the direction I pointed, then stops, laughing. "You'd better call the ambulance, there must be something wrong with me, I *like* that vegan cake."

He sits down and shovels more in like he hasn't eaten in a week. Somehow, judging by his full cheeks, I doubt that.

"So what's your name, Ham and Eggs?"

He looks up, a crumb of cake on his lip. "Steely Dan."

My Gramps listens to Steely Dan. He likes their song "Cuervo Gold."

On the restaurant's speakers "She's Not There" by The

Zombies comes on. Skye Duncan, the manager, insists on playing oldies from the '60s, '70s, and '80s, (no '90s, sadly). She wants the G-Spot to have a "friendly, comfortable vibe" when people walk through the door. Especially people who wouldn't normally patronize a vegan food establishment. She figures if she can hit them with a little good-feelin' nostalgia, they'll check it out, especially the locals. Most of the songs on the mixes Skye makes are pretty good. They remind me of Gramps listening to his oldies rock station in his Chevy. Funny that it's this song. It's the title of my book—the manuscript I gave to Lois. Wherever she is, and if she's still alive.

"Your name is seriously Steely Dan?"

He can see I'm not amused. "Dan," he says. "Dan Simmons. 'Steely Dan' is just a nickname a friend gave me. Kind of stuck."

"Dan Simmons. That sounds familiar for some reason."

"Well, it's *not* the most unique name."

"And why are you nicknamed Steely Dan, exactly?"

"When I see something I like, I close in and get it—cold steel focus."

"Something like what?"

He finishes his cake. "It's weird to say this, but I think that hit the spot."

It's five minutes past closing but I don't rush him out the door. He's kind of entertaining. And this is one of those cold, rainy kinds nights where I could use some entertainment.

"So where are you from, Mr. Simmons?"

"You mean it's obvious I'm not from around here?"

"You could say that."

"Well, I come from a little town called Fairvale. Fairvale, California."

"And you're just passing through?"

"That obvious too?"

"Most people don't come to Pickman Flats unless they have a specific reason—like wine tasting. It's pretty obvious you're not one of those."

"Seems you're a pretty good judge of character."

"Just observant."

"Yeah, I stopped to gas up and get a bite to eat. Was going to try to make it to Seattle tonight, but that rain was beating down pretty hard. Makes for some slow driving." He notices that my face is an expression of unanswered questions. "I'm what you might call a traveling salesman. Mostly computer hardware and software. Have a big account up north I'm hoping to make bigger."

"You never answered my question."

"What question would that be?"

"You said when you see something you like, you get it with a cold steel focus. My question was 'something like what?'"

He grins and snaps his fingers. "Clients. Clients mean sales."

He did have a thick wad of cash. "Well, you seem to be doing pretty good at it."

"Yeah, I make a pretty honest living." He shrugs. "I'm just a guy from San Bernardino."

"You said you were from Fairvale."

"Oh, yeah, that's right," he says. "Fairvale," and then he shakes his head as if to confirm it to himself.

I then have the strangest conspiracy theory yet of my young life.

What if this is the guy who's been watching me?

The one who's given me the feeling of being watched?

The one who kidnapped Lois J. Cain?

What if, sitting across from me, is Thomas A. Keller from Ravensdale?

And what if he's playing some kind of psycho game with me?

57

My mouth goes dry. This smiling guy across from me is the kidnapper of my favorite author, I'm pretty sure of it. Dan freakin' Simmons, the author? Are you kidding me? *That's* his fake name? And I've never even heard of Fairvale. Sounds like another steaming, stinky load he's shoveling me. When I turn my back to him and act like I'm wiping the counter down with my cleaning rag, I quickly Google "Fairvale California" on my phone. The first thing that pops up is that it's a fictional town created by Robert Bloch for his 1959 novel, *Psycho*, which was also used a year later in the Hitchcock film. *My intuition was right—bullshit!*

The only weapon I have near me is a steaming pot of coffee. The knife I cut the cake with is out of reach. Though I could hit him with the boiling liquid first and while that's scorching his fake, smiling face I could then go for the knife.

INT. THE GARDEN SPOT — NIGHT

Clare and "Dan Simmons" have a nice chat.
They're really into each other. Maybe he a
little more so. On the restaurant speakers,

"Aquarius/Let the Sunshine In" by The 5th
Dimension plays.

"DAN": You're really only seventeen?

CLARE: That's what it says on my credentials.
"DAN": Heh, if you show me yours, I'll show you
mine.

Clare's clearly creeped out by this man who's
too old to know better but clearly doesn't
care.

CLARE: Well, I've never been too modest.
She grabs her backpack and pulls out her ID.
CLARE: Bring yours out. We show at the same
time.

"DAN": You drive a hard bargain.

He fishes his wallet out of his rain slicker.
They show each other their IDs. Clare's careful
to keep her finger over her address.

"DAN": Well, I'll be. May twenty-first. Same
birthday as Jeffrey Dahmer. He certainly was no
vegan.

CLARE: That's an odd fact to have memorized.

"DAN": My mind is like a steel trap. When I see
something, I commit it to memory.

She looks at his ID.

CLARE'S POV — "Dan's" driver's license. *Dan*

Simmons, Fairvale, California. Age 50. Ht. 6 ft. Wt. 195. Also, it looks like a really elaborate fake. No watermark. The ink on it is a little saturated in the paper.

She hands it back to him.

CLARE: So, I showed you mine and vice-versa.
"DAN": Well, you didn't show me all of yours. You hid a little bit.

CLARE: You don't get to know where I live until I know you a little better. First date rules.
"DAN": (nodding head) Fair enough, fair enough.
CLARE: So, "Dan," I have to say, you're not the man I thought you were. But isn't that just like a guy, always lying about what he's got underneath his raincoat?

His laughing, sunshiny demeanor changes. She has deflated his manly ego.

"DAN": Huh?

The song hits the halfway moment (best part) where it breaks into the chant *"Let The Sunshine In"* like a bright, LSD-induced mantra. *FWOOSH!* Clare splashes a pot of boiling Sumatra blend fair-trade coffee into her creepy customer's face. He grabs his eyes, blinded, screaming, and falls off the stool.

"DAN": My eyes! My eyes! You little bitch! You whore! You goddamned whore! You blinded me! I'll kill you!

Like a well-oiled machine, Clare grabs the cake
knife with one hand and then grabs the counter
with the other -- and launches herself over
like some comic-book superhero with a cause!

Dan, hearing her, gropes for her blindly.

"DAN": I'll kill you—I'll goddamned kill you!

CLARE: Ladies first, Dan, don't be rude.

She plunges the knife into his throat all the
way to the hilt. He grabs the handle of it,
scarlet streaming through his fingers, blood
babbling from his mouth like a brook.

Dan tries to speak but the blood only makes
gurgling noises. She backs up so she doesn't
get blood on her favorite pleather vegan shoes.
He drops dead, blood expanding around him like
a gruesome angel's halo that he never had in
life.

CLARE turns to the CAMERA, breaking the "fourth
wall" in *Ferris Bueller*-style.

CLARE: Wait a minute. If I kill him, then I
won't find out where Lois is... Can I take it
all back? Of course, this is Movie Magic,
bitches! (snaps fingers)

IN REVERSE

The entire bloody tableau plays in reverse with
the blood pooling back into "Dan," him rising,
and Clare pulling the knife from his throat.

FREEZE FRAME

On "Dan" holding his face after Clare sloshed him with the boiling coffee.

CLARE: Let's try that again.

FORWARD MOTION

Resumes. This time, Clare drops the knife and foot sweeps the blinded "Dan." He crashes onto his back. Using a Krav Maga move, she then wraps her legs around his neck and locks his left arm into an arm-bar.

Her victim can't move, pinned to the ground, as she can either choke him out and/or break his arm.

CLARE: OK, you bottom-feeding brown trout. Where'd you take Lois and why? And why did you try to pin it on me?

Dan gurgles, trying to speak.

CLARE: Talk!

58

"Did I say something to freak you out?"

My only customer in the restaurant is looking at me like I'm crazy. Takes one to know one.

"Or maybe you are some kind of daydream believer?"

Yeah, I tend to get distracted by violent fantasies that play in my mental movie theater.

"Only thinking about all the stuff I have to do before I close," I say, covering my brief escape from reality.

"Yeah," he says. "I'd better get on the road."

And I'd better follow you. Might as well go for the direct approach.

"Staying at the Cayuse?"

"Naw, too expensive and fancy for an ordinary ham-and-egger like me. I'm out on the highway at the Motel 6."

"So you *know* the Cayuse Hotel then?"

"Of course, I'm a traveling man. I've got an app for all the places to hang my hat for the night."

Is there an app to find out just how full of shit you are, too, "Dan?"

He picks himself up off his stool and heads for the door.

"The rain's let up a little," I say.

"A little."

He gets an escort from me to the front door. "Try to stay dry," I say, letting him out.

"Vegan food ain't too bad. Might have to stop in again."

"So, I'll be seeing you around?"

He winks. "You can count on it."

After he leaves, his dark slicker disappearing into the night, I quickly lock the door and turn the OPEN sign over to CLOSED. Then I run into the back and shut down all the lights. Counting the till and cleaning up will have to wait until I get back. Grabbing my coat, I head out the back door and jump into the Leaf. Gotta find out what he's really up to. Later, I'll call Grams and tell her I went over to Julie's to study.

The streets lie empty. Pickman Flats rolls up its sidewalks early every night. Earlier when it rains. Pulling up to the intersection near the restaurant, I sit and wait. One of the cars parked out front should spring to life and back out. Come on, come on...

Ah, it's an Escalade with California plates. Guess he wasn't lying about being from California.

The black Escalade rolls past. Yes, I can barely make out "Dan," but it's him.

He doesn't see me. After he passes, I pull out behind him but keep my distance. He doesn't need to know he's being followed. With my phone, I snap a picture of his license plate for future reference. "Tinseltown Swimming in Blood" by Destroy plays on Sirius XMU, my chase music.

"Dan" is heading down the right road to hit the highway exit, so maybe he was telling the truth about that. No, he's so full of bullshit he should be wearing horns.

The rain pattering against the window, and the Leaf's wipers futilely fighting it, makes it hard to see. Damn it, where'd he go? It's so dark out tonight and that midnight black Escalade isn't helping matters.

Ah, there he is—up ahead in the darkness!

He seems to be heading toward Highway 5, which leads out of town. Well, if he takes a left. If he takes a right, the Motel 6 is about a mile away. He sits there for a long time, and I slow, so he won't see me following.

He quickly bolts right and hurries off. Damn, maybe he saw me. But how would he know what kind of car I drive? Unless he's been watching me.

Hitting the gas, I take off after him. Problem is, the Nissan Leaf isn't the fastest car on the market. Passing the Motel 6, I slow down. The Escalade isn't in the parking lot. He either lied about staying there or he has another errand to run.

Fifteen minutes more of driving around in circles, all the way out past the old stockyards on Highway 5 and back to the motel, no sign of the black Escalade.

Damn. He wins this round.

Creepy Guy: One. Clare: Zero.

59

Just to make matters worse, on Wednesday, I lose my best friend, Julie.

Yes, it's true, people die around me—I seem to attract death like moths to a flame. But death doesn't always have to be physical. And after it all, I feel a sense of loss. Just like someone died. For someone like me, who doesn't exactly have emotional attachments to things, it can still hurt. What Julie represented to me was a kind of guide to get through life. To not feel like such an outsider. Sometimes I even picked up how she would react to things so I could engage my reactions accordingly to seem like "one of the group."

This probably comes across like I was using Julie to navigate my way through my world of Pickman Flats, and part of that is true; I'll be the first to admit it, at least here, in this long-winded confession. But I also had an attachment to her. Well, as attached as anyone like me can get to another. Up there with my grandparents. More than I had felt about my parents certainly, who I co-existed with for fourteen years. The only thing I could expect from them was anger and abuse from my mom (when she paid attention to me and wasn't in Vodka Blackout Mode) and my father, who was just indifferent.

As a creature of ritual, Julie really helped keep the beast at bay. Especially after my grandparents scraped the money together to get me the Leaf. Our morning journeys to school helped to prime me for the day. And Julie's devil-may-care attitude toward things helped to distract me from my own internal bullshit. She was like Disneyland for the emotionally challenged.

Now that's gone.

And with a potential stalker following me, plus being watched by the police for a crime I didn't commit, it feels like my little raft of safety is burning at the edges and will be engulfed. Soon, I'll be drowning in an ocean if I'm not careful.

Here's how it went down.

And it ain't pretty.

This morning, I made a mocha with MCT oil, free-trade organic coffee, vegan butter, and cacao powder all frothed together. Then I went to pick up Julie. As usual, she was running late, looking a little bit frumpy and unironed (which I love about her as opposites attract, you know). She was going on about how she had to work late because Anita, one of the main cutters at Furry O'Malley's Pet Salon, was caught skimming money out of the till. So she had—and will have—to cover Anita's shifts until a suitable replacement can be hired and trained, which will take weeks. She already works max hours for someone who goes to school—and this just may have put her over the edge. It's not like at the G-Spot where it's practically dead and I can fill in the lull doing homework. Furry's is busy all the time and Julie rarely has a spare moment to even take a bathroom break. Apparently, there are a lot of people in Pickman Flats, particularly of the retired set, who have nothing better to spend their money on than pampering their pets.

So Julie is more than pissed. She's also pissed at her mom who's happy that Julie has the extra hours. That means more income since Julie's helping keep the family of four afloat. Julie's mom, who quit school at our age, thinks that education is a waste of time. It's better to make an honest living as soon as you can. However, Julie has dreams of higher education, the house, the spouse, the pedigree dog, and the picket fence. And she feels like that's even further off now than ever.

"I mean, I'm already on the borderline for failing Advanced Algebra," she says. "It's not like you can just show up and do the assignments. That shit is hard. It's like learning another language."

"Well," I say. "I can help you with that."

"That's not the freakin' point, bitch hole," she says, her face getting flushed. "You can help, sure, but if I don't learn this on my own, I can kiss any other school goodbye. I don't want to be stuck in this town forever."

"Like your mother?"

"Are you *trying* to piss me off?"

No point answering. She's worked up. So I sip my morning brew and keep driving.

"Why don't you drink normal coffee like everyone else?"

It's obvious she's looking for a fight so I'm not taking the bait. Time for some deflection.

"We're almost to the Goats." And then I add, "The coffee of norms awaits you."

After pulling up in front of the Dancing Goats, which is slammed with locals getting their morning caffeine enema before going to work, Julie and I climb out of the Leaf. Instantly, I feel watched. Again. No sign of Detective Zang or Keller. Gazing up to the vacant building, where Keller was probably watching me before, the curtains are closed. He's not there. But he's *some*where.

"What the hell are you looking at?" Julie says, grabbing the gold handle of the coffee shop door that looks like a goat's hoof.

"Just because you're not paranoid doesn't mean that they're not after you."

She rolls her eyes and heads inside.

As we make our way to the end of the line, Lana Del Rey sings about every time she closes her eyes it's like a dark paradise. Yeah, I'm with you sister, except the darkness behind my eyes isn't exactly a paradise. More like a comfortable hell with cheap furniture and tacky decor. Speaking of cheap and tacky, what am I going to do about "Dan?" Do I go to Detective Zang with what I have? But what *do* I have? Can he even be a suspect? Can I prove anything he's done? He's definitely shifty and weird, but yeah, so am I. All I have on him is that I saw a California driver's license that looked fake and a blurry shot of his license plate. Not exactly the evidence to clear myself. And I know that's exactly what Zang will say. Could I convince her about Keller? Say that he's posing as this "Dan Simmons?" If I could get more info on him. If he *did* kidnap Lois, the chances of her still being in town are good. If she's alive, that is. But if she is alive, he's got her close. Someplace that's private and where she won't be discovered. A house? A vacant business? A—

Julie punches me in the shoulder. "Did you even hear what I said?"

"About what?"

"You're always doing this, aren't you?"

"Doing what?"

"Marginalizing me."

"Excuse me?"

"It's always about you. Lots of times I think you hang out with me because you've got nothing better to do."

"Uh, we are in public here."

"I don't give a shit. You've been acting weird. You barely respond to my texts or calls. And I feel like I'm a huge burden to you, Saint Clare!"

"You probably have low blood sugar, and you're mad about your job. When you eat something, you'll—"

"Don't oversimplify this to my inadequate glucose levels. This has been going on for the past year. And has gotten worse in the last few days."

People are starting to turn and look at us. I wish they had cranked Lana a little louder to drown out our drama.

"Can we talk about this, uh, later, like in the car?"

"You're always putting me off."

Lowering my voice, I go into shout-whisper mode. "Well, I was a little busy being dragged into the police station for doing something I didn't do and now some creep is stalking me. Excuse the hell out of me."

"What are you talking about?"

"My life has shit going on too," I say. "It's not about you and your pathetic little life." Wish I could have left off that last statement.

"My pathetic life? *My* pathetic life?"

We finally make it up to the counter. The barista is looking at us like one might watch a couple of fighting alley cats. "What can I get you?" she asks.

"How about someone who treats me like an actual friend instead of a science experiment."

"If you're trying to push my buttons for exercise," I say, "you can continue your workout by walking to school."

"Fine," she says. "Give me a triple mocha latte and a pumpkin scone." She turns to me. "Give me your keys so I can get my bag."

"Are you serious?"

"Did I stutter?"

She throws down a dead Hamilton on the bar, grabs my keys, and storms out the door. The barista looks at me, almost afraid to speak.

"Uh, nothing for me, thanks," I say and retreat to the door. Everyone in the place stares at me like I just yelled, "I'm a vegan serial killer living among you but I have a keen fashion sense."

Julie walks back in. "Think fast, bitch." She throws my keys at my face. Lucky for my quick reflexes or they might have marred my makeup.

"Are you seriously going to pull this poor-little-me martyr shit?" I ask.

"Really?" she says. "We're done—I'm so sick of your disrespectful ass."

Plum Adams, bright pink hair, bulky Hello Kitty pullover hoodie, lip ring, and sketch pad in hand, shuffles over to us in her frayed hem jeans and beaten-up Converse. Think the look she's going for is Gender Neutral Coffee House Chic. "Is everything OK?"

"No," Julie says. "Does it sound like it is?

Plum bites her lip. "Uh, do you need a ride?"

Julie looks at her, then me. "*Yes.*"

And that's pretty much it.

I haven't heard from Julie Gabriella Ramos for days. She hasn't replied to my calls or texts. At first, I think she's trying to delay, get back at me for not always responding. But maybe she's serious.

Does losing your best friend happen this quickly?

Later, I learned losing Julie was the least of my worries.

Murder came knocking at my door. Again.

Why the hell am I always home?

60

Though the trail went cold for Thomas A. Keller, maybe I can see where he's been. The first time I'm sure he was looking at me was in the vacant building across the street from the Dancing Goats. After a long and excruciating day at DeFeo Catholic High, it's time to check it out and see if there are any signs—or if he's even there. In case he is—and Lois could be too?—I arm myself with some weaponry.

In my cedar hope chest at the foot of my bed, I keep a few wares. Right now, I have a four-inch collapsible knife, as well as a Taser that Gramps got me last Christmas and the matching pepper spray that Grams got me. I also have some nylon zip-ties (in case I need to bind someone) that I bought at the downtown Army/Navy Surplus store, along with a new penlight that can double as a weapon, striking vulnerable pressure points, if need be. Also, a roll of duct tape, which is good for all occasions (mostly muffling said bound person).

Hopefully, I won't be walking into the lion's den when I break-in, but if I do, I have the tools to declaw that cat. (Oh, a note from your friendly, neighborhood vegan—don't declaw your housecats, it's cruel. How'd you like the first digit of each of *your* fingers hacked off?)

The day was excruciating because Julie avoided me in our classes. She sits right beside me, and she kept looking forward as if I wasn't there. This has gone on for days. When I tried to speak to her during Social Studies, she asked Sister Mitchell if she could move closer to the front as she was having "trouble hearing." Word got around about us at Goats. Other students were chuckling and leering at me when Julie picked up her books and bag and relocated. To get back at her, and everyone else in class, I keep my expression neutral (not exactly hard for a psychopath) so they couldn't read me. If I'd have flown into a rage or tears, it would have fed them, like throwing bloody bait to sharks. But my non-expression didn't give the onlookers much to chew on.

Now, I'm climbing into my Nissan Leaf, which looks especially bright and blood red on this cloudless October day, and I'm about to pull out when—

Amity jumps into the passenger side and nearly throws her bag on my lap. "Oh, my gosh, did you hear about what's going around school about you and Julie?"

"Uh, Amity, I'm hitting the gym and then heading to work. I also need to make a stop in between, so I don't really have time."

Apparently cosplay Clare, who's looking creepily more and more like me every day, didn't hear. "Everyone is now saying that you and Julie were, like, secret lesbians, and Truman kind of 'vag blocked' you both. Now Julie's dating Plum Adams."

"That's complete bullshit," I say. "You know how rumors circulate around school. The more bullshit they're full of, the further their stink carries."

"I so didn't know you were into girls, Clare," she says. "I mean, I think it's kind of... I don't want to use the word 'gross'... but, uh, not really my thing."

"It's not my thing either. It's not gross, everybody's different." Don't I know it. "I just prefer guys. At least for now."

"You do?"

"What's going around school is only a fraction true. Julie and I aren't friends right now, but it has nothing to do with lesbianism or any other kind of 'ism' for that matter."

"So where are we heading?"

"Well, I have an appointment," I say, "and you need to climb into your own car and take yourself...wherever."

"Daddy dropped me off today," Amity says. Then she pauses as her lower lip curls, her eyes turn red, and a single tear trickles down. "To tell you the truth, I don't feel like anyone likes me anymore."

Oh, you mean because your best friends Mercy Franks and Hope Dalquist are pushing up daisies in Pickman Flats Cemetery up on the hill?

"Well, I'm not exactly on the Popular Students List so you should probably cry to someone else."

"But you always seem to be, you know, OK. Doing your own thing."

"That's because I don't depend on anyone to make me happy. That comes from within, you know. That's your responsibility, not someone else's."

I read that on an Internet meme on a vegan website. Apparently, Amity never heard that obvious and rather ubiquitous advice as she's nodding her head like she was Moses coming down from Mount Sinai with the Ten Commandments after talking to God.

"So, I have to be my own person?"

Yes, and you can start by not trying to be me.

"That's right. Dance to the beat of your own drum and all that."

"Wow."

OK, you can leave now—I have an author to find and a creep to apprehend.

"Can I go with you?" she asks. "I'll buy you a coffee or something."

My patience is growing thin, and I'm about to say something cruel that will cut her to the quick when I realize that Amity Liston might prove useful. Maybe it was God's plan to have her jump into the car with me today. Thanks, God.

"Well, I'm good on coffee, but there is something that you *could* help me with," I say. "Should only take a few minutes."

"Count me in," she says, wiping a tear away and beaming at me. "What do I have to do?"

"Exactly what you're doing now," I say. "Just be me."

If I was the type of serial killer to give one of those evil laughs like you see in the movies, this is where I would be chortling like a devil right now.

Damn, I'm a clever, clever bitch.

Evil, sure.

But clever as a devil during the witching hour.

61

"What you're doing is not only amoral," the dead postman says from the backseat, "But just plain ol' wrong."

As Amity is yammering on about something, I'm searching for calm inside my skull before the inevitable storm, and now Bob has to pipe in. Is this kick around Clare week or what?

Maybe if I just ignore the decaying mail carrier in the backseat, he'll go away. Pretending to wipe off a phantom spot on the side of my lip in the rearview mirror with my middle finger, making sure the recipient sees it in the back, I turn away from his disgusting reflection. Out of sight out of mind, as they say.

"Try as you might, moron, you can't ignore me."

He's trying to troll me. He pulls this shit all the time.

Amity's mouth is moving a mile a minute. Unlike Julie, she doesn't seem to care that I'm tuning her out (or trying my best). She's going over everything that happened today at school like she's trying to verbally commit it to some diary. Why doesn't she just take snapshots of her mediocrity and post them on social media like everyone else? Her followers might actually care.

"It's bad enough that you're going to commit yet another series of crimes by breaking into private property, but you're also including an innocent accomplice."

Give me a break, innocent? Last year Amity and her two friends were trying to knock my head in. Not exactly innocent. For the record, I'm not getting revenge. I'm using Amity in a way that she'll be useful. Yes, I used the word "use." That's exactly what I'm doing. Julie was different, I cared about her as much as I could. She offered me something—a way into the social maze of Pickman Flats and the halls of DeFeo. Amity brings nothing to the table except for a cosplay version of myself with an incessant need to chatter like a chipmunk after a triple-shot espresso.

"You do realize that what you're planning to do with Amity will never work."

"It will," I say, gritting my teeth.

"No, and here's why—she's only pretending to be you. But the real crazy, that's in you and you alone. You'll always be a scheming, murderous little scamp, and nothing more."

"What a minute, did you actually use the word 'scamp'?"

"Say what?" Amity says, taking a break from her litany of scholastic woes.

"When I'm driving and thinking," I say, "I sometimes like to go over dialogue in my head."

"Dialogue? Are you doing another play like we did with *Deathtrap* last year?"

"No, I'm writing a novel. Well, *another* novel."

"Oh, really?" Amity says. "I didn't know you wrote fiction too. Is there anything that you can't do, Clare?" She lowers her voice conspiratorially. "Is it juicy? Is it about me? Can I read it?"

"Uh, that's a triple no. I don't like to share my work until it's done. You know, edited and polished. And I'm really slow at that part. Laborious, in fact."

"You mix truth with lies so perfectly, like a cocktail, you might as well bartend," the dead mailman says.

"Stick it in your postal box, Bob!"

"Oh, man," Amity says, "that's hilarious. Are you writing about a mailman or something?"

"Yes," I say, "that's right. And he always shows up at the

wrong time and the wrong place, then he dies." I almost laugh. "It's called *The Postman Rings No More.*"

Amity nods, seriously considering the title of my lie. "Huh."

"Well." I shrug. "It's kind of a working title."

"Remember that mailman who died under Lowell Bridge a couple of years ago?"

"How can I forget?"

"Is your story about that?"

"Nope."

"That was weird, that whole thing. The police were never really sure if it was an accident or foul play."

"Oh, it was foul play," Bob yells from the back. "By a foul strumpet walking around town just trying to seduce older men."

"In your dreams, dead man."

"Is that another line?" Amity asks.

"Possibly another title," I say. "Titles are the hardest for me."

So is the truth.

62

When we pull up to the business building with the FOR RENT sign, I can tell Amity looks nervous.

"Don't worry," I assure her. "I wouldn't be doing this if it were dangerous."

"Liar," Bob yells from the backseat.

Ignoring the dead mailman, I climb out of the Leaf and take a long look at the building, slinging my backpack full of defense essentials over my shoulder.

"Is what you're doing legal?"

As if on cue, a police car approaches, lights flashing and siren blaring. My shoes plant in the concrete and I mentally count to ten, hoping this isn't Officer Alvarado or Detective Zang and they've been somehow tipped off to my, uh, illegal activities of breaking and entering. The police car passes, and I relax.

"Of course, it's legal," I say. "In fact, I'm part of a special task force."

"Really?"

"Yep. Remember when I was pulled out of school the other day by the police?"

"Who doesn't?"

"Well, I was pulled because I have special knowledge of a dangerous perpetrator operating right here in our little town."

"Someone dangerous in Pickman Flats?" Amity scans around cautiously. "This place is getting so scary. Is he as bad as, well, as that horrible detective that tried to kill...us?" She starts shaking and her eyes start welling with tears.

"Calm down," I say, placing an obligatory hand on her shoulder as I've seen people do for comfort. "No, this guy is kind of a peeper. He watches young girls and messes with their heads. He's playing some kind of, you know, wicked game, and he has to be stopped."

"Like that song 'Wicked Game' by Chris What's-His-Name? That's one of my mom's favorite old songs."

"Uh, sure," I say, fishing for my lock pick kit. Paid $9.99 for it at the Army/Navy Surplus. In cash, of course.

"And," I say, "for the record—this is a top-secret investigation. If you breathe so much as a word of this to anyone, Amity Liston, you could be indicted and face jail time. Got it?"

"Uh...yes."

As I'm working the lock, Amity gives me a worried look. "I've watched enough cop shows to know that this is called 'illegal search and seizure' or something like that."

"Keep watching the street," I say. "Remember what I said about top secret."

"Why do I have to keep watching the street if all of this is legal?"

"What if Mister Peeper shows up?"

Amity shudders.

The lock surrenders with a click. *Mardi Gras!* I swing the door open. There's a flight of stairs straight ahead, and a corridor to the first floor off to the left. Keller was watching me was on the second floor, so that's where we're going first. Well, that's where Amity is going. She's on point. That will also make her an accomplice if we're picked up. Yeah, it's kind of a bitch move, but then, so am I.

"That way," I point.

"Up the stairs?"

"Slowly and cautiously. No unnecessary talk or questions at this point. Total stealth mode."

"I'm scared."

"Don't worry, I'm right behind you. Nothing's going to happen." Reaching into my bag of goodies, I finger the Taser. "Go!"

Amity tiptoes up the stairs and I follow. The place is gloomy and smells of dust, decay, and something acrid. Obviously, nobody has been interested in renting out this space. Can't blame them, it's kind of creepy. Nothing that a few cans of kerosene and a blow torch couldn't fix.

When we reach the landing, the curtained windows stand beyond. The smell is stronger up here. The ammonia stench of urine stings my nostrils. There's cardboard on the well-treaded carpet. Crushed beer cans. Candy wrappers. Chip bags. An old, ratty blanket. Someone's been squatting here. Have we found the rat's nest of Thomas A. Keller? Could Lois J. Cain be somewhere in the shadows and grime?

"This place is gross," Amity whispers. "Stinks worse than my cat's litter box."

"Shhhh."

He could still be here, hiding. We've got to remain quiet.

My cell phone blasts Radiohead's "High and Dry"—*Don't leave me hiiiiigh; don't leave me dryyyy.* It's Truman. Dammit, I was so distracted by Amity, I forgot to silence my phone. I'm about to mute it, but I'm always muting him. Dammit.

"Hey," I answer, hanging back from Amity, keeping my voice low. "What's up?"

"How are you doing, babe? Why are you whispering?"

"In a library. They kind of frown on phones. Gotta bounce."

"I was just calling because your grandma invited me for dinner Friday night."

What? Why? "Uh, OK."

"Did *you* put Grams up to that?"

"Uh, well, yeah," I lie. "Thought it'd be nice."

"Should I bring anything?"

"Only your hot bod and your sexy, forlorn expressions. Gotta go, love. Kisses!" Hanging up, I silence my phone this time.

Amity frowns at me. "I thought you said to be quiet."

"When love calls, you answer."

A moment later, a shadowy figure lunges at us. He brandishes a knife in his hand—the blade glinting off the dim light from the window.

The figure goes for Amity.

Now, for the second time in her life, I'm going to have to save it.

And not get killed myself.

63

"Teresa!"

That's what the man shouts. The man with the knife. The man from the shadows. He goes after Amity, since, you know, I kind of planned it that way in case there was somebody waiting. This also gives me a second to drop my phone, shove the screaming cosplay Clare out of the way, and parry the knife out of shadow man's hand.

He gets a knee in the balls and a foot sweep, which sends him on his back. His breath reeks of sour beer.

I throw a knee onto his throat.

He doesn't move, clearly still reeling from my rapid assault.

He has piercing blue eyes and a face full of hair. The rest is grime. He's wearing a black and red Portland Trail Blazers stocking cap over his dregs of ratty brown curls. His patched overcoat is about two sizes too big for his skeletal frame. Bet this guy doesn't weigh much more than me.

He just stares at me, not saying anything. A look of horror on his face.

His "knife" was a tin toy, which is a silver, wind-up dolphin.

This is definitely not the "Dan" who came into the restaurant.

Not sure if the piss smell is him or from his contribution surrounding us.

Amity has backed against a wall, catching her breath and crying. The excitement was too much for her.

"I'm removing my knee from your throat," I say to him, keeping the Taser ready in my hand. "When I do, you're going to tell me three things: Who You Are. What You're Doing Here. And Why You Attacked Us."

I pause for effect, then: "Can you do that?"

He nods.

I release the pressure to his throat with my knee slowly, ready to blast him with the Taser if he gets frisky. He doesn't, swallowing. "StarMan... My name is StarMan."

"StarMan?" Amity says, catching her breath and regaining her composure. "Uh, did your parents not like you or something?"

"Answer my other two questions, 'StarMan.'" Clearly, it's the week for strange dudes with weird pseudonyms.

"This...is my home."

"Technically," Amity says. "It's a vacant building, dickhead, and you're trespassing."

"You're trespassing," the one named StarMan spits.

"We're undercover cops," Amity says from my conspiratorial scowl. "I was, uh, recently deputized, yeah."

"I don't truck with no cops."

"Relax," I say. "You didn't answer my third question."

"I...thought you were somebody."

"Who?"

"Somebody I lost."

"Teresa?"

"She was my daughter."

The only Teresa I knew was Teresa "Skizz" Wainwright who died last year at the hands of Truman's dad and accomplices. They were going to exploit her for underground sex films. I doubt there's a connection. She was a runaway from Grants Pass, Oregon.

"That was her favorite toy when she was a little girl." The

grizzled man under my weight nods toward the metal dolphin that grins at me with a red-painted smile.

"What happened to her?" Amity says.

"I don't know. She's lost. Trying to find her."

"What's your last name?"

"My name's StarMan."

"No," I say, pulling out the Taser so he can see it. "What's your real name, spacey?"

"Derek," he says. "Wainwright."

"From Grants Pass?"

"How'd you know?"

64

The whole thing turns out to be a total bust. I finally get the story from "StarMan" that he came up here a few months ago looking for Teresa but couldn't find her. Not having a job, any money, and a drinking problem, he found himself homeless on the streets of Pickman Flats.

"She's dead," I tell him. "She was killed by some bad men. Her remains were found by some elk hunters up in the mountains last year. It was actually a pretty big story since the police were involved."

He clutches the silver toy to his stained overcoat. "You mean she's not coming back?"

"Sorry to be the bearer of bad news." I turn to Amity. "Let's go."

"What about the investigation?"

"There's nothing."

"Do you have a couple of bucks?"

"For what?"

"Could use a Mickey's 40."

"Mickey's?" Amity asks. "Like Mickey Mouse?"

"Malt liquor," I say, fishing out a dead Jackson and handing it to him. "Don't spend it all in one place."

Yep, this after-school activity was a waste of time. Total dead end.

But as we're leaving, I happen to notice something by the window. Under StarMan's stinky blankets, a paperback book. He doesn't seem like much of a reader. I grab it. It's a weathered, water-bloated copy of Lois J. Cain's novel *Look Behind You and Die.*

Inside the book, which has clearly been read and re-read based on its worn spine and dog-eared pages, are the initials W.R.B. written in black Sharpie.

W.R.B. not T.A.K. *What the hell?*

WTF?

"This your book?" I say, flashing it to the homeless man.

"Naw," he says. "I don't read too good. It's been there a week or so."

"And you didn't put it there?"

He shakes his head.

"And you didn't, like, ever wonder who the hell did?"

StarMan shrugs his shoulders, more interested at this point in the shiny, new twenty-dollar bill he earned.

Throwing the book under my arm, I shove Amity forward gently. "Let's beat a hasty retreat."

"Come back anytime," StarMan says. "Your money's always good here!"

"You tell me if you see anybody suspicious around here and I'll make it worth your while," I say, holding up Jackson's twin brother.

"I will."

65

"Oh, man, this is to die for!"

Truman munches on the black bean and vegan cheese nachos that Grams made. She went for this whole south-of-the-border-themed dinner.

We're sitting in the backyard in Gramps's half-finished gazebo. He has the platform built and the supports up but it's lacking a roof. Good thing the November rains are still a month away.

"If you want the recipe for the cheese," Grams says, "I have it. It's made from raw cashews, paprika, pimentos, and nutritional yeast, isn't that strange?"

"I really couldn't tell the difference," Truman says with his casually sarcastic tone.

I squeeze his knee under the table, and he jumps.

"Clare's unusual ways of eating have certainly had an effect on all of our lives," Grams says. "Some of it is weird, this whole vegan thing, but some of it isn't bad." Gramps seems like he's trying to be extra nice to Truman, which makes me a little suspicious. It's not his usual male rival energy.

"And let's not forget Gramp's cholesterol is way down," I say. "He's also dropped some pounds to a healthier weight."

"My doctor is definitely not happy," Gramps says, "He wanted to put me on a bunch of meds that he probably owns some stock in." He winks at Truman. "Sure do miss my bacon double cheeseburgers from Burger Bliss though. Right, Gigi?"

A term of endearment Gramps sometimes uses toward Grams, especially when he's feeling playful, is Gigi. Guess it's something he's said for a million years since high school. I'm not sure of the nickname's origin, and I'm a little too afraid to ask.

"What kind of wood did you use for the gazebo here, Mr. Newberry?" Truman asks, changing the subject.

Thank you, *mon amour*.

"Well, most of your Sunday carpenters would probably use a white pine or possibly cedar, but I like something stable and longer lasting, like a majestic Redwood. It's sturdy and it will last for generations. Maybe after Gigi and I are both gone, Clare will have her grandkids sitting here having dinner too."

Grandkids, Gramps, seriously? Right now I can barely handle a boyfriend. Procreation is definitely not in my immediate future or far-flung future as far as I'm concerned. *Ick.*

"Redwood," Truman says. "That's a great choice. I also love woodworking."

Gramps's eyebrows raise. "You do?"

"Yeah," he says. "DeFeo actually has a pretty decent wood-shop. Right now, I'm building a nightstand for my mom out of a sweet piece of mahogany. Hope to have it done by Christmas."

"Well, that's good to know," Grams says. "We may have to put you to work."

"I'd enjoy that," Truman says.

"Huh, I figured kids your age only got their hands dirty touching gaming controls."

"Uh, Gramps," I say, "that's kind of an unfair cliché, and some serious small-dick Boomer energy."

Gramps picks up another quesadilla and slaps it down on his plate. "Well, I *am* a Boomer, so what do you expect? And I don't have a small dick!"

Can I die now? Please!

Truman gives his fake laugh. "Yeah, well, I don't really game. Most of my friends do. I, uh, enjoy the more tactile pleasures in life. Working with wood, holding a paperback book, collecting vinyl."

"Vinyl?" Gramps asks.

"What the kids call records these days," Grams says.

"Oh, albums," Gramps says and then studies Truman. "So, tactile, huh? Meaning hands-on?"

Truman smiles.

Don't say it. Dear Lord, please don't say it.

"Well," Grams says, saying it. "One of the reasons I had you come over here, Truman, not saying that we don't enjoy your company from what little we see you, is that we've noticed that your relationship with our granddaughter has seemed to become more, uh, serious."

"Serious?" Truman says.

"Well, she was hauled in by the police after she visited your house."

Truman peers at me coolly. "Oh, yeah, that."

"We don't really appreciate Clare sneaking out in the middle of the night," Gramps says. "Or being sneaky at all."

If you only knew, Grams and Gramps, if you only knew.

Grams places a string of condom packages on the table next to the guacamole. "Now these are not saying that what you're doing is OK, but if you are, you know, 'doing something,' I want you to be safe."

Truman's face goes as red as the salsa.

"Oh, damn," I say, squinting at my wrist, which, unfortunately, doesn't have a watch on it at the moment. "We're going to be late for that movie!"

"Late?" Truman asks. "What movie?"

"Uh, it's, uh, one of those superhero movie actiony things."

Truman really likes them. Under the table, I nudge him with my knee.

"Yeah," he says, going along with my lie. "This one is supposed to be pretty good. Like, off-the-charts, spectacular."

"Well, off-the-charts spectacular," Gramps says, leaning back, an assertion of disbelief in his eyes. "Maybe we should *all* go."

"You *hate* superhero movies, Gramps!"

"Well," Grams says, holding up the condom packets. "I hope my directness isn't frightening you off."

"Oh, no," Truman says, stumbling to get to his feet, falling over his chair. "We've got to get to the theater. It's opening night for, uh, 'Super-Spectacular Man,' and there's going to be a ginormous line!"

"Thanks for dinner, Grams!" I say, walking away. "Love you both."

Grams waves the condoms at us. "Don't forget your rubbers!"

The dark soul inside me screams.

66

The high beams of my Leaf slice through the night like a knife.

Radiohead's "Creep" plays along on satellite radio and my boyfriend sings along and taps his hands against the knee of his jeans. He's pretty cute when he does this. Completely unselfconscious. If you hadn't guessed from my ringtone of "High and Dry," Truman is quite the Radiohead fan. They're less of a band and more like a religion for him. Pretty soon I'm worried he'll start speaking in tongues. After that, Panic! at the Disco's "I Write Sins Not Tragedies" comes on.

"Damn, *another* good song," Truman says, smiling. "So now we're going to the movies?"

"Would you rather stay back at home with Grams and get the Planned Parenthood lecture?"

Truman pulls out his phone. "I'll see what's playing. Also, it's a little unorthodox that your Catholic grandparents are pushing contraceptives, don't you think?"

"Well, they're pretty progressive."

Truman chuckles. "Yeah, I've noticed."

As he's checking off movies and showtimes, I notice a car has pulled up behind me, tailgating me, in fact. Peering in the rearview mirror, I can't tell who it is as they're too close, and then the driver hits the high beams, blinding me.

"What's that douchebag's problem?" Truman says, glancing up from his phone and peering at the bright lights burning behind us.

What should I do now—drive to the theater or try to lose him?

"Hang on," I say, and jerk the wheel at the next right turn.

"Should I call the cops?" Truman asks.

"The cell signal's shit on this hill."

Truman sighs and throws his phone down. "What do we do?"

"Wait and see."

The lights ahead search the narrow, winding roadway. The night breeze has picked up, and some of the dark locust trees sway like boney fingers. Dead leaves swirl across the pavement. I floor it, losing the tailgater who apparently didn't anticipate my sudden move and had to turn around.

"This is the road to the graveyard," he says, ignoring The Smith's "Cemetery Gates," which has appropriately started to play after P!ATD.

"Well, technically, it's the road to the cemetery. A graveyard is near a church."

"Yeah, that's what I meant."

Don't even try it Truman, I'm a better liar than you'll ever hope to be.

"So, who the hell was *that*?" Truman asks. "Do you think you lost him?"

Hmmm, one guess—Thomas A. Keller AKA "Dan Simmons."

"Probably one of my many admirers."

As if on cue, I see high beams burning up the hill behind us. What's not going to happen is me going on a chase. It's gotta end right here. I pull into the Pickman Flats Cemetery entrance. Reaching into my purse, I palm my "credit card" knife (basically the size and thickness of a credit card and folds out into a blade) so Truman can't see and then I step out of the Leaf.

"What are you doing?" Truman asks.

"Ending this."

"In a cemetery?"

"Is there a *better* place to end it?"

"Huh?"

"Poetic justice is a bitch and then you die."

"What are you talking about?" Truman says, climbing out of the car with me.

Our pursuer crests the hills and slows, seeing us. No, it's not Keller, unless he switched his Escalade for a new ride. It's a BMW owned by—

"Woo-hoo," Wade yells as he rolls down the driver's side window, shouting over Laurie sitting shotgun. "Just thought I'd give you a good ol' DeFeo High cheer! Hi, Tru-Blueman!"

"That's real subtle, douchebag," Truman says. "You almost caused us to wreck!"

No, he didn't. It'll take more than Wade Braden to make me wreck.

"A douchebag calling me a douchebag?" Wade says. "That's rich—you freaks have fun!"

Wade squeals off.

Part of me is relieved that it was Wade, part of me is disappointed that it wasn't Keller so I could end it right here. Before the squabble, I instinctively extended the three-inch blade of the credit-card knife. If Truman wonders why I have a knife I can just—

"Why do you have a *knife?*"

"This?" I say, climbing back into the car, Truman following suit. "Just something I picked up lying around. Gramps always says a pocketknife is a handy thing to have."

"That's not a pocketknife—that's what my stepfather used to call a 'pig sticker.'"

He gets a cold stare as I fold up the knife and put it away. "You do know I'm vegan, right?"

Truman smiles. "Every day." He shakes his head. "What was Wade's problem? He's been acting so weird lately, especially around you?"

Could it be that I recently kicked his ass or that I am holding some serious blackmail material against him?

"Mostly I attribute it to restless male hormones," I say.

Truman shrugs. "I'm not like that."

"You wouldn't be sitting here next to me if you were."

Truman smiles and then he grabs the book I purloined from the homeless man, *Look Behind You and Die,* reading the title. "What happened to Lois J. Cain is sad. Nobody seems to know where she disappeared to or if she's even still alive. People are searching everywhere."

Don't I know it. Local authorities have searched all the parks, culverts, and abandoned buildings over the last few days. Though they must not have done too good of a job if they didn't roust the homeless man.

He thumbs through the water-swollen book. "What are you doing with it?"

"Uh," I say, "just re-reading it."

Yes, I am rereading it. The initials W.R.B. on the opening page of the book mean something. There's got to be a connection. And the strange thing is, the plot of *Look Behind You and Die* is about a kidnapping that goes horribly wrong.

It seems a little more than coincidence.

67

Flashback time:

INT. CARVER HIGH GYMNASIUM - DAY

Clare is back in the Carver High Gymnasium. At
first, it's her, looking anonymous in the
crowd, but then the lights snap off and two
spotlights from above snap on. One light on
Clare, and one burning on Lois, who stands at
her podium in the middle of the gym. She speaks
only to Clare.

LOIS: Rejection is a big part of life. Keep
holding on to your crazy. Keep it burning like
a great big cast-iron stove inside of you. Keep
poking the coals when they're only embers. Keep
the crazy fire burning even when nobody can or
wants to see the beautiful light inside you. If
you keep those fires burning, eventually
someone will be drawn to your light. Yeah, it's

obsession. But it's obsession that gets you
through those dark days and lonely nights.

Clare claps and raises her arms in the air as
if she was at a Southern-fried sermon.

LOIS: Eventually, somebody will feel the warmth
and see the smoke, fueled by your obsession.
Can I get an amen?

CLARE (rises): AMEN!

There's no problem with holding onto my crazy, Lois, no
problem at all. And obsession should be my middle name. And I
promise, I'll find out what happened to you. Because it's really
starting to feel personal. And I'm pretty sure someone named
W.R.B. is behind it.

68

The gates of Pickman Flats Cemetery stand in the headlights. The white sign with red letters states CEMETERY CLOSED AT DUSK.

"So, are we going to the movies or what?" Truman asks. "The boneyard is kind of, you know, the wrong way."

"Wrong way to the movie theater," I say. "But not the wrong way, since we're here, for what I have in mind."

In the cold blue of the dashboard lights, I give him my most wicked smile, which isn't hard for me to do.

His eyes widen. "Any particular reason you want to hang out at the deadest place in town on a Friday night?"

"You're a smart boy," I say, shutting off the car. "You figure it out."

Five minutes later, after we've slipped through the gap between the chained gates, we're standing at the headstones of my parents. My father wasn't from Pickman Flats but since he died with my mother, it seemed like he'd want to spend an eternity beside her. A head-on collision with a drunk driver in a two-ton truck going ninety with them in a tiny Hyundai, and there wasn't much left to bury. It was a double, closed-casket funeral. Grams was the only one who cried. Gramps only looked sad.

"Chloe Marie Newberry-Bleecker," Truman reads. "Born December 7, 1976, and Died 20—

Beloved Mother."

"Death makes saints of us all," I say.

"Daniel Allan Bleecker," Truman reads. "Born February 5, 1974, and Died 20— Devoted Father."

"Ditto."

"So you don't miss them?"

"Can hardly remember them, really. Little memories here and there. Most not very good." Time to change the subject. "Is your stepdad buried up here too?"

Truman nods. "Want to pay him a visit?"

"Hmmm, I'd rather chew chicken bones, thanks."

Truman gives a sardonic grin. "Just a thought."

"Yeah, a terrible one," I say. "Maybe if I have to take a piss around here someday, I might visit his grave to relieve myself."

Uh, newsflash—I already did last year after his burial. Consecrated his cold headstone with some of my warm, holy pisswater. The symbolic act was rather cathartic and satisfying, considering all the trouble crooked Detective Timmons put me through, trying to murder Amity and me.

As I'm recollecting pissing on his stepfather's grave, the corrupt cop who tried to murder me, a drop of rain pecks my cheek. And then another.

And then a downpour.

A moment later, Truman's warm lips lock against mine, his body pressed up tight to me.

The world of death seems to fall away.

69

We're soaked in October rain but don't feel the cold.

"We should go back to the car," I say, pulling away to catch my breath.

"You sure?"

"Unless you want to catch your death of pneumonia, then yeah, I'm sure."

We dash back to the car, hand in hand. Inside, I hit the ignition so we have some mood music.

The rain beats down outside like fingers tapping, wanting to get in. The windows fog. My awareness around me shrinks to but a few inches. The music carries us. It's like we're in this metal cocoon, hard and cold on the outside, entwined and warm within.

Truman leans across the seat and we continue what we started back at my mother's grave. His lips are warm and have a slight taste of salt. He smells good too. Most guys at my school don't, smelling either sweaty or of some cheap deodorant that reeks. Truman always has a clean smell, like freshly laundered sheets. Being a bit of a clean-freak, I'm into it.

Except there's another odor—a little bit like raw minerals, and a lot like decay. Maybe the mud we tracked into the car. Maybe the decay of dead leaves is stamped on our shoes.

"Lord Can You Hear Me" by Spacemen 3 comes on satellite radio. Truman's hands make their way inside my coat, and I don't stop him. His hands explore the fabric of my blouse. The fingers of his right hand finding the top button. He undoes it. Again, I don't stop him. After all that's been happening, I let go. Distraction is what I want, what I desperately need.

He undoes the second button.

The next.

And the next.

His hand starts to slide inside my shirt. He breaks contact with my lips. "Is this OK?"

He gets a nod from me.

Truman traces the laciness of my favorite black bra with his fingers and then starts to reach over the top of it to cradle my left breast.

There's a strange tingling sensation to all of this. Part of me is revolted and all I can think about is that time I was eight years old. That time the Man With The Orange Sunglasses attacked me. Almost hurt me. Almost killed me. The things he did to our den mother. The thing he was. He's long dead now but that invading memory won't die. So I try to shut it out.

No, I want this. I want Truman.

For far too long, I've held him at arm's length, and he's been nothing but patient and kind to me, gentle and understanding. Like me, he's kind of an old soul, wise beyond his teen years, like he's an explorer from another time who reincarnated himself into his body, but still remembers the previous life he had as a gentleman.

He cups my warm breast with his cold hand.

Serial killers vibrate on a low frequency which also means that things that get normal people's hearts to race don't have the same effect on us. My heart is pounding against my ribcage like a persistent fist.

Then I break the oxygen-depriving lip lock he has on me.

"Alrighty," I say. "That's far enough."

"Huh?"

He doesn't remove his hand.

"You have something that belongs to me, may I have it back?"

"I was just getting into...things."

"Little by little," I say. "Good things come to those who wait."

"But we've been waiting so long." But Truman nods in understanding and slowly removes his hand, and I button my blouse back up. It's pretty funny that half an hour ago, Grams was lecturing us on the dangers of pre-marital sex, and here we are up at the petting zoo doing some heavy petting. Maybe the thought of abstinence is what gets some people hot.

"Think of it like a really good movie trailer before seeing the feature," I tell him. "You know it's coming, you can't wait, but that excitement alone keeps you on the edge of your seat."

"I've been on the edge of my seat for almost a year now."

"When the time is right," I say, "I'll release the main attraction."

Then I give him a playful bite on the end of his nose, so he'll shrink back a little bit and give me some breathing room.

"Until then, it's just trailers."

"Ow," he says, moving over to his side of the car, rubbing his nose. "How about a red-band trailer? You know, the ones that show some of the restricted stuff?"

"This was definitely a red-band trailer. In fact, this was *the* red-band trailer of our relationship."

"Yeah, but."

"Hey," I say. "Don't be a Wade Braden. It will happen, don't worry. But not in a car. And not a moment before I'm one-hundred percent ready, got it?"

Yikes, I think a little of the Other Clare came out. Definitely triggered. Did my eyes glow red? Did my incisors grow into cobra fangs? Did my face contort into a hideous demon? Dunno, but based on Truman's bewildered expression, they might as well have.

"You know," I say. "Speaking of trailers and features, there's still time to catch the late show."

"Yeah," he says. "OK."

The rain outside rolls down the window. It's backlit from the single blue sodium arc light at the entrance of the cemetery, making somber shadows on Truman's face that look like tears.

"Cheer up, love nugget," I say. "I'll buy the popcorn and hold your hand."

"You drive a hard bargain."

"Uh, speaking of which, your zipper is at half-mast."

Even in the darkness, I can see Truman's face turn a shade of red.

In a few minutes, his face would turn red again, but not from blushing.

From blood.

Maybe we should have made out at the cemetery a little while longer.

But Death found us.

70

"So what's it going to be," I ask Truman as I'm starting down cemetery hill. "Horror or superheroes?"

The rain is coming down heavy, and I need to slow. The road's a little slick.

"Kind of in a horror movie mood," he says. "Halloween is only a couple of weeks away."

"Good choice."

A horror film (hopefully good) will get my mind off my other troubles for one hundred minutes. Nothing like experiencing other people's fictional pain and misery to distract you from your own.

Headlights blaze in my rearview mirror. They're coming up fast. Dangerously fast.

"Looks like we've got company again," I say.

Truman turns around, having to squint because of the high beams. He flips the driver the bird. "Suck it, Wade, you douchebag asshole!"

As I speed up this driver hugs my rear-end. Hitting the brake hard isn't advisable as I might skid around these wet, hairpin turns. The driver lets off when I do. It's like he's reading my mind. He's good.

"I don't think it's Wade."

"Who the hell else would it be?"

The Leaf's wound up to sixty-five, which is risky on a thirty-mile-per-hour stretch of road. It's slow on this hill for a reason. Blind hills and as crooked as a snake.

"It's Keller."

"Killer?"

"Keller," I say. "Thomas A. Keller. He's after me."

"Keller? Does he go to our school?"

"Not exactly," I say, trying to keep the car on the road. "He's a really sick individual who's capable of anything. He's the reason I carry a knife in my purse." The truck roars up on my left like he wants to pass—which is insane. If another car is rocketing up the hill, he'll be totaled.

But it's not Keller. He drives a black Escalade with California plates. This is an old, yellow Ford pickup from Washington. The blinding high beams prevent me from seeing the driver. Maybe it's some rednecks who are out having some Friday-night kicks?

He drops behind me again. *BOOM!* The pickup bumps my car. What the hell?

To stay on the winding road, I have to over-correct the steering wheel.

"What the hell is Keller's problem?"

"Don't know if it's Keller. If it is, *I'm* his problem," I say. "He wants me dead."

"Dead why?"

"If we survive this," I say. "I'll tell you."

Truman picks up his cellphone. "I'm calling the cops."

"That's probably a good idea."

"Oh I forgot—"

"There's no cell signal until we reach the bottom of the hill," I finish for him. "Try it anyway—I'm gonna try to lose this fucker."

I pull into the center of the road. It's a little risky, but this way it's harder for that jackass in the Ford to try to ram me.

BOOM! He hits me again in the ass.

The jolt makes me swerve all over the road. One side of the

road is the hill with a deep ditch, on the other, a sheer cliff that vanishes into the night. Either way isn't much of a choice.

"He's going to make us crash," Truman says, still trying to get through to 9-1-1.

"Not if I can help it," I say.

After regaining control again, I slow down, staying in my lane. Gonna try something.

As predicted, the yellow Ford pickup comes up on my left again. This time, though, I tap the brakes. As the Ford whooshes past me, I try to see who's inside, but I can only see the silhouette of a head. It's one guy.

Now I'm behind the Ford—so I hit my high beams to give the asshole a taste of his own pain.

"What are you doing?"

"It's called defensive driving."

The bottom of the hill is rushing up. If I can try to run this bastard off the road, I will, but if I can't, at least we won't be going off that sheer cliff.

"Hey, I'm getting a ringtone."

The Ford tries to slam on his brakes and swerve so I'll rear-end him, but that's an obvious move I anticipated.

If you want to drive insane, buddy, you picked a crazy racing partner.

"If I just stay on his ass," I say. "I'll follow him into town. I've got the plate memorized CQB 503.

"Hi," Truman says. "This is Truman Quick. I want to report an attack. We're on Cemetery—"

Blood and glass explode against my windshield. Bastard lobbed a Mason jar full of blood. What an aim!

Truman freaks and jerks my arm, making me turn the wheel. The gravel on the edge of the road grabs my wheels. I try to over-correct, but the rocks pull the Leaf over the edge of the hill.

A moment later the Leaf is rolling for a tree. There's no steering.

BAM! A naked locust tree stops our fall.

The airbags inflate.

But not before the shattered glass slashes Truman's head.

Something strikes me in the head. A flash of white.

Like when the Man with Orange Sunglasses kicked me with his boot.

Near as I can tell, the Leaf is wrapped around a tree. My birthday present.

W.R.B. W.R.B. W.R.B. W.R.B.

What do those letters mean?

Something warm and sticky runs into my eyes.

But before I'm blinded, before things go black, I look up the hill.

The man in the Ford pickup who threw the jar of blood peers down.

Pretty sure he's laughing. Or he's just really happy.

Can't make out his face.

Are his initials W.R.B.?

This I contemplate until...

Blackness overtakes me.

71

When I open my eyes again, some woman looms over me. She stands about twenty feet tall. Red lights flash on her face that make her appear to be an angry demon. Cold rain pelts my face. Everything in my body screams in pain, especially my neck, shoulders, and back. I'm lying on the side of the hill.

"Quite a ride," the woman says to me.

The hood of the Nissan Leaf is folded around a locust tree. My brand-new birthday present now looks like every other old junker out at the Pickman Flats wrecking yard.

Truman is being carried out of the twisted metal mass on a stretcher up the hill. He looks worse than I feel.

Seems like half the town's police precinct is here, red and blue lights flashing like fireworks. Let's not forget the ambulance and the EMTs in white running around. It's like somebody tweeted about having a flash mob of people running around in uniforms right here on the side of the hill.

Somehow this all connects to me, but I cannot remember how.

"What happened?"

"That's what I'm hoping you'll tell us, Ms. Bleecker," the woman in the white linen suit says. She seems familiar. Think she's a cop. Yeah. A detective. Oh, I know, Detective Jaqui Zang, that's it.

Officer Alvarado, I believe that's his name, strolls up. He stares down at me like I'm a bug, chewing his gum. He then speaks to the detective like I'm not there. "Car went off the road at a high rate of speed as the tracks indicate."

"Clare, were you two speeding down the hill in the rain?"

"I don't remember."

"Speed kills, you know. Especially in inclement weather."

Was I speeding? Was there a reason I was speeding?

"Were you drinking?"

"How's Truman?"

"He's going to be fine," Zang says. "He's a little worse off than you, but he'll live. Now answer my question."

Question. She asked me a question? My head won't stop ringing.

"Question?"

"Were you drinking?" the detective asks. "Or doing any kinds of recreational drugs?"

As I start to shake my head no, I have to stop as my neck screams in pain.

"No." My mouth is as dry as the Yakima desert. "Water?"

"Hey," Zang says to one of the EMTs. "Can we get her some water?"

"We're going to be pumping an IV into her in a minute," says one of the EMTs as they wheel up a gurney, load me on, and start rolling me away from my wrecked car. Another ambulance up the hill has already loaded Truman, and he's off into the night. Then I start to recall the evening's events. The drive up the road. The cemetery. The rain. Us kissing in the car. His hand on my breast. My heartbeat. And then some asshole chasing us. What a strange night. After the nice Southwestern dinner my Grams fixed.

"My grandparents," I say.

"They've been notified," Zang says. "They'll meet you at the hospital."

"Did they sound, you know, worried? Grams worries too much."

"You'll have to ask Officer Alvarado, he made the call," Zang says. "But you have *other* things to worry about."

"What other things?"

Zang doesn't answer right away. Instead, she motions the EMTs to cart me around to the back of my destroyed Nissan Leaf. The trunk is wide open. Somebody wearing rubber gloves and a laminate tag that reads Pickman Flat Police Forensics is snapping pictures of whatever's in the trunk. Whatever it is, they seem awfully concerned about it.

"What's back there?" I ask.

"You don't know?" the detective says.

"Just my spare tire. Maybe my gym clothes. And they're probably pretty funky."

"That's not the smell."

Zang's right. The smell that's coming from the trunk isn't stale sweat, it's death. And I've smelled death before. It's a sickly-sweet stench, and it's always the same.

"A few days ago, you had a fight with this boy, Max Williams, from Carver High School, who went missing twenty-four-hours ago, and now he's in the trunk of your car."

She's right. It's big ol' Moosey. He's wearing the same clothes, in fact, from when I saw him. There's something troubling though.

In his chest, right through the "I" in the Metallica logo on his shirt, is the hilt of a knife.

It has an avocado-colored handle and says *The Garden Spot* on it in ivory letters.

And the handle is sticky with old blood.

72

"Whose fingerprints are we going to find on that knife, Clare?"

A forensic investigator, this one with patches of gray hair and wearing a really ugly shirt printed with antique cars, is dusting the knife handle for fingerprints.

Detective Zang asks me the question again.

Maybe I should plead the fifth here as I'm certainly in no shape to take on Zang. Hell, I'm not even in any shape to walk at the moment.

"Think I'm going to need that lawyer that you offered me before," is all I say.

"I think you're right."

Zang follows me to the ambulance. The EMTs take me inside. Zang sits down next to me as the EMTs check me over. Zang has a slight smile on her face, like the kind of smile a crocodile might have after eating a warthog.

It's going to be a long ride, and crocodile tears.

73

At General Hospital, I get the once-over with Zang standing there the whole time. Apparently, she's waiting to see if I either spill the beans or bite the dust. Though I have some lacerations, it's nothing too serious. They give me some pain meds. Truman, on the other hand, sustained a concussion, bruised ribs, and a broken left wrist. Poor Truman. All I want to do is see him. And my grandparents, who I saw waiting for me outside as they wheeled me into the emergency room. But Zang is like my Mother Confessor. She's worse than Sister Prudence Head back at DeFeo. Always watching me in silent judgement, waiting for me to slip up.

She's got me handcuffed to the bed. She says I'm a flight risk. *Seriously?*

"You know," I say, "I'll save you the trouble right now of trying to blame me for a murder that I didn't commit and a kidnapping that had nothing to do with me."

"Don't you want your lawyer?"

"Well, I've been thinking. Why do I need a lawyer when I'm telling the truth?"

"Go on."

"There's this creep named Thomas A. Keller. He snuck into

Lois's room once and tried to take pictures of her. He did three years in jail. He's back in town. In fact, he came into the Garden Spot under the name 'Dan Simmons.' I know it's him. He's playing some kind of sick game with me, and I don't know why. Maybe he was at Carver High School when I was there. I don't know. But I do know this- *he's* the one responsible."

"And you can prove this how?"

"I've been doing my research, it all fits."

"Yeah," Zang says. "It all fits, if it could fit, but it's not Keller. We followed up this angle already. Do you think some seventeen-year-old girl with an Internet connection is going to do a better job of looking into leads than a police detective?"

"And why do you say it's not Keller?"

"Because Keller died a year ago."

That next sound you hear is my jaw dropping to the hospital floor.

74

"No way did Keller die," I say, "it'd be on the Internet."

Zang smiles at me. "Well, maybe you missed the part where Keller legally changed his name to Steve Gruben."

This has to be a joke. Tell me it's a joke. But I'm not laughing.

"Gruben died last winter on Snoqualmie Pass in a weather-related traffic accident."

"He what?"

"And even if the freak formerly known as Thomas A. Keller were alive, why would he bother with somebody like you?"

Because he has a devious mind. Because I know something about that. No matter how much I try caging that tiger, that jungle cat wants to hunt. But I know this—I didn't do it. The Other Clare, the beast within me, didn't do it. Jesus loves me this I know. And I also know that I didn't do this. It's not my style, or the Other Clare's style. Somebody is playing a dangerous game. What about those initials W.R.B. Is there a connection?

"Then it's somebody else," I say. "Some other sick fan of Lois M. Cain's who has a twisted mind and is willing to do terrible things."

Zang's eyes light up and she leans in closer to me. "And who might *that* be?"

She means me. She's not going to let me go.

"For the record, I did not kill Moosey, uh, Max Williams, and stuff him in my trunk, and I did not hurt or kidnap anyone else. Give me a lie detector test if you don't believe me. I'll pass it with flying colors, and then you can stop harassing me and go after the *real* culprit who's running around Pickman Flats."

Except I want him as much as Detective Zang does, so I'm not going to reveal the initials W.R.B. That's the proverbial ace up my sleeve. And I'm not playing that card unless I have a really shitty hand at the poker table. Which, of course, it's looking more and more like I do. How can this game get any worse? I'm in the hospital, accused of another murder, my boyfriend's smashed up in another room, my favorite author's kidnapped, and my car's a total wreck?

It's been said that life sucks and then you die. But I'm not dead. Maybe this is God's punishment—just making everything suck for me but keeping me alive long enough to suffer for it before I'll face my final punishment in the flames of everlasting Hell. Maybe.

Or maybe I should just relax and try to get Detective Jaqui Zang off my back? And kill the one responsible for my suffering? Make *his* Judgment Day happen sooner than mine? There's a real divine plan...except I don't kill anymore.

Wow, I picked the wrong week to stop being a serial killer.

A lot can happen in a short span of time.

Forty-eight hours later, I'm out of the hospital with a neck brace and some pain meds. Later, down at the police station, I successfully passed a lie detector test. This was to clear myself of the murder of Moosey, er, Max Williams. Skye doesn't have any video monitors in the Garden Spot, so Detective Zang had to take my word for it that the guy that I suspect is behind this, "Dan Simmons," is still out there, throwing Mason jars full of blood (Max Williams's blood) at windshields and driving teens off the road.

My grandparents weren't too happy about the Nissan Leaf being destroyed. But they're happy that I'm safe and sound. Well, the latter might be arguable. The insurance company is investigating the accident on Cemetery Road to see if it's my fault, which, you know, it wasn't.

I've also visited Truman at the hospital. He's a little better now, and he's going to go home in a few days.

But there's still a killer on the loose. A murderous animal.

No, not me.

Him.

Bye, baby bunting, daddy's gone a hunting.

Listen, I abhor hunting. I'm a Level 5 vegan after all. If you don't know what that means, I don't even say the word "honey" because it's not vegan, got it? No animal products. Ever. And don't even get me started about hunting. Since I live in a small Eastern Washington town tucked into the Walla Walla Valley with the foothills and Blue Mountains surrounding it, there are a ton of hunters driving around in pickup trucks with appalling stickers like IF IT FLIES IT DIES, EAT MORE FAST FOOD, and WITH BEER, DEER, AND PICK-UP TRUCKS, WHO NEEDS WOMEN? Talk about being triggered. People who prey on the innocence, whether it be animal or human, is a huge pet peeve with me if you haven't noticed. Yeah, I kind of get fighting mad.

But are these hunters like me? Are they fighting some homicidal impulse that makes them want to kill something every autumn when hunting season rolls around? Does the impulse keep them from sleeping at night? Do they need to kill simply to kill? What they're killing isn't dangerous—deer, ducks, and pheasants never murdered anyone. Never sexually assaulted somebody.

There's nothing sporting in killing something defenseless with a big gun from twenty yards away. No, they're not like me.

How does your friendly neighborhood Clare go hunting? Well, first you need some bait. And since this deceptive stalker asshole seems to want me, who better than to lay in the trap? This guy seems to know my every move. After all, he planted a body in the trunk of my car, (I am guessing when I was at work or maybe at the cemetery) so he's probably tracking everything I do. If he's not, I'll make it easy for him. I'll make sure the bastard knows my whereabouts.

It's slow at work, and I'm tired of wiping down the same five tables ten times each. One can only clean a coffee maker so many times and scrub the restrooms like they were up for a military inspection. Like I'm some kind of pufferfish on display in an aquarium, I try to keep myself out in the open, near the big window. Also, don't eat pufferfish, they're poisonous. And so am I. Since it's dead in here, I crank the music up too—my stuff, not the tunes the manager wants. L7 is shouting over the speakers who's made their "Shitlist."

Grabbing my phone, I text Grams what I'm doing immediately after work. She's usually slow about texting me back, but her text pops back only moments after I send mine.

GOING TO THE GYM THIS LATE AT NIGHT IS A BAD IDEA. COME HOME.

Of course, I assure her that I'll be fine. (I still have my bag of goods—knife, Taser, pepper spray.) Grams texts back a big, long rant I won't bore you with, and so I only respond with DON'T WORRY. Then I ignore my phone.

Yes, I realize that going to Iron Works gym is kind of stupid not only because there's a homicidal maniac stalking me, but I also got in a bad car wreck and I'm not exactly one hundred percent. My neck and shoulders still hurt. But maybe pounding a bag will make them feel better. Or maybe, in my own Catholic way, I'm punishing myself for being so stupid and naive. Maybe I need a little pain to sharpen me up again.

Also, there's a good chance that my own personal stalker will take a stab (pun intended) at showing up at my house.

Last year, I had to save Grams, Gramps, and Truman from three armed men coming into the house to kill us—hired guns from Detective Timmons. I barely lived through that, and Grams had to have the carpet on the stairs and in the living room replaced because of all the blood.

No more bloodbaths at the grandparents' house, m'kay?

So, here I am, like a mother robin, feigning an injury to lead the predator away from my babies back at the nest. In this case, though, my injuries aren't feigned, they hurt like hell.

Bye, baby bunting,
daddy's gone a hunting,
to get a little rabbit skin,
to wrap his baby bunting in.

Always hated that lullaby. Here's a better version:

Bye, baby bunting,
Clare's gone a hunting,
to get a stalker-killer's skin,
to wrap her vengeance in.

Hey, it's a work-in-progress. Don't judge.

77

Going to the Iron Works at this time of night is ideal. The gym should be completely dead.

If this creep is watching me, he'll know this.

He may make his move.

This I'm counting on.

Of course, thinking from his point of view, which is essential if you want to be a successful hunter, always think of what your quarry may do. He may know that I'm laying a trap for him. Even if that's true, I'm counting on his over-confidence. Hey, I'm basically a 129-pound, seventeen-year-old girl. He's a stocky, 205-pound bastard. Also, I have the home-field advantage. And I doubt he's spent much time in Iron Works, so I know the gym layout. Yay, me.

In the alcove of the florist shop, a girl in an Army coat huddles on a piece of cardboard. Next to her is a sign that says SPARE CHANGE? GOD THANKS YOU. She stares straight ahead. The deep mascara around her eyes makes her look like a raccoon. She's shivering. The girl doesn't look much older than me, same color hair too, and we look similar in many ways, and could possibly be sisters. She's so thin and underfed.

"Hey," I say. "Are you all right?"

"You got any change?"

"What's your name?"

"Why do you care?"

Fishing into my wallet, I pull out a dollar—the smallest bill I have—and hand it to her. "This is all I've got."

"Thanks."

"If you ever want a hot meal, stop by the Garden Spot over there." I point. "Come just before closing time at nine."

"OK."

"You know," I say. "There's a homeless camp on the edge of town. It might be safer than being downtown. There's a lot of creeps around here lately."

"There's a lot of creeps at the camp," she says, stuffing the dollar in her army hoodie. "I'll take my chances."

Then I nod and start to walk off.

"Katie-Ann," she says.

"Huh?"

She smiles. "My name. You asked."

"Nice meeting you, Katie-Ann. I'm Clare. Come by the G-Spot tomorrow."

"G-Spot." She smiles. "That's pretty funny."

"Yeah," I say with a wink.

"Didn't mean to give you attitude," she says. "There's just a lot of cold people around here. I'm saving up enough money to kick this town's dust off my shoes and skedaddle on the Greyhound to someplace like Portland."

"A dollar isn't much, I know, but I hope it helps," I say. "Goodnight."

Iron Works is another block away. Of course, my stalker could attack me while I'm en route, but somehow, I doubt that. He had that opportunity many times before. It's like he's planning something. But what?

Still, I look around, scanning every dark corner not illuminated by streetlights. This part of town is dead at night. It would be a good place for him to ambush me. A lone girl walking along a dark street. Can I make myself more appetizing as bait?

As I'm turning the corner to head up the stairs, a guy tries to grab the sleeve of my hoodie. Quickly, I knock his hand away and am ready to follow it up with a throat punch, using the keys in my hand to drive them into the soft flesh under his chin.

78

But I stop.

'Cause I know him.

It's Davis Craig. He's a semi-regular at the Custard Freeze, a popular hamburger joint about a block from here. Most people go to the old Custard Freeze, which is one of the reasons the Garden Spot Café is doing so badly. Davis also does a lot of odd jobs around town. I've seen him doing yard work outside the school. Pretty sure he's harmless. Just has a life-long habit of bad judgements.

He also reeks of stale cigarettes and cheap whiskey.

"Hey, baby," he says, slurring his words. "You look familiar."

"Hey, bro," I say. "You *smell* familiar—from a few hundred yards away."

"Why you got to be like that?" he says, trying to paw me again. "Just wanna talk to a girl."

"First," I say. "I've got places to be and heavy bags to fuck up. Second, if you touch me again, I'll skip the heavy bag upstairs and work you over instead. Dealio...Davis?"

He shakes his head, his matted, curly hair falling into his face. "You're so aggressive."

In return, he receives my wickedest of smiles. "Frankly, my

'aggressiveness' as you call it, which is completely justified by the way, is simply a defense mechanism for dealing with stellar assholes like yourself, sir." Then I start to tromp up the stairs.

"You—you're crazy."

Turning around, I shoot him a death stare. "You have *no* idea."

He seems creeped out by this and hurries off.

"Happy Halloween," I say after him, wagging my tongue.

With the key fob on my keyring, I buzz myself into Iron Works. Gym members can come and go 24/7 using the fob. Just to make things easier for my stalker, I pick up an old popsicle stick off the stairs. Making sure Davis isn't hanging around—the coast is clear—I place it between the door jamb and the door. That will make for easy access. The stairs are old and creaky. It's virtually impossible to climb them without making noise. And I'll be waiting.

Will he come to kidnap me or only to kill?

Hope he'll at least try.

A girl can only give a guy so many signs that she's available (said the black widow to the courting spider).

;-)

79

Damn, there's someone else here working out. A couple. The guy, around college age, is helping his girlfriend with a bench press.

Having them in here might short circuit my plan.

In the changing room, I slip out of my work clothes and into my workout garb as fast as possible. Then I have a thought. What if he's already inside the building waiting for me? This is a good time to strike. Outside, I can hear the girl giggling at something funny her boyfriend apparently said.

Truman pops into my head. Yeah, I miss times like that. Laughing together was the best part of our relationship. Snap out of it. Thinking about anything else but Mr. Stalker Pants will get you killed. Get your head back into the hunt, killer.

After I change, I keep my Taser in the waistband of my black yoga pants covered by a baggy gray sweatshirt. It looks like a phone. I also have my credit card knife stashed in my sock. A place I can get to it easily.

Lacing up my bag gloves, I go to work on the heavy bag for a few minutes. Not doing any kicks, just punches as I don't want to jar my hidden knife loose. The couple, who I'm watching out of the corner of my eye, are doing more socializing than lifting. She's looking at her phone and showing him some pictures. He laughs.

OK, this is going to have to end as I can't get anything done with them in here. Plus, c'mon, this is a gym, not a nightclub. Work the hell out!

Walking over to them, I point to the bench press bar. "You guys using that?"

Other times when I've used this approach in the past, it makes people go away.

"Yeah," the guy says. "But you can work in a set. Need a spot?"

OK, that could have gone better. "Sure," I say.

The girl, wearing a t-shirt with Rihanna on it and the tail of it tied at her hip, glares at her boyfriend, who's smiling. His perfectly white teeth are a sharp contrast to his cinnamon skin. His girlfriend narrows her eyes at me. "Want me to *drop* some of the weight plates for you?"

Oh, kitten's got claws.

"No," I say. "It's super light and will be nice for a warm-up set."

Eat that, kitten.

The girl makes a *pfft* sound and backs away from the bench, folding her arms.

Sliding under the bar, I adjust myself on the bench and grab the metal.

"Need help yet?" the girl says.

Ignoring her, I heft the forty-five-pound bar off its cradle with two 25-pound plates on either side, and knock out eight reps. Two more than I counted her doing.

The guy goes to grab the bar and help me.

"Hands off," I say.

Then I bang out four more and drop the bar back into its cradle, rising.

The guy raises his hand to give me a high-five. "That was awesome."

Ignoring his hand, I stare at the girl. The death stare that I only reserve for a few, like Davis Craig outside. It's the one that tends to make people's blood turn cold. It's nothing mean looking, not a scowl, only emptiness, like me inside. A clear window into my empty soul. It reflects nothing back to the beholder, and it tends to unsettle them.

"C'mon," the girl says, grabbing her boyfriend's arm affectionately, and then kissing him slowly on the cheek to let one lioness know to another that the papa lion is theirs. "This place is starting to stink anyway."

"Really?" the guy says, not registering any of the female subtlety. "Thought we were working another set."

"I'm good," she says, glancing at me again, but not holding a stare, not daring to.

"Yeah," I say. "Forgive the smell—I had tofu tacos for dinner."

"Gross," the girl says, grabbing her hoodie and storming off toward the front door.

"Hey, Amber," the guy says. He stops and smiles at me. "I'm Tane, by the way."

"Nice meeting you, Tane," I say, not taking the hand he offers.

"Tane means God of the Forests."

"Think your *girlfriend* needs you, forest god." Stressor on the feminine noun.

He looks forlornly at his gal pal. "Yeah." Then heads out.

They're going to go down the stairs and out the door, moving my popsicle stick. Now I'll have to replace it.

Amber and Tane leave. Opening the door, the small stick lies discarded on the stairs.

Then a thought. *What if Mr. and Mrs. Wonderful didn't move the stick when they left?*

What if my stalker's *already* inside?

The creaking coming from the locker room jolts me back to reality.

I'm not alone.

Pulling out the credit card knife from my leggings and snapping it open, I grab my Taser in the other hand and go to check it out.

Yeah, I know, it's stupid because he's trying to lure me in there.

But I'm ready.

All the showers are on in the women's locker room. That was the creaking noise I heard, all of the hot water faucets being turned on. A layer of damp, oppressive fog hangs in the air. Steam has misted over all of the mirrors. On one mirror above a sink is the drawn emoji of a frowning face with X'd out eyes.

Glancing in the mirror, a form looms behind me, coming up fast. I turn and the three-inch blade of my credit card knife slides into the neck of my attacker.

She gasps.

It's the homeless girl, what's her name? What's she doing here?

WTF?

The homeless girl in the army coat stumbles back, clutching the knife in her neck. She has a claw hammer in her hand, and she drops it. It makes a metallic sound on the slippery white tiles. She falls over one of the benches, cracking her head on the floor.

Holding the Taser in one hand, I pick up the claw hammer. Why did she come after me with that? I wait. Maybe my stalker sent her ahead as a distraction. The mist in the bathroom grows thicker, and it's hard to breathe in all the steam's heat.

When I rush over to her, I ensure that my back is to the lockers. This way I can see the entrance, well, the obscured shape of it, if somebody tries to enter. The girl is dazed. Blood trickles from her mouth. If I pull the knife out of her neck, she'll bleed more. What do I do? If I call an ambulance, I'm sure to go to jail. This is my knife, and I did stab her. But can I let her die?

"Why did you attack me?"

As she tries to talk, she spits up some more blood.

"He gave me...money. Said that you killed his daughter. Would give me more money if I hit you."

"Who?"

"A man."

"What did he look like?"

"Am I dying?"

"No," I say. "I'm going to get some help. Hang on. Will you tell everything you told me to the police?"

"Did you kill his daughter?"

"Hell no," I say. "He used you to get to me."

"I'll tell them," she says. "Help me up."

Grabbing a gym towel off the rack, I tie it around her neck, leaving the knife in place.

"Pull it out," she says. "It hurts."

"If I do," I say, "you could bleed to death. My car is five minutes away. The hospital is another five minutes away. Can you hang on?"

"Yes."

I help her out of the locker room and down the gym's stairs. She nearly takes a tumble. I get her on the steps outside.

"Wait right here," I say. "I'll be right back with the car."

As I turn to run, I trip over somebody lying in the doorway of the building. Over his feet. It's Davis Craig. He's dead. Somebody strangled him with something like piano wire and there's a thin red line around his neck. His bulging eyes stare at me in a sick kind of judgment.

By the time I get Gramps's Camaro and bring it back, the girl on the steps is dead. She's slumped over like she's been drinking too much.

What do I do?

Now I have two corpses that I didn't kill but I will be framed for, no doubt. My knife is in one person and I'm pretty sure that's my grandma's treble piano wire is wrapped around Davis's neck. Call it an educated assumption.

Only thing I can do is get rid of the bodies. No bodies, no crime, right?

No, I'm not thinking straight, but it's the best I can do.

I load the girl in the trunk. And I stack Davis, who's a bear to lift, on top of her.

If somebody happens by, I'm done for.

With the bodies in the trunk, I do a quick clean-up of the stairs and locker room, wiping everything down using some cleaning products from the janitor's closet. When that's done, I throw the bloody towels in the trunk with the bodies.

They'll have to be burned.

The towels, I mean.

What do I do with the bodies?

Rain pelts the windshield. As I'm driving out of Pickman Flats, not really sure where I'm going, the road ahead looks like it's out of a dream. I try to put all the pieces together. Why would somebody be playing this game with me? What did I ever do to them to deserve such torment? And how am I ever going to find out?

Grams texts me and wonders where I am. I should have been home an hour ago.

I don't have anything to text back. I'm all out of excuses. So I just write back, EVERYTHING IS OK. BE HOME SOON. Then I shut my phone off.

"Is everything going to be OK?" the decaying postman in the passenger seat asks. "Because you've really blown it this time, psycho girl."

"If I wanted your opinion, Bob, I'd beat it out of you."

"No, in my case, you strangled me."

"Had to do something to shut you up."

"What's your next move, huh? Dump the bodies off somewhere like the serial killer you are?"

I say nothing.

"It's funny, the more you deny to yourself who you really are, the more that's who you become. The irony is delicious."

"Don't you have somewhere else to rot, Bob?"

"No." He reaches for the radio dial. "Don't you listen to real music?"

"Don't touch that dial," I say. "It's Arcade Fire's 'Electric Blue'—it's one of my *calming* songs."

The dead postal worker ignores me and changes it to an oldies station. It's the "Please Mr. Postman" cover by the Carpenters.

"Ugh," I say. "Are you serious?"

"Serious as a homicide."

"You can't even change the knob, you're not even really here."

"But you're here. There are two bodies in the trunk. And the Carpenters are the greatest musical group of all time."

"Well, two out of three."

About a mile past the old stockyards out on Highway 5, I arrive at my destination.

In the darkness, the sign appears in my headlights.

"Oh, Cold Creek Park," the postman says. "Good call. It's only one of the most *visited* county parks in the area."

"Yeah, and?"

"You want people to find the bodies? Isn't that kind of *not* the point?"

"I don't answer to dead postmen."

After switching the satellite channel back to Arcade Fire's "Electric Blue," I sing along, ignoring my dead companion riding in the front seat, and the two corpses stacked in the back. I sing along with the chorus until that's the only thing I can think about, like a mantra. Thank God Gramps updated this old Camaro with satellite radio when he restored it. It's like a miracle this song is playing. Maybe it's even a sign. It's the Universe telling me that it's going to be OK. It's all going to work out. That what I'm doing is right.

Once the song is over, I climb out of the car. After three days of rain, it's muddy and swampy. Great, just ruined a perfectly good pair of cross-trainers.

Opening the trunk, I grab Davis Craig. He's definitely the heaviest. Might as well get the hardest part done first. And to think, I was going to go to the gym for a workout when all I needed to do was be out here in the middle of a cold, moonless night in the middle of the rain and pull dead bodies around. Take that, crossfit!

This dude is heavy. As I drag him along the walking path, I try to figure out where to put him. *Where? Where? Where could you go?* I could try to hide him or leave his corpse out in the open. Then I get an idea. A demented little idea that makes me smile.

Once his remains are placed, I go back for the other one.

She's much less heavy, probably around my weight. I'd fireman carry her, but she'd get blood all over me, so she also gets dragged along the muddy footpath. Guess it's just as well that these shoes are ruined. They're going to have to be burned anyway, along with these clothes, in Gramps's workshop stove. Another night of me burning my stuff and climbing the trellis outside the house up to my bedroom window in the buff, then taking a cleansing, midnight shower as quiet as possible. Fun times.

OK, girlio, your place of rest has arrived.

After I place her carcass in a bed of wildflowers, I pull out my credit card knife from her neck, fish in her pocket for the dollar that I gave her, and remove the bloody towels. She appears that she's taking a snooze in these beautiful autumn flowers. Davis sits propped against a tree nearby, standing watch over her, his hands resting in his lap. He doesn't get wildflowers. Oh, what the hell, I put one in the lapel of his jacket. Yes, much nicer. Davis's puffed purple tongue sticks out at me as if he's criticizing my choice of adornment for him.

The story will break soon, no doubt. There are plenty of early-morning walkers and runners who come up this way. Once I heard the expression "for the news of the dead travels fast" from somewhere. Yes, true, very true. This will be the breaking story after the disappearance of Lois J. Cain. The tiny little town of Pickman Flats is getting a real rep as being a murder capital. And it seems that I'm involved in every case, either directly or indirectly. This sleepy little town might be too hot to live in with so many murders.

And then there's Detective Jaqui Zang. Will she be up my ass about these two killings too?

There's nothing to link me to them hopefully. Back at Iron Works, I did a thorough job of cleaning up. Thankfully the old, rickety place doesn't have security cameras, or I would have to break into the office and try to hack into their system. That would have been a whole 'nother pain in the ass.

Peeling off my bloody gym clothes and shoes in the rain, I stuff them into a plastic grocery sack. Luckily, I still have my work clothes, so I put those on. I'll burn the goods after I check in with Grams, who will no doubt be waiting up for me. Then after she's asleep, I'll have a secret clothes-burning party.

Only thing to do now is get home.

As I start the car, it's LCD Soundsystem's "How Do You Sleep?" Another favorite. The stars, wherever they are hidden in the rainy night, are shining down on me tonight, at least musically.

I shove the '67 Camaro into first gear and let out the clutch. Nothing happens. The rear wheels spin in the mud.

Seriously?

Then I slam the car in reverse. Nothing. I try forward and reverse, trying to rock it back and forth. "As idle as a painted ship upon a painted ocean" as the Coleridge poem goes.

Damn it!

Some headlights cut the night down the road, heading my way.

Are you freaking kidding me?

Wow, what couldn't be more conspicuous than a silver '67 Chevy Camaro out in the middle of a rainy night. And two dead bodies not more than three hundred feet away.

After trying to rock the car with no success, I jump out, ruining my good shoes in the mud. Who cares! What would Gramps do? He'd put some traction under those tires.

Searching along the edge of the trail, I locate a couple of pieces of rotting wood and drag them back to my car. The headlights are burning brighter, heading my way. Oh shit, it's a cop. I can see the siren on top of it.

Maybe I should give up. He's got me dead to rights.

NO!

I stuff the pieces of wood under the rear tires—I'll back over them. Hopefully, this will work.

Jumping back in the car, I give it a go. The Chevy's rear tires are spinning, trying to gain traction on the wet, rotting wood. The headlights are closer—so close I can see the outline of the white police car, the sirens on top of the roof.

Tromping on the gas pedal, the Chevy rocks and thumps over the wood. The tires grip terra firma—I'm free!

Spinning the wheel, I shift into first gear. The Chevy stalls. Damn, I'm not good at driving a stick yet. I start it again. It doesn't matter. The car is right up on me. Then it turns off. That's when I notice it's not a police car at all but an ordinary car with a ski rack on top.

My heart slows.

Thank God for small favors.

84

Back at home, I torch my bloody workout clothes and muddy cross-trainers in Gramps's woodstove. On his worktable is the cedar chest that he's refinishing for Mrs. Maitland. It's almost finished—and he's done a beautiful job.

Often, I've wondered if I'll grow up to be a ripe old age like him and have nothing to worry about in my retired life. Like what if the worse problem I have is deciding what kind of old furniture to strip and refinish? Certainly, I can hope for a cozy future such as that.

In my underwear, I don't feel like climbing the trellis on this cold and rainy night, so I'll risk it by going in the back door. In the laundry room, I have my robe that's hanging up. I don't like to dry most of my clothes in the dryer, it's too hard on them. So, I slip on the pistachio-colored, eco-friendly cotton robe, and wander into the kitchen, tired and weary. This night has been truly a nightmare.

And I still have a stalker out there.

And Lois J. Cain's missing.

And Truman's at home busted up.

And my best friend Julie's no longer talking to me.

And a detective's looking to lock me away for life.

All of those worries slip away when I enter the warm comfortable surroundings of my grandparent's kitchen. It smells of baked bread and kindness. Sure, I've got ninety-nine problems but being home isn't one of them. This has always been my sanctuary of peace and solace.

The house lies dark and still. That's a good sign. Maybe Grams grew tired and went to bed. Heading up the stairs, I tiptoe, skipping the steps that creak, like playing a silent sonata with my bare feet, avoiding the noisy keys of the piano.

Gramps's snores echo down the hall for a minute, then it's interrupted. Probably Grams elbowing him to turn over. All good.

When I enter my room, I notice my desk lamp is on. Grams sits on my bed, her eyes bloodshot. She's been crying. Wrapped in her faded pink chenille bathrobe, she doesn't make a move to rise. *This is bad.* She's a hugger by nature, a bear hugger, if truth be told. Her not offering to hug me immediately is a grim sign. She clutches her phone.

"You had me so worried," she says, her voice shuddering and cracking. "I've called you and messaged you and you didn't pick up or answer."

My mind searches for a thousand casual lies to hide the cold truth of my night's murder and mayhem.

"You weren't working out," she says, her voice increasing in volume. "Where were you?"

"Actually," I say. "I was doing just that. And I ran into Tane and, uh"—can't think of her name—"his girlfriend, Tiffany"—good enough name—"at Iron Works. We sorta lost track of time."

"You've never talked about Tane and Tiffany before."

"They're just, kind of, you know, casual gym buddies. Like gym rats. They're always there. Anyway, Tane is a personal trainer and was showing me some moves. Tiffany and I were talking about"—what do normal girls talk about?—"uh, fashion tips and shoes and video games. We kinda got carried away."

"You weren't with Truman? Didn't go to his house?"

Why does her line of questioning now sound like a cardinal heading up the Spanish Inquisition? Am I going to get a red-hot poker shoved up my ass if I'm revealed to be a lying heretic?

"Well," I say, choosing my words carefully, "no. I thought about it. But I figured he probably needed his rest. He needs to get well."

Grams starts crying again. Carefully, I approach her. I really don't want her to see my—

"Where are your shoes? And clothes?"

"Oh, I parked right next to a mud puddle and jumped in when I got out of the car. They're, uh, drying downstairs."

Grams blubbers some more. So I sit on the bed and comfort her, rubbing the soft texture of her bathrobe. This is the kind of thing I've seen Gramps do when Grams is upset, a gentle hand on the back.

"What's really going on?" I ask.

After a few more minutes, she gains her composure. "It's not just me being worried about you. That's a lot of it. But I'm worried about Ellis. He's been acting so strange lately. And he's been snoring a lot more. The other day, I saw him stumble in his shop when I was taking some coffee out to him. He said he was fine, but I know he wasn't. He won't talk to me. He seems to avoid me, like I'm a stranger."

"Maybe he's going through some weird kind of man-o-pause or something. You know how fragile guys are, all weird and stoic. They all seem like they're trying to hide the little boys in them or something. Even somebody as old as Gramps. We must be the strong ones."

"For your age, you see a lot."

"Well, I guess, I'm just, I don't know, observant."

Grams smile fades and she looks sad again. "I don't know what I would do if anything happened to you or Ellis. I love you both so much."

Yeah, that makes two of us, Grams.

"We're going to be fine," I say. "We're all going to be fine."

Then I notice something about two inches in diameter on Grams's leg. At first, it looks like the pattern of her flannel pajamas, but I know it's not.

"Grams," I whisper. "Don't move a muscle."

"What?"

"Don't move."

Carefully leaning across my bed, I grab my empty water glass from the nightstand.

"What are you going to do with that?"

"Just relax."

She tenses up. "It's not a—spider?" Grams is an arachnophobe.

Shake my head no.

With a quick flick, I swipe up the foreign body into the glass and lid the glass with my hand. The hobo spider, aggressive, fights his new, transparent surroundings, trying to get at Grams and me.

Grams screams and jumps off the bed. "Kill it! Kill it! Oh my god. Kill it!"

"There, there," I whisper. "That's a big boy." It's getting cold, and the spiders are coming inside due to the chill in the autumn air.

Since I was small, I've always had a kinship with spiders. They terrify most people, but not me. They're different; they're hunters. If people really took the time to understand them, they would find them creatures to be admired, not feared. But fear over understanding is easiest for people.

"Clare," she says, backing against the bedroom door. "Don't mess with that—they're deadly poisonous. Kill it!"

"He's not going to hurt anyone," I say. "He's just looking for a safe place. Just like we all are."

"I do not want that horrible thing in the house."

Rolling my eyes. "Fine."

Holding the glass carefully, I open my bedroom window and let the big spider go on the trellis outside. Sorry, boy, it's going to be a chilly night for you. Not my choice.

Then I close the window.

"Why didn't you kill that thing?"

"Have you met me? I don't kill innocent things."

85

Making my morning protein mocha, "Death By Chocolate" on page twelve of my recipe book (ABP: Always Be Plugging), Gramps informs me that he needs the Chevy, so he's going to take me to school.

"My own personal escort," I say.

Normally, teens are mortified to have their parents, or grand-parents in this case, drop them off in front of school. Not me. My gramps is as cool as they come. In light of last night's nocturnal activities, I should be nervous about him wanting to take me in the Camaro. After all, I did have two dead bodies stuffed in the trunk.

But no worries there.

After Grams finally went to bed, I switched off the driveway motion-detector light, snuck outside, checked on all my clothes and the shoes I burned up to make sure they were ashes, and scrubbed the trunk and car clean. The credit card knife I stabbed Katie-Ann with had to be soaked in bleach, then placed into the fire. Then its undestroyed remnants were buried in the crawl-space under the house. (Sad, as I loved that knife.) Bleach and lots of scrubbing removed any blood from the trunk, too. Those towels and rags were also burned. When I have to, I clean up pretty nice.

Last night I only clocked maybe three hours of sleep.

Really *needing* all the caffeine in this mocha. Stack a guarana supplement on top of it. Guarana seed extract, a stimulant the Brazilians have been using for centuries, has a weird effect on me as it makes me all smiley and warm. It gives me an unrealistic feeling of well-being for several hours. Normally, I don't take guarana as I'm too annoying to be around when I do. Today, though, as tired as I am, I'll be like a corpse that's been reanimated and forced to smile and be friendly to people.

Gramps tells Grams he's not hungry and only has half a cup of coffee. Grams looks at me, conspiratorially, as if this confirms that he's been acting strange as he's not having his usual breakfast of Scottish oats and turkey bacon. I just shrug, meaning, boys will be boys.

"Planning a big day?"

This I ask Gramps as he's driving me to DeFeo.

"Not really. Just need some more materials for the gazebo and I hate driving Arleen's Camry. Miss the old Silver Stallion here." He cranks up the '60s station on the satellite radio. Dion warns the song listeners about a girl who gets around town named "Runaround Sue."

Wow, an old song about slut-shaming. Nice.

Gramps sniffs the air.

"What's up?"

"Dunno. Smells like bleach."

"Oh, yeah," I say. "Had to pick up some produce and other supplies at Williamson's Market for the restaurant and some beet juice spilled all over."

"Beet juice?"

"Yeah, I know, right?" I say. "That stuff is the devil to get out. But I did it. Luckily you had the plastic mats down. It didn't stain the carpet underneath."

"Glad to hear it," he says and gives me a wink. He takes a hit of his coffee from his stainless steel travel mug that says WORLD'S GREATEST GRANDPA. It was a birthday present from me a couple of years ago. He kind of winces as he does so. Then I smell it—the stench of bourbon. This isn't like him.

"Are you OK, Gramps?"

"Yeah," he says, rather gruff. "Why wouldn't I be?"

At that moment, there's a brief silence as the song changes to "Mother's Little Helper" by the Rolling Stones. Gramps has a little helper today too—in the form of Wild Turkey, the bourbon he used to drink. I don't want to embarrass him about it or put him on the spot about what Grams said about him stumbling or acting weird, but I need to know. This is the person I love most in the world. Well, care for, love is a little hard for a person with my unusual psychological profile.

"I noticed that you didn't eat breakfast," I say. "You usually can't wait to dig in."

"Haven't been too hungry lately," he says, taking another hit of his whiskey-laced coffee. "Nothing taste's good." He shrugs. "Maybe my taster is going down the crapper along with the rest of me."

"Are you, uh, feeling bad?"

"No, why?"

"No reason," I say with a casual shrug. "Just what you said about the crapper."

"It's only an expression, you don't have to take it literally."

"You know, if you can't taste anything, you should eat some more zinc foods like nuts, beans, and seeds. They could help with that."

Gramps snarls his upper lip. "Beans make me fart, and squirrels and birds eat seeds."

Um, OK, forget I said anything "grumpa."

As we're pulling up to DeFeo, I notice the spot of blood on the mat in front of me about the size of a dime. And then I see Detective Zang climbing out of a car.

Really? But I cleaned the Chevy. Thoroughly. How did that get there? There's no way I overlooked it.

Gramps glances over in that direction, so I strategically drop my backpack down on the stain.

Zang is going to nail me as soon as I step out of the Camaro, I know it. And if I move my backpack, what am I going to do about covering that spot? Either way, the blood is going to raise questions from somebody.

"Oh, you know what, I forgot my English book back at home."

"Can't you look on with somebody else?"

"There's a test," I lie. "I *need* it."

"Then you certainly won't need your English book."

"It's an open-book test."

Gramps looks annoyed. For the first time, I think in my entire life, he seems to want to get rid of me. He turns around in the parking lot and starts to head out. Zang waves us down and stops us.

"Her again?" Grams grumbles. He pops a few spearmint Tic-Tacs into his mouth and rolls down his window. "Can I help you...detective?"

"Good morning," she says in her bright and also condescending manner. Her bright white linen suit looks a little too starched and stiff. "Decided to play hooky today?"

"You didn't answer my question," Gramps says. He's not usually this abrupt.

"I would like to speak to Ms. Bleecker," the insistent detective says.

Oh, here it comes. Be cool. You expected this.

"About what?" Gramps asks. He pops another Tic-Tac.

"Tic-Tacs," the detective observes. "Nice."

"I've had lifelong halitosis," Gramps says. "Count yourself lucky I have them."

What? That's an out-and-out lie. Gramps doesn't have chronic bad breath. He's covering up the Wild Turkey stench.

"I won't stand too close then," the detective jokes badly and gives a forced chuckle.

"You didn't answer my question."

"I want to talk to Ms. Bleecker about something."

"What's that?"

"Well, I would like to do it in a more conducive environment," the detective says. "Not standing here freezing in a school parking lot."

"Well, I'm her legal guardian—what's this about?"

"There was some suspicious activity last night at Cold Creek Park," the detective says. "And I'm checking in with the usual suspects."

"My granddaughter is a good kid. She's not a suspect."

"Well—"

"In fact," Gramps says, interrupting Zang, "after work, Clare came home and brought Arleen and me one of those vegan tiramisus. They're really good if you can get over the fact it's not made with butter and cream. Goes nice with a cup of black coffee. Though I have decaf in the evenings as I get a tad jumpy and restless if I sip the leaded stuff. Then we all binge-watched some *Virgin River* on Netflix. Pretty much a standard family evening. The kind of evenings I cherish, in fact."

"You're saying she was with you after she left the Garden Spot restaurant *all* last night?"

Gramps nods. "In so many words."

"And she didn't go out," the detective asks. "Maybe after you and your wife went to sleep?"

"I'm a light sleeper."

The detective looks past Gramps and glares at me. Not knowing how to respond, I give her a smile and a wave. Zang narrows her eyes. She burns with a cold fire under that pale linen suit.

"Thank you, Mister Newberry," the detective says, enunciating her words for effect. "I'm sure we'll be talking more soon."

"Hope not," Gramps says, peeling away, flipping a U-turn, and heading out of the parking lot. He flips the knob of the radio up and rather appropriately, "Born to be Wild" by Steppenwolf plays. He's gone from age seventy-two to sixteen with the jerk of a steering wheel.

"Gramps," I say. "Take it easy."

Wow, now I've officially become the adult here.

"What's the use of driving a fine automobile like this if you're not going to ring it out once in a while?" He laughs. "Blows the carbon buildup out!"

Yeah, Gramps, you're blowing the carbon out. But something tells me you're projecting yourself onto the car. Just an observation.

Twenty minutes later, when I returned to school, with my English book (which, of course, I didn't need), everyone was talking about what happened at the park. Mostly rumors. It's going around that Katie-Ann strangled Davis Craig and then killed herself in a jealous love tryst. Ridiculous. And a few other theories. At least those theories don't involve me. Maybe I've gotten away clean?

Their murderer is out there. Yes, I killed Katie-Ann, accidentally, but it was Mr. Stalker who put her up to it—and he definitely killed Davis!

Julie's in my English class and peers through me like I'm not even there. *Whatever.* Not that I care right now.

Currently, I'm busy trying to figure out what this bastard's next move is.

It's going to be major.

Gramps said he'd pick me up after school at 3:15 sharp. Waited a half hour.

He never showed.

First time ever he's never fulfilled a promise to me.

"I'm worried about Ellis. He's been acting so strange lately. The other day, I saw him stumble in his shop when I was taking some coffee out to him. He said he was fine, but I know he wasn't. He won't talk to me. He seems to avoid me, like I'm a stranger."

Last night, Grams words cut through me like a knife.

Have we both become strangers to the man we love?

Amity offers me a ride in her daddy's BMW, and I accept. Better than sitting here and waiting like a miserable idiot.

We stop by the Dancing Goats. Pretty sure she can tell I'm depressed, and she buys me my usual—sugar-free vanilla latte with almond milk.

Plum Adams, who is usually hanging out drawing, is now hanging all over Julie.

Julie has now dyed her hair green. She must've done it right after school. WTF?

Plum still has her plum-colored hair. They're making out in one of the overstuffed wingback chairs with Julie sitting on Plum's lap. Yeah, I've never been a fan of PDA, and this is beyond ridiculous. They should be charging admission. Part of me feels like Julie's putting on a big show now because she's dyed her hair and is kissing a girl. She's wearing a black and white Ms. Fits t-shirt over her DeFeo skirt. Guess she's going full secular school now. Good for her. Julie glances over at me from the corner of her eye, and then attacks her plum-haired girlfriend with a new, passionate vigor.

Before I stroll out with my latte, I give them a loud and steady golf clap. Call me a bitch.

This warrants no reaction from the newfound lovers. They're too tongue-tied with each other's tongues.

What the fuck ever.

"Do you need to swing by your handsome beau's house to drop off his daily lessons?" Amity asks with a wink. Truman does need them but more importantly, I need to find out what happened to Gramps. Calling the house, I talk to Grams to find out if he's there. She said he's not home and not answering his texts or calls, and she's worried about him.

Quick stop to Truman's, and then to find Gramps.

Amity pulls up to the Timmons's house. Good, his mom's car isn't here. Ever since I killed her husband in self-defense, it's been a little awkward around us, as you might imagine.

"Wait here," I tell my Clare cosplay chauffer. "I'll just be a minute."

"I'd love to see Truman, too."

I shoot her a sour look. Today's not the day.

"Tell him hi then."

After I knock on the door, it takes several minutes for Truman to answer. His hair is disheveled, and his eyes are heavy. He seems out of it.

"Oh, hey," he says, rubbing his fingers through his dark hair. "I must've fallen asleep. It's these damn pain pills."

The cast on his arm is pristine white. Nobody has signed it.

I raise my backpack. "You left your social studies book at school, so I brought it."

"You can come in," Truman says. "It's kind of a mess though."

I shake my head. "I've got something to do."

"Yeah, right, of course."

"What's that supposed to mean?"

He clears his throat. "Nothing."

"C'mon, you said it. Own it."

"It's just that you're always running off to parts unknown and not telling anyone. It's like you're a superhero or something hiding your secret identity from me so you can go fight crime."

Well, yeah, if you want to put it that way. I shrug. "*Batwoman* and I have never, ever been seen in the same room at the same time. So there's that."

"It'd be funny if it wasn't so frustrating and sad. I just wish you'd let me in. I feel like I'm single or something. Couples are supposed to share their personal bullshit, good or bad." He stops. "Can I tell you a story?"

"If it's a quick one. I seriously have to run."

"When I moved here with Mom four years ago from Aberdeen, I thought Pickman Flats was going to be boring. I mean, in Aberdeen, at least I had my friends, even though they were mostly shitheads and troublemakers. And you could go to the ocean whenever you wanted. Mom enrolling me in DeFeo and marrying a police detective felt like the end. Then I met you, and I felt like I wasn't alone with all of my weirdness and pain."

"Uh, thanks, I guess."

"I was reading this self-help book that Mom had lying around called *A New Earth* or something like that. The author talks about pain bodies, and how if we're carrying around a pain body, we are attracted to others who might have the same. It all has to do with our egos. We fall in love with people and things that reflect our own egos in some way."

I check my watch. "There's a point to all this, right? I really need to go."

"It's just when I met you, Clare, I thought you were it for me. Nobody else in town was as fascinating as you. Guess I was attracted to your mystery. But now I live in mystery wondering what you're doing. And I feel like I have to play detective and interrogator to get anything from you."

"Are you saying that you want to break up? Because I heard this same kind of spiel from Julie before she pulled the plug on our friendship and it flatlined."

"No, I didn't say that. What the fuck?"

"For your information, Gramps is missing, and I need to go find him. He hasn't been well, and I'm worried. There, now you don't have to play detective." I hand him the book. "I really have to go."

"Yeah," he says. "I know. Loved seeing you."

He leans over and kisses me. I kiss him back.

"Sure you can't stay?" he says, softer.

"I need to find Gramps. You need to get better. I'll call you later."

He nods, then waves at Amity in the BMW, and shuts the door.

After that, I make Amity drive me all around town.

There's one place I think he might be. A place Gramps has told me about when I hang out with him in his shop as he crafts his next woodworking project. He's always the most candid with me without Grams around. Like we were two old war buddies swapping secrets. (Except I let him do all the talking and secret-revealing). A place that Gramps has mentioned more than once.

Amity takes me there.

Henry's Place is a little hole-in-the-wall joint one block off Main Street in the more run-down part of Pickman Flats. It was built sometime in the 1930s post-prohibition as a kind of cozy-looking Irish pub, and the last time it was renovated was probably about the time Ronald Regan was president. Henry's doesn't look like a place you want to spend much time in, it mostly looks sad, just sad, as if it stood still as time moved on around it.

The '67 Camaro, AKA The Silver Stallion, is parked around back.

Amity waits but I tell her to leave.

In my mind, it goes like this:

```
INT. HENRY'S PLACE — DAY


CLARE enters the establishment. Haggard REGU-
LARS slouch on barstools. A single light shines
on her GRAMPS and his golden chalice, as he
sits at the bar. The whole thing plays like
something out of MAN OF LA MANCHA.


Clare goes to remove her grandfather from the
```

```
stand but the grizzled MEN and WOMEN from the
bar join in to sing the chorus of what happens
next...

A spontaneous rendition of "The Impossible
Dream" explodes on-screen in a random musical
number. "To dreeeam the Impooossible
Dreeeam..."

And then, at the end of the clumsy rendition,
Clare edges her forlorn Gramps, like Don
Quixote who has lost his way chasing windmills,
out of the depressing establishment. She has
rescued him from his prison. Victory!
RETURN TO SCENE.
```

Ignoring the sign that says NO MINORS ALLOWED, I walk into the dingy den. There are a few patrons, that look like regulars, attached to bar stools. Gramps sits at the counter nursing a drink. I get a few nasty glares from some of the haggard-looking men, but they don't say anything. Colorful Christmas lights are strung up, perhaps to make the place look cheerier. It isn't working. The TV above the bar has September Jones on *Top Talk* wondering what happened to Lois J. Cain. The TV host is taking some insane theories from deranged locals.

Ignoring this, I sidle up to the familiar old man at the bar. "Ready to saddle up and head out, cowboy?"

He turns to me. He's shit-faced drunk and his breath reeks of sour mash.

Gramps slurs his words about not being a cowboy and then wonders what I'm doing here. At least, that's what I can decipher from his whiskey-tinged speak.

"Hey," the sharp-tongued bartender says. "You can't be in here, sweets." She's wearing a sausage-skintight sequin shirt with an American flag on it that barely covers her pallid muffin top that hangs over her too-tight designer jeans that went out of fashion around the time Journey first sang "Don't Stop Believin'" on the radio.

Ignoring her, I grab Gramps's arm.

"Hey, you little chippy," the woman insists. "Get the hell outta here."

She receives my patented death stare.

This only seems to antagonize the woman. "You got something to say to me?" She waddles around the bar and over to me, fists clenched.

Don't escalate this, Clare. Don't. "Just grabbing my grandpa."

"Maybe he don't wanna leave," the tawdry woman says. "It's a free country."

Gramps pulls loose from my grip. "I've been drinking here since before you were in Pampers."

Normally my smart-ass self would make a joke about adult diapers in correlation with geriatrics, but I hold my tongue. The Other Clare is itching for a fight but not here, not now.

I breathe, speaking slowly and clearly. "You're either coming with me, or I'm calling Grams and she can pick us both up. Which is it going to be?"

The woman, who I peg at maybe sixty-two, closes the space between us. OK, this isn't quite going like the "Impossible Dream" number I had imagined. Why can't life conform to my craziness instead of the other way around?

"You got bee's wax in your ears, bimbette?" she says. "Get the hell out of here or I call the fuzz."

She reaches for me, and I parry her hand away.

"Did you just try to hit me?" the woman says, staring daggers.

"Don't touch me," I say. "Gramps, let's get out of here. Please."

The woman tries to reach for me again and I slap her hand away, harder this time. "I am a minor."

"A minor that's trespassing."

She lunges for me again, but Gramps rises from his stool and stands between us. "Give it a rest, Delores."

He stumbles and I grab him. He's heavy. You can bench press

and squat at Iron Works gym all you want but try lifting a rambunctious septuagenarian who's been knocking back the Wild Turkey all day. That's a whole 'nother challenge.

"Next time you slide in here, Sparrow Tits," Delores says after us, "I *will* call the damn five-oh."

Sparrow Tits, really? There won't be a next time, dumpster fire queen.

And as much as this whole episode at Henry's Place sucked, it wasn't as big of a problem as what came after.

89

Gramps rides in the passenger seat of the Camaro, slumped over. My first thought is to drive him around until he sobers up so he won't have to deal with the wrath of Grams Arleen, but I'm not going to protect him. She'll know. He smells like a distillery anyway.

Can't wait for the family drama.

Not only is my favorite author missing, my boyfriend's banged-up, my Nissan Leaf's totaled, I have a murderous stalker coming after me, and now I've gotta deal with Gramps coming home drunk. Had to deal with this with my mom, the vodkatarian. Really thought I'd gotten past this in my life.

"Hey," Gramps says, his words slurring. He points to the dime-sized spot of blood on the floor mat in front of him. "Is *that* blood?"

Holy hell. In all the distraction, I completely forgot about that spot.

"Uh, no. Remember when I told you about the beet juice I spilled?"

"That don't look like no damned beet juice," he says. "It looks like blood."

He starts leaning down to touch it. The blood has dried, of course, but it clearly looks like blood, not beet juice. Any idiot can see that. Even a drunk one.

Think fast, Clare. Think fast.

As if God is watching out for me, a gray squirrel darts in front of us, and I swerve.

Smack! Gramps hits his head on the dash. "Ow, what the goddamned hell!"

"Sorry," I say. "Had to avoid hitting the squirrel. You OK?"

He leans back in the seat, rubbing his forehead. "I don't give two damns about no squirrel."

Well, at least he seems to have forgotten about the blood. Thanks, God.

"That's why I'm here," I say. "To take care of little things that can't take care of themselves."

Gramps's sour face crinkles into a smile. "Like you're taking care of me now?"

"That's right," I say, patting his shoulder. "Now hold it together, we're almost home. Grams isn't going to like this."

"Don't worry about Gigi," he says. "I've been hiding snorts of Wild Turkey from her for years."

Years? WTF? Guess I'm not the only one who's been keeping secrets in the family.

"Can I ask you a question?"

"Shoot!" Gramps says.

"Is there a, uh, reason that you've started drinking?"

Gramps turns and looks at me a moment like he wants to say something, then stops. "Because I need to sometimes. Good enough reason?"

No, Gramps, not really. I had the feeling you were going to tell me the real reason, then froze. What is it? Why? I can't take him being this way.

Pulling into the driveway, I slide the Camaro into park. "Need help out?"

"No," he says, waving me off. "I'm an old pro at acting too."

Wow, what's Gramps mean by *that?*

The moment Gramps stumbles through the kitchen door and takes a look at his wife, he pukes on the floor, splashing Grams's shoes in bile-colored vomit. The sour stench of used Wild Turkey Bourbon's in the air.

It doesn't get much better after that.

90

The next day at DeFeo, the shit hits the fan at precisely 3:15 p.m. And it has changed some lives for the worst. And it all started with a note.

In Sister Molly Walsh's English class, I sit behind Laurie Meeks. Usually, I sit in front, as I'm that annoying student who often has all the answers. However, after Wade Braden started dating Laurie Meeks, I've moved back a few seats as I wanted to keep an eye on them, especially Wade.

During class, Wade snuck his phone out of his pocket. Phones are expressly forbidden in class and using one will have your ass shepherded to Sister Aileen's office, led by creepy Sister Prudence Head. He quickly texted a message to Laurie. Her silent phone vibrated with message received as Sister Walsh was yammering on about dangling participles, interrobangs, and diphthongs.

With a fake yawn and stretch, Laurie covertly slid her phone out of her jacket draped on the back of her chair. With all the expertise of a pickpocket, she snatched out her Android and read the message. And so did I. Wade wrote: BELL TOWER AFTER SCHOOL?

Laurie responded back with a yes, a kiss emoji, and a few others too nauseating to describe here.

So, the bell tower, huh? DeFeo looks like an old Spanish-style mission, that's why there's a bell tower. A year ago, Wade ushered me up there under false pretenses. Having the best biceps in school, I was kind of taken with him for about fifteen minutes before I found out what a complete shitheel he is. He'd tried to take advantage of me. Mercy Franks was trying to record him molesting me as some lame way to "slut shame" me. (In the twisted world that it is, I'd be the one blamed, not my aggressor.) Mercy ended up dead, tumbling over the railing and splatting on the concrete below. They hadn't counted on the Other Clare crashing the slut-shaming party.

So, Wade's trying to get his bell rung again up in the bell tower? Fine. We'll see about that.

However, the Other Clare isn't invited to this little tryst.

This is strictly me, your friendly neighborhood Clare.

Yep, Clare is going to handle this. Part of this new Clare handling things would involve going straight to a sister and telling them about the afternoon delight Wade had planned on school grounds. But that would mean getting Sister Prudence Head involved, and that's not happening. There's no chance of me getting on her good side since I don't believe she has a good side. It's all rocky and craggy like a sheer mountain face.

After school, I keep on Laurie like a six o'clock shadow on a summer's day. Most of school is clearing out, so I hang back. But one of the advantages of everyone dressing alike is you can remain anonymous out in the open. Laurie says goodbye to her friends, which involves me tying my shoes for about fifteen minutes, and then she heads into the janitorial area in the back of school.

When Wade took me up there last year, which is expressly off-limits, he knew where the key to the bell tower was. However, it didn't matter, as it was the *wrong* key and I ended up picking the lock. After Mercy fell and died, a new padlock went onto the trapdoor. Did Wade somehow have a key for that since I wouldn't be around to pick the lock again?

Following Laurie now is a bit more challenging as the students have left, and it's only her and me. I duck into shadowy corners and doorways, synchronizing my steps with her. If being a serial killer has taught me one thing, it's that I'm an excellent tracker of prey. Pretty ironic, I know, since I'm #veganAF. But yeah, mad skills in the tracking department. Another irony, if you're into that, is I'm tracking Laurie like prey when I'm trying to protect her. This girl has no idea what a piece of shit her boyfriend is. He's absolutely the worst kind of human being.

Laurie slinks up the dusty, winding stairs to the top of the bell tower. Tracking her is going to be difficult here as the old wooden stairs creak like ancient bones. I'll have to wait until she's up there in the tower before I can begin my ascent. After she knocks on the bottom of the unlocked trap door, it opens, showering afternoon light on the gloomy stairwell. So I duck out of sight like a vampire afraid of the sun.

Once Laurie vanishes and the door shuts, I make my way up the stairs, staying close to the wall and the edge of the stairs, taking light steps to avoid the creaks and groans. It's slow going, but I avoid conducting the wooden stair orchestra and alerting the lovers of my music. On the landing of the stairs, it's a ten-foot climb up a wooden ladder to the trapdoor. This also creaks, so it's going to be tricky.

Then, a godsend. Muffled voices and giggles from the other side of the door, followed by a couple of thumps. Dear Lord, what are they doing up there?

Climbing the ladder, I move to the sound, and suddenly freeze on the creaky wooden rungs when the noise abruptly stops. It's their silence that worries me the most. Can Laurie Meeks from Colfax really be this stupid? Well, she's with Wade and she seems to be in love, so I guess the answer to that is in the affirmative.

You can never account for a person's taste—or lack of it.

Poor little stupid farm girl whose shoes still smell like wheat chaff and cow shit. There are some Big Bad Wolves in Pickman Flats who eat Red Riding Hoods for snacks. At least there's one wolf who keeps tabs on the pack—this she-bitch!

What are you going to do, Clare? Huh? You have to keep your

Fitbit in check. You can't let it go above 150. This is a potential conflict situation that could trigger The Other Clare. In fact, it's pretty much guaranteed. No, you're going to control this situation and not unleash that monster. You're going to be rational and use your words. *Use your words.* We're not savage beasts (well, most of us), we can use communication and language. Everything doesn't have to break down into animalistic violence when human interaction is lost.

You're just going to inquire about what's going on, I tell myself. *You're just going to inquire and tell them this is not a good idea.* Yeah. Interrupting them is enough. They'll stop. They'll know that you know. Just tell them that if they stop and come down now, you won't go to Sister Prudence Head. Them being up here —doing an illicit act on school grounds in a place expressly forbidden by *anyone* to go—is grounds for expulsion.

Reaching the top rung of the ladder, I hold tight with my left hand and gently push up the trapdoor with my right. The view becomes clearer—Wade and Laurie are writhing in a hot and heavy embrace on a threadbare green wool blanket. Part of me wants to yell at them and part of me wants to watch—to see how far this will go.

What's wrong with you? You didn't follow Laurie up here for a peepshow, sweetie. You followed her up here to protect her from Fuck Dodgers.

Wade starts unbuttoning Laurie's shirt while she has her head rolled back and her back arched—did she see this move in some kind of bad, Victorian period, bodice-ripping movie? Then I can't help it, I laugh. And I laugh. And I laugh. And I can't seem to stop.

Wade and Laurie turn toward me, horrified that I've found them.

Well, since the cat's definitely out of the bag now, I throw the trapdoor the rest of the way open and join them on top of the bell tower platform. The panoramic view up here of Pickman Flats is spectacular.

Something happens that I wasn't expecting. Wade and Laurie start laughing as Laurie rises and buttons her blouse.

At first, I can't figure out what they're laughing about, and then I see Jeremy Herrera. He is waiting behind the trapdoor, so I don't see him until it'ss too late.

And he's pointing a pistol at me.

91

Wade checks his watch, making a big theatrical gesture of it. "Wow, it's 3:15—look who showed up right on time."

My focus isn't on Wade, though, it's on Jeremy, and the pistol he has leveled at me.

Don't Hulk out into the Other Clare... Don't Hulk out into the Other Clare... Don't Hulk out into the Other Clare...

Stealing a glance at my Fitbit, I see it's slowly rising: 106... 110... 117... 127... 136... Just about to hit the breaking point.

"What's this about?" I say, stalling. Fighting to keep calm.

"You tell us," Wade says, smiling like he's the villain in some kind of James Bond movie who has trapped the super spy. "This little party is in your honor."

A trap. I should have suspected. Laurie made it really easy for me to see the message. They had anticipated me taking the bait. They know I'm the kind of obsessive freak who would. Seems like the other wolves of the pack have just called out the alpha. *Bravo!*

No, you're going to hold your shit together, Clare. Somebody's going to die here if we're not calm and careful. You don't want to end up splatting face first on the Lord's Prayer seal on the stoop of the front stairs like Mercy Franks did a year ago. And you don't want to kill anyone, accidentally or on purpose. This is Clare remaining calm... calm... calm... Zen AF.

"You're going to have to clue me in," I say.

"Oh, so you deny attacking us the other night at Lamb Hollow?" Wade says.

"That was some Carver dudes."

"No," he says, edging up inches from my grill.

Calm, calm, calm. Calm, calm, calm.

"It was you," he says. "I've *always* known it was you."

"Yeah," Jeremy says, keeping me clocked with the pistol, pointing to his nostrils with his free hand. "This nose can smell a no-good bitch from fifty yards."

"Um, I do *not* smell." Yeah, had to defend my honor.

"Shut up," Wade says, his face reddening and a drip of spittle flying from his mouth and landing on the lapel of my navy blazer. Guess I'll have to burn it. A shame, it's my favorite. "We're talking here. The adults are talking."

Really? Who writes this guy's lines? Strictly B-movie, pulp paperback at best.

"You're going to do two things," he says.

"If one involves me touching you, Fuck Dodgers, that's definitely out."

"Shut up—you think I want your diseased meat?" He narrows his eyes. "You know what I want—that flash drive of the video. That one you stole from Mercy."

"And the second?"

"After you give it to me, you stop following me, stop leering at me, and stop taking up oxygen near me."

"Or?"

Jeremy points the gun. "Or I put a cap in a bitch."

"OK," I say. "May I speak? You know, like a rational adult?"

"Make it quick."

"First, I don't have the flash drive on me, it's at my house. Second, we should really not be here. If we're discovered, we're all done here at DeFeo..."

"And third?"

"Space Cadet here is threatening me with a deadly weapon on school grounds and that's a pretty hefty charge. I've been meeting with the police a lot more than I would like and I know what the stakes are here. Think it over, Fuck Dodgers and friends."

My reasoning seems to throw Wade for a loop. He wasn't expecting this. Maybe he was expecting me to lose my cool? When you're a person whose rationale replaces emotion, a cool head generally prevails. But I can feel that Other Clare climbing up my leg with a knife between her teeth. She's itching to jump and stab. Gotta keep her reigned in. Don't need her to get this done.

Calm, calm, calm. Calm, calm, calm.

"First," Wade says. "Stop calling us Fuck Dodgers and Space Cadet. I don't know what that even means. Second...if you don't give us that flash drive, right now, you'll meet with an accident," Wade says. "You won't know where or when. Since you're so popular with the police, I'm sure they wouldn't lose much sleep over your permanent disappearance."

"I sure as shit won't," Jeremy says with a smile. "Hell, I'll sleep like a baby."

Going for Jeremy's gun as it's jammed in my face is a mistake. Somebody could get killed. And if it's me, it would be the most tragic and you would be sad my story ends here. One thing I've learned in my seventeen years—when you're forced to do something you don't really want to do, agree, in fact, seem happy to do it, and then when they relax a little bit, go off and do your own thing. Most people simply want servitude and compliance from you. It's a power play. It's rarely backed up by action. People are too distracted with their own lives to keep tabs on you 24/7. And I'll go along with these morons. When they think they have me, I'll decide a different recourse. No, not as the Other Clare—that bitch needs to stay in the kennel with a muzzle on. Nope, I'm going to come clean to my special friend, Detective Jacqui Zang. Tell her everything that's been going on with Wade and his friend. They'll lie about what happened here, three witnesses to one. But recorded footage doesn't lie. And I have it of him attacking Julie at that party when she was passed out. Wade's going down. If it doesn't get him thrown in jail, it will wreck his sterling reputation in this town. His family, who are on the Pickman Flats city council and on the board for charity events, will be crushed that their "good son" is a serial abuser of teenage girls. And I'll make it my personal mission to make sure that information goes out as far and wide in the world as possible. I'll definitely be calling back September Jones for a special return to *Top Talk*.

So, I nod. "All right," I say. "Follow me to my house, and I'll get the flash drive."

"No," Wade says. "It goes down like this—you go with us in *my* car, you get the drive with Laurie going in with you, you bring it back out to the car, we check it on Jeremy's laptop, and if it's what I want, you're free to go. If not..."

"Guess you've one-upped me here, Wade," I say, really piling on the sarcastic compliment. "You should play chess, you're always five moves ahead—you'd make Bobby Fisher look like an amateur."

"Who?"

And then, just like that, call it happenstance or God's divine grace, I notice what looks like a glistening diamond out of the end of the pistol Jeremy is holding. In the afternoon light, it gleams. A single droplet of liquid.

It's a water pistol.

92

When you're facing a loaded gun—and trust me, I have—two questions go through your mind. Do you act or do you submit? Do you risk getting shot or wait to get shot? When you have a choice like that, that's not much of a choice, it's called a dilemma.

Now, I was facing a dilemma a few moments ago when I had a pistol waving in my face. But now the factors have changed, but the game is still the same. Since I'm not going to Clare Out on this guy—and I really have to give myself credit for not doing that and for keeping my FitBit from rising to the tipping point—I must weigh my options. The easiest one would be to inform Jeremy that he's holding a kid's toy, not a weapon of mass destruction. His options would be to smile and do nothing (unlikely) or grab me (more likely). At that point, my Other Clare will pierce through my pores. It's inevitable. Somebody would end up seriously hurt. Probably dead or at least maimed. Probably wouldn't be me. Detective Jaqui Zang already has a girl boner for me the length of the Walla Walla River, so why entice her any further?

Yes, I know you're disappointed. You want me to freak out. You want me to kick ass. But dammit, I'm telling you as a born-again serial killer who's trying to quell the homicidal urges, and who's challenged at every level of self-control, that you can "turn the other cheek." Just like it says in the Bible. You can appeal to the better angels of your nature. In a way, this would be giving Jeremy and Wade exactly what they want. Sure, the Other Clare would come to my aid and most likely win the battle. But would she win the war? No, this would only prolong things.

So, I'll act like I didn't see that ridiculous water droplet out of the end of that pistol and go along with it. Buy myself some time. The potential stress of my beast woman emerging has lessened anyway. Mind over matter will certainly make matters better.

"OK," I say, making a concentrated effort to not look at that pathetic toy that Jeremy is pointing at me. "Let's go for a drive."

"Wow, Clare," Wade says. "Always knew you were smart, but you surprise me—you should try to beat the next rocket scientist out of his Nobel Prize!"

Now it's Wade's turn to lay on the thick, sarcastic compliment. Ah, mine was better, it rolled easier off the tongue, and was less forced. Kudos for Clare.

"Lead the way," I say with a gesture like a courteous door handler at a luxury hotel.

"Who's up there?"

That piercing voice that makes the warm afternoon air turn to ice and the chirping finches and starlings in the nearby tree take flight and flutter away can only belong to *one* individual.

"It's Sister Prudence Head," Laurie whispers.

The faces of all my colleagues turn to a shade of ash as their blood drains away. Guess I'm not the only one that she instills terror in.

Jeremy stands there with a dumbfounded expression like he just got hit in the face with a soccer ball. The squirt gun now dribbles water.

"Put the gun away, stupid," Wade hisses at him.

Everything after that happens in a series of flashes, like snapshots.

Sister Prudence's hands, which are more like vulture talons with frail human flesh stretched over them, starts to climb up the ladder. Each talon grabbing a rung and pulling her dark form up and up. The wind that rushes through the bell tower and down the trapdoor makes her black habit flow around her like some kind of demon emerging from hell.

"I saw you," she says, climbing one rung at a time, out of breath, her voice becoming ragged like the sound of tearing paper. "All of you, when I was outside. You're all going to report to Sister Aileen. And I suspect all of you sinners will no longer have a future here at DeFeo."

Laurie and Wade stand there, unmoving.

Jeremy is slow to put his gun away.

And then I kind of blurt it out. "Sister, look out, Jeremy has a gun!"

Yes, I've always had an impulse control problem—I'm a sociopath, sue me!

"You bitch," Jeremy says, covering the short distance between us at an alarming speed. With the gun no longer a threat, the dilemma no longer being a dilemma, the choice has been made. I side-step him and strip the toy out of his hand. It rattles to the ground, betraying its plastic makeup. Using Jeremy's momentum, I grab his right arm with both hands and swing him into Wade.

Swinging his big arms, Wade knocks Laurie back. Thankfully she just falls on her butt instead of over the edge of the tower like Mercy did. Wade takes a step forward to right himself, but he steps in the open space of the trap door. He falls on Sister Prudence Head, and they tumble the ten feet with Wade on top of her. Somewhere in that mess of boy and nun, I hear something that sounds like dry twigs wrapped in cotton snapping.

Peering over the side of the trap door, I can finally see what broke as Sister Prudence Head's right arm is twisted at a rather sickening angle like the broken wing of a crow under her dark habit. And she's making this low moan, like a wet cat that was caught out in an ice storm and begging to be let in.

It's the most pathetic sound I've ever heard.

Then I wonder if that's the same sound that the kid who broke his arm made when running away (or pushed) down the stairs by Sister Head.

Jeremy stands there like a stump with his mouth agape.

Sitting on the wool blanket, Laurie stares at me a moment, and her face contorts like she's going to ugly cry. "You're—you're evil."

Yeah, I smile, I can't help it. "You don't know the half of it, bitch."

93

The epilogue to that little adventure went like this. Wade and Jeremy claimed that I forced them up in the bell tower at gunpoint. They told this to Sister Aileen and Officer Alvarado. Their reason didn't any make sense. They said I was trying to make them jump off the top of the tower. This was their revenge for my unsuccessful assault on them at Lamb Hollow.

However, Laurie folded under questioning and revealed what had happened. She confessed as all good Catholic school girls do. The way I'm confessing to you now.

For once, I got off easy. Fuck Dodgers and Space Cadet couldn't prove I was at the hollow, not to mention the police didn't buy it that somebody with my size and build could hurt two strapping young men (sexist). Laurie ended up being my savior, though she failed to mention the flash drive. Wade and Jeremy were expelled from DeFeo Catholic High School. Laurie and I are still attending, thank God. Laurie's parents, so I'm told, made her break up with Wade for being a "bad influence."

As far as Sister Prudence Head, that ended well for me, too. After she had her arm reset and cast at the hospital, she decided to retire. Apparently, the sister had enough as a disciplinarian and found kids today "too unmanageable."

All in all, not too bad for me.

Except Wade. I knew he would exact revenge. Fuck Dodgers in the 21st Century wasn't done with me yet.

It seems this was the eye of the proverbial hurricane, too. As a total, merciless shitstorm blasted me right after that.

94

And finally, we're up to the day my life went to complete shit.

How did this happen? Was it God punishing me? Was He testing me like Job? Or do I just have shit luck?

It went like this.

School just got out and Amity (looking more and more like me every day) asked me for a ride home. At first, I told her no, that I had to get to work. But she bribed me, saying she would like to buy a whole vegan blueberry cheesecake from the G-Spot.

Yeah, I can be bought. And so can you, suckers, so don't judge!

The moment I pull up at the restaurant, The Raveonettes crooning "Dead Sound" on the satellite, my phone rings. It's Grams. Usually when she calls, she wants me to bring some groceries home from Williamson's Market since she doesn't like to drive anymore. It's odd how you miss boring and banal things like that when life takes a sharp turn for the worst. You wish you had those comfortable feelings again. The past doesn't have teeth that bites as sharp as the crushing jaws of present-day reality.

"Ellis fell in his shop," Grams says, fear in her voice. "We're at the hospital. You'd better get here, quick."

Those last five words hang in the air and echo in my brain. *You'd better get here quick.*

"What happened?"

"Just get here," Grams says. "Stop by the house first and get his medication. I couldn't remember what he was taking. The doctor wants to know. Grab all the insurance forms out of my little file cabinet too. You'll see them."

"Is this serious?"

"Yes."

Forgetting Amity is in the car, I pull away from the G-Spot in the Camaro, nearly hitting a Subaru station wagon from Montana. Damn tourists!

Amity asks me what's going on. Her voice sounds distant, like she's shouting from the bottom of an elevator shaft.

"It's Gramps," is all that parts my lips.

She offers me words of assurance and comfort, but she might as well be blowing bubbles because I'm not listening or deciphering any of it.

We pull up to the house. Amity asks me why. And so I tell her I need to get some stuff and that maybe she needs to get out of here, as I'm going to the hospital after this. Amity says she wants to be here for me. Then tells me to wait in the car, she'll get whatever I need.

So I tell her where Gramps keeps his prescription bottle (in the medicine cabinet above his bathroom sink) and the insurance papers (in a little black plastic file cabinet in the den).

Amity runs inside the house.

All I can think about is Gramps. His smile. His warmth.

It all plays in my mind like a movie clip on a loop.

Then a huge *BOOM!* rocks me, a flash of light, and a sheared and burning post from the porch hurls in my direction and impales the front window of the Chevy.

95

The house isn't there anymore. It's now a roaring fire and pillar of black smoke rolling up into the pale October sky.

The post from the porch sits lodged in the front seat where it missed my head by inches.

Through the broken windshield of the Camaro, I can feel the heat from the roaring flames.

Amity.

She was in the house.

She looked like me.

She's dead because of that.

This was on purpose—that I know.

This was him.

96

Ten minutes later every fire truck and police car in town are at the burning wreck of my grandparents' house. The only home I really ever knew. The firefighters, wearing their yellow jackets and helmets, are hosing down the flames but it's like an incendiary bomb went off.

Detective Zang is there. And I'm telling her that I need to get to the hospital. But she won't stop asking me questions. Like why did I send Amity into the house instead of going in myself? Why did I come home instead of going to work?

Excuse me, bitch, but why the hell would I blow up my own house? My sanctuary? The only place in the world I've ever felt love? And felt safe? Why?

For the first time in a long time, tears wet my face. It's an odd feeling. At school, I see girls cry all the time about the stupidest things, mostly over boys. Crying has never made sense to me. These are real tears. Even Zang seems surprised.

Wade could have a revenge motive for what happened at the bell tower.

But it's not in Wade to do this.

This was the work of *him*.

It's then I finally admit to Detective Zang that somebody out there is trying to destroy my life, bit by bit. He's kidnapped my favorite author (and made it look like I did it), nearly ran me off the road, planted a body in my car (and made it look like I did it), sent somebody (Katie-Ann) to try to kill me (this I don't reveal), and now blowing up my motherfucking house. Is he responsible for Gramps too? Did he make him fall? Somehow, I doubt it. Maybe the intention was to kill all of us. Maybe Gramps getting hurt and not being here was what saved his life. Irony is a weird maiden.

After the flames are doused, the firefighters remove Amity's remains in a black body bag. It's odd that a year ago, the God Squad—consisting of Amity Liston, Mercy Franks, and Hope Dalquist—tormented Julie and me and made our lives a living hell. Now they're all gone. All because of me. I didn't kill any of them, but they died because of their proximity to me. Julie's even gone. She's still breathing, thank God. But I feel like she's gone forever.

And now my grandparents lost their home (because of me).

And Gramps is hurt and in the hospital (because of me?).

Part of me wishes I could walk into Gramps's work shed (which is still standing for the most part), pour a can of gasoline on myself, and walk into the smoldering fires of my former house and self-immolate like a Buddhist monk. Maybe if I'm out of the way, this stalker bastard will stop hurting everyone I care about.

A hulking fireman with a red face, gray handlebar mustache, and wearing a yellow, soot-stained jacket, carries something in his glove—it looks like the broken neck of a wine bottle. He shows it to Zang and me.

"Know what this is?" the fireman asks.

"Looks like a melted part of a wine bottle," I say.

"It's an IED—improvised explosive device. It was rigged to some wine bottles filled with gasoline. Basically, a firebomb."

"It was *him*."

"An IED is rigged to a cellphone signal and a 9-volt battery—at least this one was," the detective says. "Whoever set it off was here at the time. They had eyes on the target."

"He thought Amity was me. He was trying to kill *me*."

The detective cocks an eyebrow. "Why would somebody be trying to kill you, Ms. Bleecker?"

"Maybe he doesn't like me. Maybe he's playing some kind of sick and twisted game. How the hell should I know?"

Zang only stares at me—through me.

My phone rings—it's "Love is Like a Butterfly" by Dolly Parton. Grams's favorite song. Normally, I'd ignore this. But this isn't normal.

"Grams?"

"I need you at the hospital—now!"

"Did something happen to you?"

She starts to sob. "It's Ellis."

97

At General Hospital, I find Grams in the waiting room. Her eyes are the color of tomatoes. She's been crying non-stop. She doesn't know about the house. Detective Zang drove me. The police left it to me to tell her. Being back here is weird as I was just here for the crash—and my grandparents were here to see me.

"Why do you smell like a campfire?" Grams says.

"How's Gramps?"

"He's stabilizing," she says, wiping her bloodshot eyes. "He had a heart attack in his shop...and then had another heart attack when we got here."

"Can I see him?"

"He's in intensive care," Grams says. "They're doing every-thing they can."

98

After what seems like a day and a half, the doctors let us see
Gramps. They say he's stable and needs rest. He's under careful
observation. Grams hugs and kisses him, practically climbing on
top of him in the hospital bed. An annoyed-looking nurse wearing
SpongeBob SquarePants scrubs has to pull her off.

"It won't happen again," I reassure the nurse. "It's just a hard
time for us all right now."

The nurse gives an indifferent nod before she leaves.

"Can I see him?"

Grams wipes her eyes and nods.

Pulling up a chair, I sit down next to Gramps and hold his
hand. For the second time today, tears fall down my cheeks.

His skin appears so milky pale. It's hard to tell if he's only
resting or dead. He seems thinner than he did a couple of days
ago. Like he lost twenty pounds overnight. His usual full cheeks
look sallow. His thick fingers seem like brittle winter twigs that
can snap in a breeze. His breathing is so shallow, I can't even tell if
he's doing it.

He cracks his eyes open a quarter inch. For some reason, it
reminds me of a turtle slowly pushing his head out of his shell, like
he's unsure of the gesture, cautious and confused.

"Babe," he says, though it's hard to decipher his thick-tongued words.

"I'm here," I say, holding his hand tighter.

"Those tears for me?"

Quickly, I wipe my eyes. "No."

He cracks a smile, which seems to break his frail face. The action causes him to moan.

"Try not to get so worked up, cowboy," I say.

He gestures for me to come closer. First, I glance over at Grams, whose eyes burn with fresh tears, then I move closer. He tries to speak in my ear. His breath is cold and has a metallic smell.

"I-I know who you are," he says.

"What?" I whisper.

"Know who you are...really."

"I don't know—"

"I know everything." He coughs. "Who you really are. The blood in the Camaro. Everything."

"How?"

"Was going to fix up your hope chest. Surprise you. Found the hidden drawer."

For once in my life, I'm speechless. What can I say? So I just nod in understanding.

"It's OK," he says. "Nobody's perfect. But you've always been...in my eyes. You're-you're my baby girl."

If I had a heart, it would be breaking right about now.

"Take care of Arleen."

"Yes," I say.

He smiles again, and then relaxes. The heart monitor flat lines and an alarm goes off. Within half a minute, a doctor and nurse burst through the door screaming Code Nine. They try to resuscitate him with the paddles. It doesn't work. He doesn't respond.

And the whole time, it's strange. Gramps looks at peace.

With a smile on his face.

99

After Gentle Meadows Funeral Home came and picked up Gramps's body, and Grams had to sign it away, she wanted to leave the hospital. She wanted to go home.

"There's...no home to go to," I finally have to admit.

"What are you talking about? Please, Clare, I'm too exhausted."

"It's gone. Completely burned down." And then I have to explain it to her. Could this day suck any worse?

The shock of losing Gramps and our house in the same day shakes Grams to the bone. She has a nervous breakdown and has to be hospitalized herself.

Not having any place to go, I stay with her all night, sitting in the uncomfortable plastic hospital chair next to her bed. After the day I've had, the darkness and quiet in the room is a much-needed solace.

The indifferent nurse in the SpongeBob SquarePants scrubs gives Grams a sedative in her IV drip. It's good Grams is asleep. While she is, I field texts from everyone I know, including Truman, asking me what happened. And so I tell them what I know. My texting thumbs feel like they're going to fall off. So much for the solace part. Surprisingly, I received a text from Julie too. It simply reads: I HEARD ABOUT YOUR HOUSE. AND YOUR GRAMPS. SO SORRY. When I text her back, she doesn't respond. Guess she said all she needed to say.

The insurance company, I am told, will conduct an investigation to see if our house exploding into a raging fireball was arson or malicious intent by an outside party. Can you believe that? Why would my grandparents or I torch our house that we love?

Detective Zang, as far as I know, doesn't suspect me—if she did, I'd be down at the police station right now. But talking to her, there is doubt and suspicion in her dark eyes. Since Hope Dalquist and Mercy Franks died in proximity to me, the natural logic would go that I was finishing off the former God Squad for good by setting up an explosion, sending Amity into the house, and setting it off remotely. It's outrageous. If I had wanted Amity dead, I wouldn't have saved her life a year ago from Truman's bad cop stepfather.

"Ellis?" Grams says as she stirs.

Leaning over in my chair, I tell her to go back to sleep.

"I can't sleep without my Ellis," she says in a drug-induced delirium. "Make him come back to bed. It's cold in the house. Could you turn up the thermostat, Clare honey?"

"Consider it done," I say, and throw an extra blanket on her, tucking her in.

We have no more house; we have no more Gramps. The two things Grams and I loved most are now gone. It was in Gramps's will to be cremated and to have his ashes spread in the backyard by his shop. After the funeral home picked up his body, I wonder if they took him back there and cremated him right away. Is he just ash and tiny fragments of bone now? Just like our house? Did the warmth and security for Grams and me go up in smoke? Has it burned away like spots on the sun? Every day I pretend to be like other people, normal people who have a heart and empathy. Right now, though, I'm glad I don't, or I'd be in a bed next to Grams with sedatives coursing through my veins.

Grams's gray eyes pop open and stare into the dark. At first, I think it's a reaction to the sedative, but she seems to have a second of clarity.

"He's gone, isn't he?" she says.

"Yes, Grams."

"And our house?"

"That too."

Grams's eyes well up with tears. "What are we going to do, Clare? How are we going to make it?"

"We're survivors," I say, holding her hand, which feels like nothing more than a cold, limp rag right now. "We're going to rebuild. Or rebuy. We're going to get on with our lives the best we can. We're women. *We're* the strong ones, remember?"

"It's going to be OK?"

"Yes."

"And you'll stay with me, all night?"

"All night."

100

Grams spends one more day in the hospital, and I stay with her, having been excused from school. I still have my school clothes on from yesterday. It's odd to realize that everything, every article of clothing I own, I'm wearing.

Then Detective Zang and Officer Alvarado visit. They come around 11 a.m. and offer their condolences about Gramps after they learn about his death. At least that's one death that the detective can't try to pin on me. Insidious bitch.

Was there a break in the case or are they coming to arrest me again? Am I going to spend another session in the interrogation room with Zang while unknown people watch my every move behind one-way glass?

"We're going to need you to come with us, Clare."

"But I'm keeping an eye on Grams."

"She's in good hands," Alvarado says.

"Am I under arrest?"

"Not at the moment," Zang says. "Come with us to the station."

Guessing that not taking me away in handcuffs again is a good thing. Though the two tight-lipped authoritarians don't make idle chit-chat as I casually try to glean details. What's waiting for me at the station?

Ten minutes later, Zang sits me down in a room with a few plastic chairs and a big picture window. On the other side of the glass are two familiar things. The interrogation room where I've spent some time across the table from the detective—and a man I've met before.

"What's he doing here?"

"We've gotten a confession," Zang says. "And I'll have you visit the observation room. Sergeant Alvarado will keep you company."

"Terrific," I say.

The officer stops chewing his spearmint gum and nods. Zang disappears.

"Why do you chew so much gum?"

"Because smoking was killing me." He offers me a green stick. "Want one?"

"And deny you a fraction of something that seems to give you so much pleasure?" I say. "I'm not the sadist you think I am."

The officer gives me a miffed look. He returns his spearmint back into his pocket like a magician hiding a white rabbit in a black top hat.

Zang reappears in the pale, sterile interrogation room I know too well. Zang has two Styrofoam cups of what I assume are coffee. Doesn't she know that Styrofoam is bad for the environment? Can't she use something reusable?

The man reaches for the cup and that's when I see the shackle on his right wrist. He's chained to the table.

"State your name."

"You've already asked me that."

"State your name again. Please."

He sighs. "StarMan."

Now it's the detective's turn to sigh. "Your *actual* name."

The man sips his coffee and seems to think about it. "Derek," he finally says. "Wainwright."

"You were found driving a Ford pickup and carrying a burner cell phone in your pocket."

"Didn't know either were a crime."

The detective rises and leaves the room. "Enjoy your coffee."

"You believe he's the one?" I say to Zang as she steps back into our observation room.

"Do you recognize this man?" she asks.

Well, yes, of course—I kicked his ass in a vacant building when Amity and I accidentally discovered where he was nesting. But I can't tell the detective that. And I can't let Derek Wainwright see me either. Then I could be the one back in the interrogation room.

"Think I've seen him around town."

"I meant did you recognize him when your car went off the road?"

What I remember when my poor Nissan Leaf went off the embankment and smashed into a tree nearly killing Truman and me was a Ford pickup on the road. A man standing there watching us, but I only saw his silhouette. The details were fuzzy at the time, like my aching head.

"The man I saw was only a dark shape," I tell the officers. "Can't be too sure."

"Didn't you say a beat-up yellow Ford pickup ran you off the road?"

"Yes."

"So why'd this man run you off the road and blow up your house, Ms. Bleecker?"

You tell me. He's the father of Teresa "Skizz" Wainwright. Last year, I killed all the men who made the last hours of his daughter's life a living hell. If anything, Derek "StarMan" Wainwright should be pinning a medal on me and showering me with gratitude.

"Your guess is as good as mine," I finally say.

"I've only gotten his confession," Zang says. "But I want to know the *why*. And I want you to be here for it."

"I *want* to be here for it."

Zang does something I've never witnessed before. She smiles. At me. *What the actual fuck?* I don't smile back. First, the Pickman Flats police are treating me like a criminal. And now like I'm their ally working on a case? *My* case? The weird world we live in just grew a little weirder. Not even a psycho like me can comprehend life's craziness.

Like a skilled illusionist, the detective in the white linen suit disappears from our room and reappears in the interrogation room.

"Good coffee?" she asks the suspect.

"I've had better."

Zang sets a burner phone in a plastic evidence bag down on the table. "This was found on you. It was used to detonate an improvised explosive device that destroyed a private residence and killed a schoolgirl. You also were found in a beat-up yellow Ford pickup that fled the scene of a hit-and-run that nearly killed two people. The scratches on the fender match the paint of the victim's car."

"Wasn't me."

"But you were driving that Ford. A Ford, I might add, that's not registered to you and was reported stolen."

"I didn't steal it. Just found it with the keys in it." The man's hands shake.

"You do a lot of drugs, Mr. Wainwright?"

"No."

"Methamphetamines, perhaps?"

"That stuff will fry your brain."

"Did you maybe steal that Ford to sell it and buy more drugs?"

"Maybe I need a lawyer," he says, pushing himself back from the table as far as he can. The chain stops him.

"You waived your right to a lawyer earlier."

"Yeah, I guess I did."

"Why did you blow up the house at 237 Straw Street and murder Amity Liston?"

The man's hands shake more as he speaks. "Yeah, OK, yeah... Y'got me. I did it all. I kidnapped Lois Cain. I planted the boy in the trunk of the car and ran it off the road. And I blew up that house because that girl attacked me. So I was going to teach her a lesson. Are you satisfied?"

"Whoa," the detective. "Back up. *You* kidnapped the author?"

"Me and another person. She's dead now. And I covered my tracks. Now I wanna make a plea deal. I don't want no goddamn death sentence."

"Is Lois J. Cain alive? Where is she?"

The man's hands shake more. He looks pale.

"Are you OK?"

"Don't feel so good," he says, shaking.

"You're most likely experiencing drug withdrawals."

The man bends over at the waist. "Think I'm gonna be sick!"

Detective Zang looks toward the one-way glass and at Alvarado and me behind it.

"Officer, I'm going to need some assistance."

"Sit tight," Alvarado says to me and exits.

The thought of leaving is tempting. But the thought of killing this man who destroyed my grandparents' house is even stronger. If it *was* him. It doesn't make any sense. Why would this drugged-up burn-out try to do such a thing? What did he have to gain?

Officer Alvarado enters the interrogation room.

"Will you escort this individual to the men's room?" Zang asks.

Alvarado pops his gum. "Sure thing." He grabs a key from his belt and unlocks the wrist shackle. "Let's go, chief."

The man takes his free hand and doubles over, holding his stomach. "I'm gonna lose it!"

"For god sakes, Alvarado," the detective says. "Get him the hell out of here!"

As Alvarado goes to help the man, he turns and punches the policeman in the groin. Then he wrestles the Glock 19 from Alvarado's holster. The officer lies on the ground gasping for air.

Detective Zang goes for her firearm, but the man points the gun at her. "Drop it." The woman obeys. "Kick it to me." She does.

Part of me wants to run into the interrogation room and confront the man (except I don't have a key) and part of me wants to see what he does. I don't have to wait long.

He smiles at the one-way glass—at me—and raises his left palm. On it, drawn in Sharpie, is the familiar frowny face with the X'd out eyes. It's a message. From him. Wainwright then points the gun at the one-way mirror. I hit the floor as a volley of bullets shatter the glass, sending fragments down on me. Trying to climb back up, I stumble among the overturned plastic chairs.

Wainwright moves forward, his hand shaking from withdrawals but steady enough to shoot. He has me at point-blank range. Detective Zang stands behind him, hands raised, and appears like she's mentally measuring her options.

"Hello again," he says. "Guess I have the upper hand now."

There's nothing I can say to him. And I can't run. Looks like I get my one-way ticket punched to Heaven (or Hell) right here.

Wainwright smiles. He's got my full attention. He points the pistol at me, lining up a shot.

"So sweet," he says. "So innocent."

Then in a rapid motion, he bends his elbow and shoves the barrel of the pistol under his chin.

"See you in hell," he says. And then softly, "Teresa."

BLAM!

Detective Zang's white suit is going to have to be thrown away. No way all the blood and brains splatters will ever wash out.

101

"You have a spot of something on your lapel," Truman says an hour later.

When I look down, it's blood. A drop the size of a pinhead on my white school blouse.

"And I know you don't like ketchup."

Why lie? He's my boyfriend.

"It's blood. Some guy just blew his brains out in front of me an hour ago, my grandma is having a nervous breakdown, my grandfather died, and my house is gone. It's been kind of a shitty day, may I please come in?"

Like some kind of threshold guardian, Truman stands in the doorway. He has a pale cast up to his mid-left forearm, and he's wearing an open denim shirt. He has rigid stomach muscles underneath. It's a nice view, but I'd rather not stand on the front porch as the light is dying, and the October cold starts whispering against my bones.

"Uh, yeah, I was just about to have some Earl Grey and some Lemony-Bites."

Wow, how weird, he's eating cookies that I used to sell as a Firefly girl way back in the day. A decade, for those keeping track.

They're one of those mainstream cookies that are accidentally vegan. Now my boyfriend is eating them. Have I come full circle around the Firefly cookie?

"Sounds lovely," I say, pushing my way in. He smells like a boy who hasn't showered in a couple of days. The thin shadow along his chin and jawline betrays his devotion to the razor. The stubble agrees with him, makes him appear more rugged and handsome. If I told him that, though, he'd probably shave. He's not a guy who's easily impressed with the bravado and machismo of stereotypical uber-male characteristics. He's a bit of an emo boy. But he's *my* emo boy. Seeing him now makes me realize how much I've missed him.

The house is dim with only the light over the stove in the kitchen on. The shades are half pulled. My boyfriend even makes the house emo.

"How are you feeling?"

"Better," he says. "I'm not taking as many pain meds, so my head isn't as fuzzy." He raises his cast. "It's a good thing I do everything with my right hand, but it's a pain in the ass to wrap it when you wanna shower."

"Yeah," I say, noticing the house is unsettlingly quiet. "Where's your mom?"

"She's out tooling around with some of her church friends. They're all going to that new Jennifer What's-Her-Name movie."

"I didn't know your mom was so involved in the church."

"She wasn't...until my stepfather died. Then that changed. They're kind of her go-to support group."

"Yeah," I say. Sorry mom, for slaying your murdering psycho husband. In the future, pick a better spouse who's maybe more into busting criminals instead of being one. "Here's your social studies assignments, English test, math," I add, pulling the day-old assignments out of my backpack and placing them on the kitchen table.

"Thanks."

Then I move closer to him, putting my hand under his shirt

and against his hard stomach. "If you need some physical fitness make-up work, I'm a willing and eager subject."

The teapot on the stove whistles.

"Watch the ribs," he says. "They're still screaming."

He jerks away from me and tends to it. Not exactly the warm reception I was expecting. Hey, I'm breaking out of my comfort zone here by being more affectionate as he's wanted me to. Remember our conversation back at the G-Spot before things got so insane? Now he's making me feel like Typhoid Mary made a house call.

"Something wrong?"

He doesn't answer me for a few minutes, plopping a tea bag into each of the two mugs. One mug has a faded Monet painting on it. The other is dark blue with a badge on it that says Pickman Flats Police Department. Guess which mug Truman hands me?

Yeah, not the Monet.

Don't make a big deal of this... don't make a big deal of this...

"Nice choice of mug."

"Huh?"

I hold it up to display the faded gold badge, which catches the light of the dim forty-watt bulb over the stove.

"Oh," he says. "I didn't even think. Guess it's just a mug to me now." He offers his pale Monet. "Want this one instead?"

"No," I say, gritting my teeth and forcing a smile. *Can't believe he did that.* "It's fine."

After loading his tea with non-dairy creamer and sugar, we drink in silence like two strangers.

"Is something wrong?" I ask.

"Wrong?"

"Well, you're acting weird. Distant. Like I'm carrying some kind of disease that you're afraid to catch."

"I also have a little bit of a cold and a headache," he says. "Not really feeling, you know, affectionate. Don't want to get you, uh, sick either."

He glanced to his left slightly when he said this. He's lying.

That slight glance is his "tell." Truman would be a terrible poker player.

His phone *bings* with a text. My eyes dart over to it—it's a message from Julie. He quickly swipes his phone off the counter and stuffs it into the back pocket of his baggy jeans.

Why do I feel like I'm the center of a joke where I don't know the punchline but everyone else does? Yeah, I know. I'm a sociopath with multiple personality disorder—of course I'm always the center of attention. But this seems different.

"Who's the text from?"

"Oh, just, you know, a friend."

OK, I'm tired of beating around the bush. The bush is beaten to a pulp and my stick is hungry for fresh prey. If Truman is going to be this way—

"A friend? Meaning Julie?"

"Yeah," he says. "Good eye."

"And when exactly did you and Julie become texting buddies?"

Truman doesn't say anything for a few moments and then crosses his arms. He licks his lips. He's forming a narrative. Another "tell."

"When you were unreachable. Like always."

"What? I've been texting you. From the hospital."

"I meant before that."

"Do you have any idea of all the shit I've just been through? Sorry I wasn't able to immediately text you back when some meth head was going to blow my head off. And the dozens of times the police have been harassing me."

"Hey, calm down."

"Calm down? Seriously, my grandfather dies and you're wanting to break up with me? Bad timing much?"

"I've been wanting to for weeks," he says. "But I've never known how to put it into words."

"Weeks? Like how *many* weeks since we're baring our feelings here?"

He shrugs. "Couple of weeks maybe."

"First Julie bails on me—and now *you're* going to do the same?"

"Well," he says, "I think I had the idea originally. She just acted on it first."

"Wow, Truman Quirk, just wow. You *do* have a way with words."

"Hey, this isn't the way I wanted it to go."

Despite the boiling tea burning my lips and mouth, I suck the whole thing down in a gulp. The pain makes me feel alive. It makes me feel something.

"I'll show myself out," I say. "You have lots of homework to do. I'd also recommend taking a shower and texting back your friend. Take it from her former best friend—she gets pissed when you don't respond right away."

Truman moves toward me and puts his right hand on my shoulder. It's all I can do to not turn around and rabbit punch him in the throat. "Hey, Clare, wait."

"Get your hand off me before I break that one too."

He quickly removes it.

"Have a nice night."

"You know," he says. "I really thought... I really thought you wouldn't care. I mean, it's like when we've been together you *don't* care... It's like you're not there."

"Oh, the man's a poet and *knows* it."

"Whatever."

"Not There Clare," I say. "Yeah, I know. We all have our troubles. But I'm here now."

"I'm sorry," he says. "I care for you. But I just... I want... I need, you know, more."

All I can do is nod. "Well, I hope you find it."

Under the cover of night, I slip out of the house. The empty yard and the dark street are an appropriate welcome. A psychopath is even lonelier when nobody pretends to love them anymore.

Love, it seems to me, is like a gentle form of combat, and I'm tired of fighting.

Walking away, and had I known what would happen to my now ex-boyfriend in my absence, I would have stayed—and I would have fought for him.

And all-too-soon, the fight was brought to me.

102

Realizing I haven't eaten much all day, I make a stop at Williamson's Market. Time for a couple of Kind bars (dark chocolate cherry cashew), some organic, raw macadamia nuts, and a Cran-Raspberry LaCroix.

Where do I go now?

Grams and I are now staying out at the Motel 6 until we hear from the insurance company. I wanted us to both stay at the luxury Cayuse Hotel, like Lois J. Cain did. We both need the spa treatment, but Grams is kind of a penny-pincher. Yes, I realize that the guy who's trying to kill me, "Dan Simmons" or "W.R.B.," was staying there. But it's me he's after. Most of the time, I can feel his eyes on me. He's a stalker from hell. He "outstalks" me.

Driving the silver Camaro around Pickman Flats, which seems so much smaller than it was a few days ago, and sipping my icy LaCroix, I think about where to go.

Feels like I don't belong anywhere.

Nope, I don't want to go back to the motel yet. I told Grams I had to slip out to take Truman his assignments and that I would be right back. But that shitty little motel room, which ironically smells like stale cigarette smoke despite it being a "non-smoking" room, depresses me. It feels like the end of the line. With Lois gone, and now Gramps and the house, there are no leads as to who's been doing all of this except for a couple of fake names. I'm completely lost. There's no Julie or Truman, either. Hell, no Amity. Hell, even Bob Rextor, the dead mailman, seems to be on postal holiday.

Appropriately enough on XMU Radio, MGMT's "Time to Pretend" gives way to Marshmello's "Alone."

I think about heading into the Dancing Goats, but Plum Adams and Julie with their respective purple and green hair will likely be lip-locked on an overstuffed chair. They'd do it to spite me.

Everybody is out to spite me, it seems. Is this what happens to people like me? The four percent of the population who are sociopaths? The unloved, and the unwanted? Even though we try to fit in, wear the same clothes, repeat the same lines, and even show up for charities and human (and animal) rights causes. Do we somehow not fool anyone? Is our secret eventually discovered? Are we always going to be the consummate outsider?

Yes, I realize I'm throwing the world's smallest pity party with only me in attendance, but what would you do? Oh, I know what *you* would do. You're not like me, you're one of the ninety-six percent, no doubt. You're just a tourist following me along, waiting for me to keep you entertained. You'd go to all your "normal" friends and emote. Emote, emote, emote.

Well, fuck you! You and your emoting can go cry on somebody's fucking shoulder.

The Silver Stallion leads me back to 237 Straw Street, or what's left of it.

In the darkness, the frame of the house looks like the blackened bones of some kind of *Jurassic Park* dinosaur that died there and burned away, leaving only the dark ribs poking up. Yellow tape warning DO NOT CROSS is wrapped around what remains of the Newberry residence. Climbing out of the Camaro, I cross the lawn, slip under the flimsy barrier the police and firefighters left, and head toward the back with my snacks in tow.

The unfinished gazebo stands out like a sad little island in the backyard. A gazebo that will never be finished. The man's hands who created it are probably ash now, particles of dust. Maybe if we get enough insurance money, Grams and I can have the house rebuilt? Maybe I can finish this gazebo?

I doubt that will happen though.

Everything seems impossible and futile.

Truman once said he'd help Gramps finish the gazebo. All words lost on the wind.

Yes, yes, yes, I realized that I've dragged my solo pity party from the Camaro into the backyard of my old residence. Sue me.

As I eat my raw macadamia nuts, I bring up Spotify and play Arcade Fire's "Electric Blue." My calming song. I'd share my Spotify playlist of songs that calm me, aptly called Clare's Calming Songs, but why bother? This is the only song that matters right now, and it's on a loop. Sitting here at the table, trying not to think of Truman, Gramps, Grams, and past me sitting here a couple of weeks ago. Awkward, yes. But happy. At least as happy as a psycho like me can be. All gone.

Now it's only me. A lone survivor, so to speak.

Usually, my phone is blazing with texts from Amity, Truman, and Julie, even Grams. But it's quiet. Only Arcade Fire is keeping me company. My electronic companion.

P-A-T-H-E-T-I-C.

Then I get an Instagram notification. It's from Lois J. Cain!

WTF?

Quickly, I open the private, view-once message and it's a video. It wasn't shot by Lois, but by somebody who's obviously hijacked her phone. The video pans to the right and there's Lois J. Cain. Tied up. She looks dirty and tired. Dressed up like a Firefly den mother. She has a cardboard sign tied around her neck. And scrawled in black felt marker:

CALL THE POLICE AND SHE DIES.

Then the camera pans right again, away from Lois, to another sign hanging on a brick wall.

COME JOIN THE FUN SOON, HAPPY CAMPER!

103

Come join the fun where? He didn't say. Where is he keeping her? How long do I have? It could take all night to scour the town. Pickman Flats, with less than twenty-thousand people, isn't a large place, but large enough for one girl working alone. And say if I do find it, what then? Will he let my favorite author go? Is this in exchange for me? Or will he kill both of us? God, I hate dealing with crazy people.

A text bings. Maybe he's going to give me a time and a place.

WHERE ARE YOU AT, IT'S GETTING LATE? I'M WORRIED.

Grams. Good timing (sardonic font).

My head's starting to buzz. First, I was alone with nothing to do—and now I have to keep a person I care for alive. That bastard W.R.B. is punishing her because of me.

RUNNING SOME ERRANDS. WATCH SOME TV AND STOP WORRYING. SEE YOU SOON. (KISS ICON).

That will keep Grams occupied for a little while so I can think.

Entering the side door into Gramps's darkened shop, I half

expect him to be there, standing over his lathe making a table leg or hunched over his band saw cutting out some design for a bird-house. The only way he'd be here now is as a ghost.

A year ago, I killed a man, the last of three, who followed me in here, who would have hurt my family. It was my last reprieve. Now it's all that remains of the house. It seems I did a terrible job at protecting my home and those I love. Once, I locked Truman, Grams, and Gramps into a walk-in closet so I could fend off those murderous jerkoffs who were playing the home invasion game. Now Gramps is gone, and Truman is, well, gone too, in his way. Yeah, terrible job. The silvery light of the full moon makes my shadow long and willowy over the dusty concrete floor. The Other Clare of sorts. My FitBit stays steady, but my mind is awhirl.

In the bathroom, I relieve my bladder of the LaCroix. Washing my hands, I catch my reflection staring back at me in the bluish-silver light, shadows pulling at my face. Moonlight invading the bathroom window. Who am I really? Who can I ever hope to be?

"*Think*, you stupid bitch," I scream at the Other Clare in the glass. "Where would he take her? He'd need time. He had to keep Lois there."

"Not necessarily, stupid bitch," the Other Clare answers in the dark mirror. "He could have moved her to another location. He could have been moving her around town. Don't assume—it makes an ass of you and me." The glass girl squints. "And I'm not the ass."

"The last thing I need is to have you horn in on this too—I can handle it."

"You can handle it? You can fucking handle it? Oh, that's rich!"

My FitBit steadily climbs.

"Kiss my ass."

"You're pathetic. All you can do is try to keep me contained because you know *I'm* the strong one. I'm the one who handles shit when there's a crisis. You'd just stand around holding hands with that pathetic excuse for a boyfriend and working a lame job. In the world of fight or flight, I'm the former and you're the latter."

"Nice speech, Shakespeare."

"You're a weak-assed bitch. Pathetic and weak. You're the one that needs to be locked in the cage. Weak-assed, pathetic bitch. Go cry about your roasted grandpa. You turned him into ash anyway. He'd be alive without you in his life."

"Fuck you!"

My world flashes red. And my fist goes up before I can stop myself—and I shatter the bitch in the mirror with a left cross. Glass rains down in the sink and onto the floor, glinting and sparkling in the moonlight. My left fist drips with blood, which looks black in the darkness. The familiar, mineral smell of copper taints the air, a stench I know all too well. Broken fragments of myself stare back at me.

"You're going to have to get no-holes-barred bloody on this one," the bitch growls to me. "And that means not spilling your own blood. That means gutting that son of a bitch who's been ruining your life from stem to stern, throat to balls. Gut him like a fish."

"But I'm a vegan."

"Fuck that bullshit label. You're an animal, *we're* an animal. And animals kill when they're backed in a corner. Now let me the fuck out so I can do some good. Stop trapping me."

My FitBit is escalating close to the breaking point.

"Stop looking at that piece of shit. Take off that collar and let the wolf run free."

Instead, I reach for the bandages behind the broken mirror, and I wrap my fist in gauze. The blood leaks through and I look like a boxer who's been going at it too hard in the ring.

"Take off that collar."

The FitBit keeps climbing.

So I rip it off my wrist and toss it in the toilet.

"Smart move, dumb bitch," the broken Clares in the mirror say in unison.

The stockyard.

It's got to be the stockyard out on Route 5—the old slaughter-house is there. That makes sense. That bastard could hide out forever and nobody but doves and mice would know. He knows that I would never set foot there. In Lois J. Cain's book *Look Behind You and Die*, the finale plays out in an old textile plant. Yes, that's right. The killer does exactly the same thing. He lures the plucky heroine, Destiny Cameron, there. Then what happens?

She dies trying to save those she loves. It's the one book of Lois's with a total downer ending. The suck-ass movie gave it a fake-ass happy ending. But Lois, what she was saying, is that sometimes, most of the time, in fact, evil is strong and evil wins. People don't want to acknowledge that. They want happy endings so they can feel good about themselves, about life. They need romance books to feel better about love and Disney movie endings to feel better about the world.

But darkness prevails. Always has through the annals of human history.

Does that mean I'm gonna die like the ill-fated Destiny Cameron does to save those she loves from the Roseville Butcher?

"You could die right now," the girl in the slender length of glass says from the sink. "You could pick me up, slash open those wrists, and bleed out. You could make all this stop in a couple of minutes."

And then Lois J. Cain would certainly be dead.

She'll die anyway and you know it.

Nobody gets out of that slaughterhouse alive.

And you know it.

Once, I saved Meghan Greene at the G-Spot from dying.

If I'm going to die, it's going to be so that my favorite author, my friend, can live. So that Lois J. Cain can bestow another great novel into the world.

No, she will live.

Maybe I'll die—but so will that sonofabitch with my last breath! We'll both leave the slaughterhouse in body bags.

Yeah, I'm fine with that.

More than fine. I get to die the hero.

"Wise choice," the Other Clare says from the reflection. "Glad you didn't bitch-out."

104

The Other Clare turns away from the sink, crunching the glass under her pleather shoes, and heads out.

If it's time to get bloody, if it's that time to kill, weapons are needed.

Many weapons.

The Other Clare grabs a shop flashlight and turns it on. The old man probably had some kind of weapon around here. The workbench, where a few tools are scattered, won't work. Can't go to a gun fight with a ball-peen hammer. Surely you have a gun or a knife stashed, you old fool.

She searches through his toolbox. Nothing.

Maybe he stashed a pistol between all of his *AARP, Reminisce,* and *Reader's Digest* magazines in the bathroom stacked next to the toilet. She checks. Nothing.

Wait, what's this in the medicine cabinet, behind the broken mirror?

It's a ring. A familiar ring.

It's a class ring. One that belonged to Bob Rextor. That dumb Clare bitch had it stashed in her hope chest. But the Other Clare's the one who strangled him under Lowell Street bridge. The one who made sure he hit his head on that rock in the stream. And the one who took his ring. Almost took his wallet too, but TOC wanted it to look like an accident, not a robbery gone wrong.

So how did that old fool end up with the dead guy's ring? It's labeled *To Bob, from Doris.*

The old man had to know that his granddaughter had something to do with it.

That dumb Clare bitch didn't kill him because the Other Clare would know about it. She's the one who handles shit when goody-goody can't. She just goes to sleep like the dumb, lazy bitch she is. She keeps the Other Clare locked away like a junkyard dog until she's needed. Well, guess what? She's the one staying locked away in the cage. It's been too long. The strong one has emerged.

She slips the ring on. It looks kind of nice.

What's this also in the medicine chest?

Certainly not medicine.

It's a pint of Wild Turkey. Guess the old bastard had a funny idea about what kind of medicine he liked to take. Maybe that's what offed him.

Might as well take it for the road. No sense in wasting good whiskey.

No weapons here, but there's got to be a place to find some.

The bitch's phone bings. It's a message.

WHERE ARE YOU?

It's the old lady.

She's going to be a pain in the ass, isn't she?

I'M WORRIED. PLEASE COME BACK TO THE ROOM.

Room? What room? Hotel? Motel? Hospital?

What if she does something stupid, like call the cops? She needs to be silenced. She'll fuck this up for everyone.

WHERE ARE U? TOC texts back.

WHAT?

TOC texts the same question again.

AT THE MOTEL 6. YOU'VE FORGOTTEN?

She asks the old lady for the number. Got it.

A quick errand to silence her. And then the weapons. Then somebody dies.

105

It's a quick drive in the Camaro across town to the Motel 6. There's a bag in the back seat, it looks like a gym bag. Maybe there's something in there. The Other Clare has gotta make this quick.

She heads into the room. The TV is blabbing some cooking show and the old lady is on the bed, watching. She sits up.

"There you are!" the woman says. "Where have you been?"

The last thing TOC needs is a police interrogation. She hates answering questions.

TOC sets the gym bag on the other bed, the empty one. Unzips it. Nothing but some sweaty workout clothes. Well, they're better than this blouse and skirt combo.

She slips out of those and puts on the workout clothes.

"You're not thinking about going out again?" the old lady says.

"Yep, going to Iron Works to *work* off my aggressions."

"No, please don't leave, Clare, I need you to stay. I don't like being alone."

Shut up, bitch. Quit the whining. Whining will not be tolerated.

Part of the Other Clare wants to tell the old bitch off and part of her wants to simply walk out the door.

What would that dumb bitch Clare do? *Think!* She crosses to the bathroom.

"Clare?"

"What?"

"You're not acting like yourself, honey, are you OK?"

"Fine," TOC says, closing the door. "Gotta piss."

Inside the bathroom, the old woman has some prescription pills. Looks like some sedatives. *Hmmm.*

Exiting the bathroom with two plastic cups, TOC heads over to the mini-fridge. Ah, lucky break—there's some orange juice. She fills each cup and then hands one to the fidgety old lady.

"I'm not thirsty."

"Hydrate, old lad—Grams, you'll feel better."

TOC holds up her glass in a mock toast.

"I really don't feel playful, Clare."

"A toast. That the scary and creepy bastards of the world get what's coming to 'em. Death to the Mr. Screepys."

"That's a terrible thing to say!"

"Is it?"

The old lady squints at her orange juice. Then starts to sit it down.

"Nope, you have to drink it with me—chug it—or my toast won't come true."

"I don't feel like it!"

"*CHUG IT!*"

The old woman stares at TOC. Scared. Maybe it's the girl's eyes, which, if they were lasers, would be burning a hole in her pathetic-looking face right now.

"OK," the old lady says. And does.

Ten minutes sitting there watching some over-excited TV douchebag make breakfast burritos and the old lady is out. The three sedatives TOC crumbled up into the cup did the trick. She'll be out the rest of the night.

Heading out the door, the Other Clare catches her reflection in the mirror on the back of the door. She's wearing a smelly black t-shirt that says VEGANS MAKE BETTER LOVERS in lime green letters, some black leggings, and green gym shoes. Can't say that Clare bitch had much style. But considering it's this or the Catholic school girl monkey suit, she'll go with this stinky shit.

Time to go, there's a dirty bastard out there.

Time to go into the night and wreak havoc.

That's what nights were made for.

106

Checking the search results on Clare's phone, there's a Waldo's Surplus shop on the other side of town. It's on the way to the slaughterhouse. How convenient.

First, though, it's a trip to the cash machine at the local bank. Cash doesn't leave an electronic paper trail like a debit card does when you purchase something. And if there's going to be blood, you don't want that leading back to you in any way. It pays to be paranoid. The Other Clare doesn't know how much Clare keeps in her bank account.

At the bank's ATM, TOC checks the balance. Figures Clare's pin number is her birthday, TOC's birthday too—0521. Yep. Hmmm, not much in checking, only about $463, but she has about $9,666 in savings. Five hundred is the withdrawal limit. So five, zero, zero it is.

As TOC is pulling up to Waldo's Surplus, parking the Camaro around back, it appears the guy inside is about to close. He's wearing a red t-shirt with a fist on it. Stocky guy with his head shaved and a salt and pepper goatee.

"Hey sweets," he says as TOC walks in. "I'm closing up shop. Gotta come back tomorrow."

She pushes past his gut. "Only need a few things—it'll be quick."

First thing she needs, if she's going hunting, are some better clothes. She selects some black cargo pants, a gray t-shirt, and some boots in her size. She slips out of that bitch's stinky workout clothes. Ugh, Boring Clare needs some better underwear. What's up with the big, white granny panties? Hasn't she ever heard of black lace? She slides into the pants, shirt, and boots. That fat, bald fuck is watching in the shoplifter mirror. King Leer much, Shakespeare?

Now it's time for her favorite part—the hardware! Baldy keeps the knives and guns up front.

She ambles up to Baldy, sets the stinky gym clothes on the glass counter, and peers at all the knives in the case below.

"You gonna leave your, uh, clothes there, darlin'?"

"You keep 'em as a souvenir." Gives Baldy a wink.

There's a large selection of knives, pistols, and rifles.

The best bet would be to buy a rifle with a scope, go out to the slaughterhouse, message the guy to come outside, and use his head for target practice. It's doubtful that that's how the dirty bastard will play this game. This is going to be CQB—Close Quarters Battle. That fucker wants Clare up close and personal. Don't need to be a goddamn psychic to figure that out. Just psychotic.

"Gonna go with that Shinto blade there, some of those Chinese throwing stars, bottle of that pepper spray..." And scanning the selection of guns. "Maybe that Desert Eagle there with a few hundred rounds."

"How old are you, sweetie?"

"How old do I look, hot stuff?"

The guy grins, showing his yellow teeth. "Man, you've got a mouth on you."

She licks her lips. "Wouldn't you like to know."

Baldy shifts in his Hi-Tek boots uncomfortably. Apparently, he didn't expect a girl to call his bluff.

"I'm, uh, I'm uh going to need to see an ID for the knives and pepper spray and gun."

"A girl can only defend herself if she's a certain age?"

"It's Washington state law, darlin', and the law could have my ass."

"A big, tough guy like you is afraid of a little ol' thing like the law?"

Baldy gulps. "I'm going to have to close."

"Let me help," she says, strolling over to the door, bolting the latch, and snapping off the neon OPEN sign. She returns.

"Now, where were we?"

"Well," he says, "I could make an exception—if you paid cash, didn't tell anyone, and did one thing for me."

She drops the stack of five hundred cash onto the glass counter.

"Name your price, 'darlin'"

Baldy starts backing up toward the room behind him.

"You want me to go in there?"

"Uh, yeah, if you're the kind of girl I think you are."

"Oh, I'm so much more."

The back office is full of shelves of overstock—knives, handcuffs, tasers. All the fun stuff. It's also littered with papers, posters of semi-nude girls holding machine guns, and a red, white, and black flag with a swastika on it.

"That yours?"

"Huh?" He glances at the Nazi flag. "That's Waldo's, the owner. He's kind of into that whole White Power thing. He was even over at that big rally in Charleston." He chuckles. "Me, I'm not prejudiced, I hate everybody."

"Every*body*?"

"Uh, well, I'm willing to make an exception."

Then she sees the mother of all knives in a box. It's a tri-blade knife that's about a foot long. It's a wicked piece of machinery.

"And what the fuck would I use that for?"

"You stick that Texas toothpick in somebody, and it'll take a team of surgeons to get it out. Not that it would matter, the poor sucker would probably bleed out before that. Austrian Special Forces use it."

"How much is that monster?"

"Unless you've got thirteen hundred bucks lying around, it stays right there."

"Yeah, whatever. Why don't you sit back and relax?"

The guy sits back in the office chair and undoes his pants. "Man, I've seen porn like this happening," he says. "But I never thought it would actually happen to me."

"Which porn?"

"You know, hot young sluts coming onto dude in offices. Shit that's on Pornhub!"

"Yeah," she says, moving closer. "Keep dreaming."

She spins him around in the chair and places Baldy into a sleeper hold. Baldy outweighs her by well over one hundred pounds, but she's got the upper hand. He tries grabbing her, punching her, waving his thick arms furiously. He gets in a couple of shots to her face, but she pulls her arms tighter, cutting off his oxygen.

"Good night, sweet prince."

Baldy starts weakening, then his arms finally drop, and he relaxes in the chair. Dead weight. She tips the chair so he's flat on his back, feet in the air. He'll remain unconscious up to about twenty seconds—she needs to move quick!

There are a couple of pairs of handcuffs. She removes them from the boxes and cuffs Sleeping Baldy to his chair. Next, she goes to the computer and deletes the CCTV video footage. Wipes it all out for the week just in case.

And then she grabs that wicked tri-blade knife—good for all occasions. She also grabs the Shinto, throwing stars, and pepper spray. And she swipes those stinky gym rags off the counter. She's about to snag the Glock and the ammo when she sees a couple of guys in hunting clothes, one wearing an NRA hat, heading from their truck to the front door. In another three seconds, they'll peer in and see her. No witnesses.

Clutching her clothes and the knives, she slips again into the back office. Baldy struggles in the chair, his hands cuffed to each arm. He can't do much more than wriggle his fat body.

"Let me out of here—you fucking bitch!"

"You're lucky I'm in a rush, 'fucking bitch,'" she says, walking out the back door. "Today I let you live."

Jumping into the Camaro, she turns it over, and she's gone like a thief in the night.

The money on the counter will cover most of what she took.

As for the rest, consider it Asshole Tax.

107

Before she heads off into battle, she needs to eat. That Clare bitch doesn't keep much in the fuel tank. On the Sirius XM, Channel 33, First Wave, Ministry screams about "Burning Inside." TOC cranks it up and takes a hard right into the Burger Bliss drive-through. She orders a double burger (rare) and a large Coke. That Clare bitch wouldn't eat here. Fine, the Other Clare is her own person.

Getting the food, she pulls over into the lot and quickly wolfs down the burger. It's gone in a few quick bites; the meaty grease mingles with blood dribbling down her chin. Sucking down about half the Coke, she pours in some Wild Turkey from the old man's stash and swirls the white plastic cup around. A little bourbon and Coke take the edge off, right?

As she's pulling out and getting ready to hit the highway—
BOOM!

Somebody hits her hard in the ass. WTF?

She can't make out the car behind her. The headlights are too bright. Her hand goes for one of the knives, just in case. She's about to get out but the driver of the car beats her to it. He strolls up to her window.

She recognizes this douche. It's that Wade Braden asshole.

Last time she saw him, she was kicking his ass by threatening to zap his balls with a crackling Taser. She knows this shit wasn't an accident.

"Oops," he says. "Sorry about that, Clare. I guess we'll have to exchange information."

"Beat it, creep," she says. "Don't have time for this horseshit."

"Oh, you hear that, Jeremy," he says to the douche on the passenger side of the window. "She doesn't have time for us."

"You know, according to driver's ed, when somebody bangs you in the ass, it's the banger's fault. Cause they weren't watching where they were going. And it's such a fine ass after all. I got, you know, carried away. So, you know, we should go someplace and talk about it."

"Clean the shit out of your ears—I have places to be!"

On the passenger side window, there's a metallic rapping. Jeremy shows the handle of the pistol that's wedged down the front of his pants. She knows that's not the squirt gun version—that's the real deal.

"You totally destroyed my life, bitch," Wade says. "My girlfriend left me, my parents won't speak to me, and you think I'm gonna get into college with what happened at DeFeo on my permanent record? For all the shit you've been serving me, it's time to pay the check, bitch!"

"Eat shit!" The Other Clare tromps the gas pedal—and the Camaro screeches through the parking lot like a banshee, smoke peeling from the tires. She hits the main drag and takes the highway exit. By the time she does, she's already at ninety. That BMW cannot keep up. She knows that's him because it's only one headlight. He knocked the other one out hitting the ass-end of the Camaro. She stomps the gas and tops out the Camaro at one-twenty; it starts to shake.

The single light of the BMW has vanished in her rearview mirror. Now she's alone.

Ministry's "Burning Inside" is howling in her ears along with the night wind—it's glorious.

She's full of Wild Turkey and Coke

And she's on the way to a killing.
Does it get any better than this?

108

"You're gonna die in there."

That's what Mailman Bob, who somehow hitchhiked a ride in the passenger seat of the Camaro, says.

"And you've been worm food for years," the Other Clare says. "So what's your point?"

"Don't go in there."

"And why the hell not, Bob?"

"Because when you die—I die. Forever!"

"Would that really be so bad, Bob?"

"You know this is a trap, right?" he says. "I know you're a bugshit crazy teen with some personality issues and some homicidal problems, but you're not crazy enough to walk into a slaughterhouse to do as he wants, right?"

"Alternatives are limited," she says. "Besides, who's going in the front door?"

"He's been playing you this whole time—kidnapping that author, killing that kid and putting him in your trunk, blowing up your house—you know he's going to anticipate that move."

"Maybe."

"He knows you better than you know yourself."

"He met that Clare bitch one time, right?"

"Yeah, I guess. But he's been watching her the whole time."

"The way you used to watch Clare, you freak of nature?"

"No, my predations, uh, intentions, were more innocent."

"You're full of shit, Bob. And you really serve no purpose to this conversation."

"Please don't go in there."

"Thought you hated Clare. Thought you wanted her to die."

"Yes, but not today."

"Ain't got no time for wishy-washy bullshit, Bob," she says, pulling over to the side of the highway. She leans over the dead mailman and opens the door. "You're not real—just a mental ghost that haunts the mind. Now take a hike."

"If I'm not real," Bob says, "then why did you stop the car and open the door to let me out? I'm a part of you, that's why. And that makes me pretty damned real, don't you think?"

"It's a symbolic gesture, asshole!"

The passenger side now sits empty. Closing the door, the Other Clare drives on to her final destination alone.

109

The old stockyards and slaughterhouse await. The moonlight outlines the old brick structure like it's an ancient castle that has fallen into shambles. An electrical fire gutted most of it about thirteen years ago, and it has sat vacant and alone ever since. Geometric rows of weathered, wooden corrals stand out front where cattle were once fattened up and herded inside to the killing floor.

Taking a left off the highway, the Other Clare heads up the entrance road, the tires crunching gravel. She doesn't get too far as there's a heavy chain across the road attached to two rusty, steel poles flecked with faded yellow paint. Guess she walks from here. Leaving the car in this spot, anyone driving past can see it from the road. Maybe a state patrol officer will happen by and check it out. That would be a first—hoping that the police show up!

She stuffs her pockets with throwing stars and pepper spray.

She attaches the knives to her belt. Well, the big one, the other one goes into her boot. It's always good for a lady to keep a few secrets.

Then she walks toward the shadowy structure. The mud puddles in the road ripple in the breeze, reflecting the moon like winking eyes.

The plan is to swing around back as he will no doubt be waiting for Clare. The moon provides some light, but it will be hard to see—and using the flashlight on the phone will draw his eyes like a wriggling moth.

The phone buzzes in her pocket.

It's another Instagram message from "Lois."

TAKE TEN MORE STEPS FORWARD AND WAIT FOR INSTRUCTIONS. DEVIATE FROM THIS IN ANY WAY AND YOUR FAVORITE AUTHOR DIES.

Fine, Mr. Caps Lock. Guess Clare's playing your game after all. But she still has a few tricks up her sleeve, or rather, in her pockets and boots. Not that the Other Clare really gives that much of a shit about Clare's favorite author. No, she's really just ready to kill a motherfucker. The beast inside has been starved too long. Like one of those ghost animals in the rotting wooden corrals.

She silently counts the steps as she walks. There's a metal table, presumably from inside, with some items on it. Looks like clothes. And something else. Binoculars?

Another IG message: PUT ON THESE CLOTHES. AND THEN TURN ON THE NIGHT VISION GOGGLES AND PLACE THEM ON YOUR HEAD. DEVIATE FROM THIS IN ANY WAY AND I BUTCHER HER LIKE A HOG.

Great, another wardrobe change. And she was just getting comfortable in these new surplus threads. Pretty smart, she guesses, as he's probably watching her, and he undoubtedly knows she's stashed some weapons. Guess she'll have to make sure he doesn't—

Another message: PLACE ANY AND ALL WEAPONS CAREFULLY ON THE TABLE SO I CAN SEE THEM. DEVIATE FROM THIS IN ANY WAY AND YOU'LL ONLY FIND HER SEVERED HEAD.

She's inclined to message him back, but what's the point? It will only infuriate him.

She removes the boots and lets the Shinto fall to the ground. She stands on it. Hopefully, he didn't see that. That's her ace in the hole. The October chill bites at her naked arms and legs, making it crawl with gooseflesh. What are the clothes he wants her to wear instead?

It's a red, blue, and yellow Firefly Girls of America uniform. Just her size.

That Clare bitch, the goody-two-shoes she has caged up, used to wear a uniform like this selling Firefly cookies door to door. And when she went on nature hikes when she was eight.

And then that fateful day when it all changed.

110

Overindulgent but necessary movie flashback:

EXT. WOODS — DAY — FLASHBACK

THE MAN WEARING ORANGE SUNGLASSES swipes up the
beret. Inside, written in Sharpie, is Clare's
FULL NAME. The man, red beret in hand, escapes
across the meadow, away from the screaming
backpackers. He's too far away for the
witnesses for them to identify the killer
except for the color of his shirt. He gets
away.

111

So now the Other Clare's a Firefly Girl of America, and she probably looks like a total douche. After putting all of her weapons down—the throwing stars, the pepper spray, and the large tri-blade knife—she grabs the instrument he provided.

She picks up the night vision goggles, studies them, and flips on the switch. Light filters out of the eye holes. Placing the googles up to her eyes, the world has become grainy green and white. The slaughterhouse stands out as clear as if it were noon.

Why does Mr. Caps Lock want her to wear this stupid outfit and be able to see in the dark?

Won't seeing in the dark give her an advantage?

And why the idiotic uniform?

The only thing she can think of is he watched the September Jones *Top Talk* episode on TV a few weeks ago where she brought up Clare's past as a Firefly girl and the tragedy. Everyone involved in that event, even the killer, Garry Lee Harding, is dead. He was shot and killed resisting arrest when the cops closed in on him in Greeley, Colorado.

So what is this, some kind of sick fetish? Is that what this whole thing is about? No doubt he was watching her change. Fine.

It's the last thrill he'll have before she bleeds him like a stuck pig. She'll make sure he dies as slowly and as painfully as possible, and she'll enjoy it.

People have underestimated Clare before—and then they got the Other her, this current version. And getting TOC was a fatal mistake for a few. She can feel the Shinto back in her boot, her ace in the hole. He didn't message her about it so maybe he didn't see her quick sleight of hand, sliding it back in when she laced her boots back up. Thankfully Mr. Caps Lock didn't provide alternate footwear—a major oversight!

Another message: LOOK FOR THE SIGNS. FOLLOW THEM. DEVIATE FROM THIS IN ANY WAY AND YOU'LL BE READING ABOUT YOUR FAVORITE SCRIB-BLER IN THE OBITUARY COLUMN.

The night vision goggles have a headset, which she fits on over her skull. Now she can walk around, hands-free. She puts the beret on after that. She probably now looks like an overgrown Firefly Girl from Mars.

What signs though?

As she heads closer, a glowing light appears.

It's his frowny face with the X'd out eyes drawn on the wall.

Lifting the goggles and peeking with her naked eyes, there's nothing there, only a dark brick wall. But through the goggles, the face burns like a glow stick. Maybe he drew it with infrared paint. Infrared shows up invisible, normally, but with something like these night vision goggles, it would be visible. Just a theory but it holds water.

Beyond the radiating unhappy face, there's another faint glow from within, so she heads toward it. She keeps watching all corners and places from where he could possibly spring. As she's walking into an obvious trap, she won't make it easy for him.

There's a second frowny face. From here, she can see a third down a hallway. This is like some twisted Easter egg hunt. Slowly, she makes her way to the third face. This place smells rank. Like old blood. And rust. And pain.

And there she is, sitting in the middle of the floor tied to a chair with a gag in her mouth—

Lois J. Cain!

And, surprisingly, she doesn't look happy to see Clare.

112

The author is surrounded by about a dozen yellow chemlights that appear like candles. They're so bright in the night vision goggles that they're almost blinding. The Other Clare shoves the goggs up onto her head. Moving closer, Ms. Cain struggles in her bonds. This joker has tied her up with nylon rope in a series of knots. The work is intricate, like it was done by a demented sailor.

As she sidles closer, Lois recognizes Clare in the warm light and stops struggling. The Other Clare makes the motion to be quiet as she removes the gag, which is the author's trademark paisley scarf, from around her mouth. Her clothes are filthy. The woman looks, and smells, like this place. Like death and slow decay.

"What are you doing here?" the author says. "He's completely unhinged—he'll kill you!"

"*Shhhh.* You've got to keep it down."

"Get me out of here! Get me the hell out of here now!"

It'd take her weeks to try to untie the kidnapped author, so she removes the knife from her boot. "Hold still, I don't want to cut you."

"Hurry," she says.

TOC can't say she's ever read one of this author's books. She knows that dipshit Clare is a fan. They're supposedly scary, suspenseful books and all that. This woman's spent her life scaring people and keeping them on edge, and now it's like the tables have turned. Wonder what she feels like now?

As the Shinto knife blade slices through several strands of the nylon rope around the woman's wrists, the phone in her Firefly vest pocket buzzes.

A yellow Snapchat message notification from JulieGabriella-Ramos16 pops up onscreen.

What does that dumb bitch want? She's in the middle of a rescue, and Julie's sending a lame Snapchat?

Fishing out the phone, she swipes right on the notice, and then punches in the passcode.

OK, *not* exactly the message she was expecting.

On screen is a video. A rather troubling video.

Julie, like the Other Clare, is wearing a Firefly girl's outfit. Her hands are tied and draped over one of those hooks they hang animal carcasses from. Like Lois, she's also gagged. Julie's struggling and wide-eyed. She's terrified. It's obviously somewhere in the slaughterhouse. Snapchat has definitely gone sinister.

Julie wears a cardboard sign around her neck.

There's the trademark frowny face with the X'd out eyes.

The sign reads: SURE U DONT WANNA SAVE HER INSTEAD?

WTF?

Then the yellow Snapchat notification pops up onscreen again. This time from Truman_Quirk. Seriously?

Thumbing right on the notice, it's another similar video. Truman, bound and gagged, is lying on some kind of bloodstained table. Whoever is recording the video moves in closer. There's also a cardboard sign around Truman's neck with a message scrawled in black felt marker.

DON'T FORGET ABOUT SAVING LOVERBOY!!!

And then the knife comes into view. It's the Austrian commando knife from Waldo's surplus store.

The bastard is filming with one hand and making stabbing

motions at Truman, whose muffled screams emanate from his gag. His eyes widen in terror. He's also dressed in a Firefly Girls outfit.

And then a gruff voice on the video says, "You can *only* save *one*. Choose carefully, Clare Not There."

113

The Other Clare's brain feels like it's going to explode. Which one? Which one? Who does she save? Who does she let die? What a choice. *Clare's Choice.* Should be a freakin' tear-jerker movie.

Like clips from a video somewhere deep in the recesses of her brain, memories of the dipshit Clare bubble up like sour-stomach indigestion.

INT. DOJO — DAY

CLARE works out with a sparring partner who's tall, thickset, and much bigger than her. The shaved-bald MAN is also more skilled, anticipating every move the young girl throws at him with ridiculous ease. On his black shirt in white letters, it reveals: ASSISTANT INSTRUCTOR. Clare throws a punch that's blocked, and as her opponent parries, her feet are twisted up and she tumbles on her butt to the red mat with KRAV MAGA stenciled across it.

Growing angrier, Clare rises, screams, and attacks the big man. (The other Krav Maga members stop their one-on-one sparring and watch, shaken by the girl's primeval SCREAM.) She fires every punch and kick she's got in her arsenal at the guy. But he outweighs her by over one hundred and fifty pounds of muscle, and he's as lithe as a deer and strikes as fast as a cobra. The man's defenses are impregnable—like a well-fortified castle. She's sweating, red-faced, tears streaming down her cheeks. Pure emotion for an emotionless girl.

Then a gentle hand drops onto her shoulder. Clare turns and goes to strike but INSTRUCTOR GEM has anticipated this and easily parries it away.

Seeing her ginger-haired female instructor gives Clare pause.

iGem: Calm down, Clare. Take it easy. You're flying blind here.

CLARE: I-I-can see...just fine.

iGem: You're not physically blind. But your rage is blinding you. You've heard of the term 'blind rage', right?

CLARE (shrugs): Maybe.

iGem: Even if you somehow beat Greg here, he still wins.

CLARE: How's that?

iGem: Because Greg controls your emotions, and therefore, he controls you.

CLARE: I'm not emotional.

iGem: You're frustrated. That's emotion. And it's useless in any match. In the streets, when it's reality, it's a game of death.

CLARE: What am I supposed to do, then, Instructor Gem, huh? Try harder?

iGem: No. Try *softer*.

CLARE: Try softer? That makes zero sense.

iGem: You're trying too hard — so stop trying. You're thinking too much, so stop thinking. *Feel*, don't think. Thinking is too slow. Thinking messes up your rhythm. Thinking will get you killed. Go with your gut. *Feel*.

CLARE: What if... What if I feel nothing.

iGem: It's not always emotion. Your body knows what it wants. Your heart does too.

CLARE: My heart?

iGem: Get out of your body's way and let things happen. Take a step back mentally and feel. Try softer. Water is soft but it penetrates the hardest things, like rock, over time. Soften yourself. Stop thinking or caring so much. Be soft and fluid like water. *Try it*.

Exhausted from her efforts, Clare goes into the "fight" again. For the most part, she's rolling her eyes and throwing out a punch here, a kick there, but not really giving a shit if they land.

WHUMP! She lands a solid fist to Greg's, the Assistant Instructor's, midsection. Not enough to hurt him, but she did it.

iGem: You see. By not caring, by not thinking, you didn't show it on your face, you didn't telegraph your intentions to Greg here. He couldn't read you. He read your thinking and your rage like a schoolbook. But nobody can stop water. Even with an umbrella, it trickles over the side.

iGem gives her favorite student a pat on the shoulder and walks away. Clare contemplates this moment.

Back to the Other Clare.

TOC closes her eyes, takes a breath, and calms. Be water, fluid and crystal clear. She knows what she needs to do now. *Focus!*

She picks up her phone and calls Julie's number.

114

And the Other Clare is not surprised to hear a man's voice. "About time you called."

A familiar man's voice. Dan Simmons who talked to the wimpy Clare back at the G-Spot. The Dan Simmons who isn't Dan Simmons. The man whose initials are likely W.R.B. He's a deep memory that's etched in the back of her mind.

"Where are you?" TOC asks.

"Have you made your choice of who lives?"

"I've made my choice."

"Who lives then," he asks. "And who dies?"

"Where are you?"

"*Some*where in the building."

"Don't be coy with me shit stain, tell me where you are."

"You have three of your friends' lives hanging in the balance and you just called me 'shit stain'?"

"That's right...shit stain."

"Maybe I underestimated your sanity. Or overestimated your intelligence."

"Save the speeches for Winston Churchill, bitch."

"So, you want to come and stop me, right?" he says. "Stop me from killing your boyfriend? You're trading your best friend and

your favorite author for him?" he laughs. "They'll be so disappointed."

"You don't get it, do you."

"Get what?"

"Clare *wants* to kill him."

"Huh?"

"If Truman's going to die, he'll die Clare's way."

"Why?"

"Because he's an asshole, and he's no longer Clare's boyfriend
—they broke up!"

"Oh," he says. "Why are you referring to yourself in the third
person?"

"Clare and Truman are gonna terminate their relationship
permanently."

The caller doesn't say anything for a long moment. He's still
there, though, TOC can hear him breathing. Maybe this was a
wrong move to call his bluff. Maybe not. You can never out crazy
the crazy.

"Turn to your right and walk forward about twenty paces,
then head through the doorway on the left. I'm on the kill floor,
appropriately enough."

"See you soon."

"And if this is your idea of a bluff, I'll gut you first, let him
watch, and then make him eat your heart raw."

"Bluffs are for pussies."

She hangs up. And then she heads out.

The woman she leaves behind struggles with the partially cut
ropes, fighting to get free. She screams for help.

Her screams go ignored.

115

To the Other Clare's surprise, the mystery caller's directions were on point. He waits on the kill floor with Truman strapped to a table like in some bad torture-porn horror movie, which, ironically, Truman used to want Boring Clare to watch. Now it seems he's the star of his own *Hostel* movie. The leading man of his own cinematic version of *Saw*. He's tied down with some nylon rope.

Whoever said life imitates art had no idea how right they were.

"Nice outfit," he says. "The second to last time we truly met you were wearing it."

He pulls out a tiny red beret and throws it at her. Inside the hatband, in black Sharpie, is scrawled CLARE BLEECKER.

When TOC looks back up, he's wearing orange sunglasses and smiling. The Man with the Orange Sunglasses. The telltale *Memento Mori* tattoo snakes up his right forearm.

"So," she says. "What's your real name, 'Dan'?"

The man behind the orange-framed shades smiles. "Baker," he says. "Wayne Ray Baker." He removes them, revealing his own piercing blue eyes. "And I'm your father."

OK, he's trying to pull some Jedi mind shit here like Darth Vader did with Luke Skywalker in Empire. *Not gonna work.*

"You're *not* my father," the Other Clare says. "My father was much better looking, which explains me."

Truman struggles on the table, trying to speak through his gag. Apparently, he's not into idle chatter about family heritage while he's strapped to the killing table.

"Maybe not physically," Wayne Ray Baker says. "But I *made* you what you are."

"And what is Clare?"

"There's that third-person reference again," he says, gazing at her in a strange kind of paternal admiration. "You're crazy, you're really crazy... Crazy Clare Who's Not There... I *like* that."

"Who gives a shit what you like?"

"You know what else I like—you're exactly like me. You're a killer, too."

"All Clare's killings were done in self-defense," TOC says. "It's public record. Clare doesn't go around butchering innocent Firefly Girls."

"Are *all* your killings public record, Clare?" He smiles. "Clare the Killer. Heh, I'm of the old adage that it takes one to know one."

She says nothing. *What's to say to this freak?*

"And now, Clare the Killer. Live up to your namesake and trim this little pussy boy like a side of beef." He laughs. "Does it count as non-vegan if it's human?"

She reaches for the foot-long, tri-blade special forces knife in his hand.

"No," he says. "The tool has someone else to fix." He points to her boot. "Use that Japanese tickler you've been trying to hide from me for the last ten minutes."

"You saw that?"

"You can't bullshit a bullshitter, Clare the Killer." He moves in close. "And like I said, it takes one to know one, my only daughter."

She fishes down into her boot.

"Pull it out, real slow." He reaches behind him into the waistband of his pants and pulls out a Browning 9mm pistol. "Deviate from the plan and you'll spoil the surprise I've been working weeks on for you. Birthday surprise!"

"My birthday's in May. It's October."

"Daddy has missed a lot of birthdays since I've been away." He smiles. "Speaking of daddies, this ol' Browning is the only thing I have from my daddy. He was a mean son of a bitch." He laughs. "Momma assumed he got blinding drunk like he always did and crashed his car somewhere out near the Texarkana state line. But I'll let you in on a little secret. Daddy was *my* first kill. My first kill at twelve-years-old. Put him down like a dog—hollow-point bullet right between the eyes. And I buried him so deep, nobody ever found him. Kept the nine-millimeter though. About the only thing left of him that was worth a shit. Yeah, I've been gone too long from your life. A really shitty father. But I'm here for you now, Clare. Daddy's home."

She pulls out the Shinto knife. Might as well try to stall him. "And where is it you've been away to, 'daddy?'"

"Did a stretch in the Walla Walla pen for some grand larceny. Eight years. But they do have a TV in there. And I saw you, last year. I'm not a religious man. I didn't go to a fancy Catholic school like you do. It's hard to doubt that there wasn't a divine hand that brought us together again. What's the possibility of us living in Colorado nine years ago, our paths crossing, and then crossing again? Yeah, I have to say, being an agnostic sitting on the fence, I might just have to go with the God team. How's that not a friggin' miracle, I ask you?"

"The Lord definitely works in mysterious ways."

He gestures with the muzzle of the Browning to Truman. "Now stop stalling and end your relationship with Emo Boy." He laughs. "Can't say as a father I approve of your taste in boyfriends."

Well, what choice does Clare have? Guess she's made her bed. If she doesn't kill that dude on the table who's writhing like a frightened animal, Baker shoots and kills Clare. And in a choice between Clare or Truman, she'll pick herself every time. It's not about being a sociopath with dissociative identity disorder who has a lack of empathy. It's just smart business. How can you live if you die, right? Pretty sure you "normies" reading this would do that same thing. And what's that make you, huh? What's *YOUR* excuse?

She marches up to the bound Truman and pulls the gag off. "Any last words?"

"Cut me loose, baby. Cut me loose. Please...don't do this!"

"You heard the man, sweets—do that and he gives Clare some lead implants she doesn't need."

"Please, Clare, please!"

"You're going to have to nut up, Truman, and take this like a man. Take death like your stepfather did...lying down."

She raises the six-inch Shinto blade over her head—

"CLARE, NO!"

—and stabs Truman, sliding the blade all the way up to the hilt.

Blood soaks the table.

He screams.

116

"Close, Clare baby, but no cigar!"

That's what Wayne Ray Baker shouts over Truman's screams of pain. "Sticking somebody in the love handle isn't a kill shot. Hell, it may hurt a little, hurt a lot from the noise he's making, but he probably ain't gonna die from that." He cocks the hammer on the 9mm with his thumb. "Pull out that blade and stick that hog again—this time in the heart. Get 'im right where he lives."

The Other Clare grabs the handle of the Shinto and pulls the knife out of the bound Truman. His blood pools on the table under him. It also beads on the stainless steel. She peers at her reflection in the silver blade. The Boring Clare, the one she's trapped inside, seems to try to plead through her eyes. Pleads to let Truman live.

"Shut up, bitch," she tells the knife reflection. "I'm driving the Camaro now—you get the back seat!"

"Talking to a knife might seem a little crazy, Clare," Baker says. "Not that there's anything wrong with that." He laughs. "Now finish lover boy off before he breaks my heart with all his pissing and moaning. It's giving me a goddamn headache."

The Other Clare raises the Shinto over her head again. In the light of a dozen yellow chemlights, on a table, with two participants, one might assume they were holding an ancient ritual to sacrifice a virgin to a pagan god. And he will die a virgin, yes, Boring Clare saw to that.

"Whoa," a voice says. "What the fuck is all this shit?"

Wade and Jeremy stand in the doorway of the kill room. Jeremy has his gun drawn.

"Dude," Jeremy says. "This is so messed the hell up."

"How the fuck did you find me?" TOC asks.

"You parked your car at the gate," Wade says. "Then left a pile of clothes."

"Oh," Baker says. "Uninvited party guests."

He whips the Browning in Wade and Jeremy's direction and caps off four rounds. Two into each of them. Jeremy drops his pistol, blood spilling from the neat hole in his forehead, the other in his chest. Wade falls on top of him, two shots in the chest.

"I told you to come alone, Clare."

"Fuck Dodgers and Space Cadet are her unfaltering fan club," she says. "Well, they *were* anyway."

Baker smiles, returning the muzzle of the smoking Browning back on her. "Well, they won't 'unfalter' anymore. From the looks of them, they're not much of a fan club." He laughs. "Fuck Dodgers and Space Cadet? Where *did* you come up with that? You kill me, Clare, you really do."

As TOC turns to attend to Truman, a shot rings out. Baker shudders, a bullet having traveled into one shoulder and out the other side, making him drop the tri-blade. Another bullet strikes him in the ribs, knocking him back. Baker grits his teeth in pain and nearly drops the Browning.

Wade, on the ground, bleeding, dying, struggles to fire a third shot using Jeremy's pistol.

BLAM! BLAM! BLAM!

Baker, a bit shaky, but still steady on the trigger, silences Wade forever.

The Other Clare throws the Shinto into Baker—hitting him in the right bicep. He drops his pistol. She vaults over the table and swipes the tri-blade knife off the ground. Baker gropes for his

9mm. TOC raises the knife and harpoons it into Baker's back—shoving it into him as hard and as deep as she can.

He gasps, blood mixing with his saliva, and he spins and tumbles on her. He punches her in the face, stunning her a moment as he pulls the Shinto knife out of his bicep and sticks it into her chest, barely missing her heart. She rocks his face with a few punches; his 187-pound weight seems to weigh a ton.

"Clare," Truman says from the table above. "Claaaaaaaare!"

She feels cold as blood seeps out of her. Cold on the killing room floor. Her ears are ringing. And Baker is on top of her, his cold blood eyes inches from her, his hot breath burning her face.

All noises, all sounds, and the light, the warm light of the chemlights, seems to meld together, become one, a relaxing blur that you could almost reach out and touch. Except for this weight on her. Which seems to grow lighter now. Everything growing lighter and hazier.

"You're a bad, bad girl, Clare," are the last words she hears from Baker. They seem to float from his stiff lips and hang in the air.

And then blackness.

117

White light. Everywhere.

It grows so bright, it blinds me, and I squint my eyes to see. And then, there she is, an angel, she's robed in white, hovering above me.

She's so beautiful. *Everything* is beautiful.

I feel so relaxed. So free. Not a care in the world.

Am I not in the world anymore?

Is this heaven?

Do serial killers *go* to heaven?

The wings of the angel flutter in the blinding light. She has icy eyes and seems, well, preoccupied.

She has a name tag, this angel, that says DIANA.

Angels have nametags in heaven, that makes sense, as this whole place is confusing. How can anyone see anything with so much light?

My eyes finally start to adjust. There's a TV on the wall. What kind of shows are there in heaven? Hopefully not re-runs of Michael Landon in *Highway to Heaven* or something like that, though Grams *loves* that old show. She would approve. Where is Grams? Back on Earth? She will be sad. Did she go to my funeral? Maybe I'll see Gramps. That would be cool. Gramps and I could hang for, like, an eternity. Maybe build a few million birdhouses and spice racks. Is there a need for that in the afterlife?

Trees wave at me outside the window. Yellow and red-leafed trees that burn with a November fire all their own.

Then I feel a throbbing pain in my chest. It's faint, but it's there, deep inside me. A dull, constant thud, like somebody cut out my heart and replaced it with a ticking time bomb wrapped in rolls of wax paper.

The angel, Diana, is wingless, it seems. Just a trick of the light.

She has some acne scars on her pale cheeks. And the tight, fixed expression on her face suggests that she could use a coffee break.

Diana's no angel—she's an imposter!

My right hand snaps up so fast, I don't realize that I'm holding Diana at the elbow, my fingers digging into her skin, my nails bone-white in an eagle's grip.

Diana gasps in surprise and peers at me, wide-eyed. She tries to break my grip. What was she doing to me, leaning over me—trying to kill me? Poison? A scalpel? Smothering with a pillow? What?

"Let me go!"

"Who sent you?" I croak, my throat cracking like cheap nail polish. "Who the hell sent you? Was it him?"

Diana grabs my hand with her other hand and breaks free—I'm feeling weak so it's no contest. She hurries out of the room, screaming.

Now I know I'm not in heaven… There's no screaming there.

118

"You really gave that nurse a scare."

That's what the police officer standing over me says. He looks familiar. Avocado, something like that. Maybe Eldorado? His name tag reads ALVARADO. Yes, I know him. Or know *of* him in a past life.

"What am I doing here?" I ask him, still croaking like a desert frog. "What happened?"

A woman moves close to me. She has tan skin in a white linen suit. She looks familiar too. "I know you're still recovering, Clare, so this won't take long."

"We just have a few questions," the officer says.

"Guess I do, too. Like first, who the hell are you two?"

The Asian woman chuckles. "I guess you're probably high on some pretty heavy pain meds. I'm Detective Zang. This is Officer Alvarado." She hands me a tumbler of water with a straw. I suck half of it down, the cool water burning the back of my throat.

"Where's Grams?"

Zang smiles. "You'll likely see her soon." She studies me like she's looking at a rare animal in a cage. "What's the last thing you remember about the event that occurred three days ago?"

"Three days?" Wow, I've been here three days. "Event? What 'event?'"

"Your struggle with Wayne Ray Baker that led to his death," the detective says. Her tone suggests she has patience, but it can be worn thin. She gives a brief sigh to emphasize this fact. "As well as the deaths of Wade Braden and Jeremy Herrera."

"They're all...dead?"

"You don't remember that?" the officer chimes in. "It's another Pickman Flats massacre...just like last year."

Zang waves Alvarado back and tells him to shush.

What do I remember? What do I remember? Very freakin' little. At some point, it wasn't me who did that. The narcolepsy took over and the Other Clare must have done it all. But how can I tell them that I don't remember anything? How can I make them believe?

"I-I don't remember much. It's all a blur, really. Think I remember some messages from Lois J. Cain. Is she all right?"

"She's fine. She's recovering. Go on."

"Basically, the messages said to come alone and if I didn't, she would die. What choice did I have?"

"And after that?"

"Well, I remember just...looking into the mirror... And wondering what to do... And then, well, waking up here."

"That's it?"

"Sorry."

"You can't tell us anything else?"

No, I really can't. You see, when the Other Clare takes over, I'm no longer in the room, I'm asleep. Stuff happens. People die. Like last year.

Another long sip of water. Stalling, hydrating, repeat. "Maybe if you could, uh, remind me of what happened, I'll...recall."

"Well," Zang says, "it's possible that the extreme shock of the event may have traumatized you."

"Entirely possible."

"You may have total recall at a later time. The memories will flood back like the Walla Walla River in February."

"I've seen it happen," Alvarado chimes in. "The total recall part, I mean. The, uh, river too."

Yes, it happens. Total recall happens. Oftentimes in dreams. Little bits and pieces from my other self. But I was asleep for three days, a deep, dreamless, drug-induced sleep. A dead sleep. And with me being away, she returned to *her* slumber, the Other Clare, sprawled out back on the floor of her tiger cage.

"Yes," I say. "That's entirely possible too."

"Wayne Ray Baker summoned you to the old slaughterhouse off Highway 5," the detective explains. "He had kidnapped Lois J. Cain. And your friends, Truman Quirk and Julie Ramos." And then she told me the rest. About Jeremy and Wade being shot. About the knife that the Other Clare stuck into Baker. "Baker got the knife and some other equipment from Waldo's Surplus. Apparently, according to the clerk working that shift, a very large man overpowered him at closing time, handcuffing him to a chair, and took the knife. Baker apparently erased all the security footage, so we only have the clerk's statement on what happened. The strange thing is that the man who hit the place left five hundred in cash."

"That *is* strange."

"Baker stabbed you in the chest. He missed your heart by millimeters. You're lucky to still be above ground. Cain managed to get free after you cut some of her bonds and she used your phone to call the police. Had Ms. Cain not called, you may have died. You saved her life—and she saved yours."

"And Truman and Julie?"

"Julie is traumatized, but fine."

"And Truman?"

"He's here too. He was stabbed, apparently by Baker. He's now in stable condition."

"What was this guy's deal? Why me?"

"We did some checking on Baker. Apparently, he was recently released from the Walla Walla penitentiary on grand larceny charges. He was involved in a series of burglaries. What's most interesting is that he has roots where you're from, back in Colorado. On a hunch, we had his DNA tested against the girls he killed. Firefly Girls. It seems he was a match. His DNA matched similar murders. It seems he was a serial killer who's cut a swath of victims from Colorado all the way to the western states. Due to some initial circumstantial evidence, the murders were attributed to Garry Lee Harding, who's in the ground. But now the authorities are finding that the evidence was unsubstantiated. It was Baker, who was a former associate of Harding. Apparently, Baker set his friend up to take the fall by planting a knife and other items on him used in the killings, and then made an anonymous call to the local police."

"You killed a real scumbag, kid," Alvarado says. "And with the wicked knife he stole from Waldo's too. How's that for poetic justice?"

Good job, the beast that lurks inside me. Good job.

"Was he responsible for blowing up my grandparent's house?"

"Yes," the officer says. "He killed a Dan Simmons from California and stole his minivan. We found the incendiary bomb-making materials in his vehicle. Apparently, he used drugs to lure Katie-Ann Jenkins and Derek Wainwright to assist him. They were addicted to meth, so he used their chemical dependencies to extort favors. He paid them in drugs. Stolen drugs he took off an alleged local dealer who's vanished, and presumably dead by Baker's hand."

"Why all the games? Why didn't he just come out and kill me? Why did he try to systematically dismantle my life?"

"That's the sixty-four-million-dollar question, kid. Baker was crazy, plain and simple. He wanted to watch your world detonate under you, and so he stood back and lit the fuse."

"What did I ever do to him?"

"You existed. You were the one who got away. We found your old Firefly Girls beret at the scene."

"Does any of this ring a bell?"

"It...it doesn't really."

Zang rises. "We're going to let you rest now. After you're released from the hospital, come see me. We'll need a statement from you."

I nod.

119

The thunder makes the room's picture window shake. Another flash of lightning is blinding, followed by another window-shaking rumble of thunder. The night rain patters the glass like incessant, tapping fingers.

"Oh," Grams says, moving away from the window in the darkness and scooting her folding chair closer to my hospital bed. "It's a bad, bad storm."

Grams Arleen is kind of cute when a storm happens. She gets as wide-eyed as a four-year-old child.

My bed's raised into the sitting position to watch the lightshow outside. "It'll pass, Grams. They always do."

Eventually, hopefully, this shall pass too—me being in General Hospital, laying here day in and day out. Believe it or not, I can't wait to get back to the hallowed halls of DeFeo Catholic High. It's been nearly a week of no school.

"Remember when Ellis would always play Creedence Clearwater Revival, that song?"

"It's called 'Have You Ever Seen the Rain.'"

"Yes, that one."

Grams stares at the wall like she's watching a faded memory

being projected there. "He'd play it on that little battery-operated tape player in case the power went out. He always...thought of things like that."

"He knew how storms scare you and he tried to make it fun."

"They do not," Grams says. "It's just that some people can, you know, get hit by lightning."

"You're safe in here, pretty sure. Safe with me."

Grabbing the extra blanket on the bed, I lean over and throw it around her. The motion makes the knife wound in my upper chest throb.

Grams starts to throw it off. "I don't need that."

"Yes you do."

Grams doesn't fight me. Then she starts to cry, so I hold her hand.

"What's wrong?"

"This. *Everything*. Ellis being gone. The house gone. You in here. All that's happened....all the death... It's like that's all life is anymore is just death. Death, death, death. I don't know if my heart can take it."

"Hey, like the storm out there, it will all blow over. Sunny skies again soon."

"We still won't have a house. Or your grandpa."

No, we won't. There's no replacing him. He's the best man I've ever known—and probably will ever know. Ellis Newberry was one of a kind, a rare breed.

"We need to find a new place to live after this," I say, trying to change the subject from Gramps.

Grams grabs a tissue and wipes her eyes. "The insurance company did their investigation. And Ellis had a sizeable life insurance policy. We'll be OK, money-wise."

"Yeah."

"Do we buy or rebuild?"

This takes me a long moment to think about the possibilities. "Well, I can't imagine living anywhere else but good ol' 237 Straw Street. How about you?"

The lightning flashes and the thunder rumbles as if to remind us it's still out there in the night.

"They say you can't go home again," Grams finally says.

"But maybe," I say, "maybe we can try."

120

Two weeks later and I'm out of the hospital. On Friday after school, I find Julie cleaning out her school locker.

It's my first day back to school since the incident.

Detective Zang had said Julie was traumatized. She didn't come to see me in the hospital. I'd heard from other students that this was her first week back too.

There had been a memorial service for Wade Braden, Jeremy Herrera, and Amity Liston. I didn't attend. I'm pretty sure Julie wasn't there either, especially for Wade. He is gone now, but what he did to her last year will be with her forever. I might've saved her life, but there's one thing that I can't do for her—I cannot take that pain away.

Julie's stuffing everything into her backpack—a blue and white DeFeo scarf, some old candy wrappers, and a pair of ratty gym shoes. She peels photos off the door of her locker unceremoniously. She starts to pull off the one of her and me—a set of four sepia-toned pictures from one of those old photo booths. In the photos, we are laughing and mugging at the camera. It was from one summer at the fair, which seems like it was a hundred years ago now. She stops.

"Not taking that one with you?" I say.

Startled, she turns. She's wearing ragged jeans and a faded t-shirt with Lady Gaga on it. Her feet are stuffed into scuffed, green Converse All-stars. Her hair is *also* green, matching her kicks. She resembles an extra-terrestrial that climbed out of a spaceship and is collecting samples of Catholic high school life to take back with her to the stars.

"Of course," she says. "I don't want to horrify the next student who gets assigned to my locker!"

Yeah, I know what she meant. Our ridiculous expressions at the camera. We weren't exactly having good hair days that day—but we didn't care. We were happy being friends and having a good time, that was it. Maybe that scares some people when you let your hair down, literally, and cut loose. I must keep that side of me curbed.

"So you're a Carver High girl now?"

Julie nods. "I register Monday morning."

"Hey, if this is about us, you don't have to go to this extreme."

Julie laughs in my face. "Not everything is about you, Clare, even though you think it is. There are some of us who have our own lives, too."

"I didn't say that."

"Well, not in your usual way. But you always make everything about you." She smiles. "That's fine, it's who you are. Going to Carver is who I am now. I've evolved from this school."

"What did your mom say? It was her idea for you to attend DeFeo in the first place."

"We had a big argument about it. She hates my hair, by the way, and my girlfriend. But she's going to have to live with who I am."

"So you and Plum Adams are definitely a thing?"

"Does that piss you off like it does everyone else?"

I shake my head. "Only a little surprised."

"How long have you known me? When have I ever really been into boys? I've had a girl crush on Daphne in *Scooby-Doo* since I was about five."

Well, yeah, I can't blame her—Daphne *is* the hottest one on the ghost-chasing team compared to Fred and Shaggy. I've always related to Velma though. Not as a crush, I only like her pragmatism—there's something badass about being a down-to-earth diva.

"Well, you did like, uh, that dead dipshit for a hot minute!"

She wrinkles her nose, which makes her new silvery septum piercing glint in the dim light. "I felt nothing for Wade. It was my way of trying to fit in—and look where that got me."

Yeah, I get the trying to fit in thing. Story of my life. He sexually assaulted me too for doing the same thing. Bastard.

"He can't hurt you anymore. He can't hurt anyone."

Julie's eyes start to water and her face flushes red. "I can still remember it, every day, like he keeps doing it. I don't know if that will ever change." She rips down the last picture of us—and hands it to me. "Here."

"You don't want it?"

"I think, maybe, you should have it."

Taking it, I slip my backpack strap off my shoulder, unzip it, and slide the picture into my book, *The Killer Inside Me*, which I finished, by the way. Spoiler alert: the serial killer is burned to death in his house. It's like Wayne Ray Baker tried to do to me but failed. Cosplay Clare paid the price instead. Poor Amity. I glide the backpack strap back onto my shoulder.

My friend shuts her vacant locker.

"Are you sure about this, Julie?"

"Juliana."

"Huh?"

"It's Juliana now. I feel like 'Julie' was my slave name while I was going here. People fuck less with a Juliana than a Julie. When the Devil can't reach you, he sends you a girl whose name ends in 'a.' I'm that bitch!"

"Wow, I like that. Now I wish my name ended with the first letter of the alphabet. Did you come up with that saying yourself?"

She shakes her head. "Saw it on an Instagram meme."

We share a chuckle, and then she and I head down the dim

hallway toward the light of the entrance. Sister Aileen meets us, who, like a shadow, is not there one moment, and then...

The nun, coming from her office, clasps her hands together. It's obvious from her expression that she doesn't approve of Julie's new look. "We will miss you at DeFeo, Julie. You were among my favorite pupils."

"Thank you, sister," Julie says. "I had a great time while it lasted."

"You're planning to stay with us, Clare, aren't you? In light of what happened?"

I nod. "Yes, sister. In light of what's happened by losing Amity, Mercy, Hope, Wade, and Jeremy. I feel like DeFeo has a little of my heart."

"God works in mysterious ways that we will never quite fathom as a sinful species," the head nun says. "Have a good afternoon, you two. I'll see you Monday, Clare."

Waving goodbye to the head nun, we exit out the double doors into the autumn sunshine.

Plum Adams sits in her plum-colored VW Bug, which was obviously custom-painted to match her hair. She's watching Tony Baker videos on Instagram. Can't blame her, his hilarious animal videos make my day, too. She has her window down and there's a song playing on the radio, "Just Like Honey" by Jesus and the Mary Chain. With my friend departing and that song jamming, it reminds me of the end of that Sofia Coppola movie, *Lost in Translation.*

Her girlfriend gazes up and seems surprised to see me there.

She has always been a little quiet, so I break the ice. "Good song."

The plum-haired girl nods. "It's my total vibe. How are you, Clare?"

"Well, I'm healing, so that's something."

"Yeah," Plum says. "Thank you for getting my girl back from that miserable piece of shit."

I shrug. "It's what I do. And I wouldn't do it for many."

"Maybe when you're feeling better," Plum says, "you can

come over for a movie night. My parents have a huge home theater set up in our basement. They even have one of those old-timey popcorn makers. Bring Truman, too."

"Uh," I say. "I think he and I are, you know, terminal."

My green-haired friend shakes her head. "It doesn't have to be that way. Go see him. Talk to him. He's good for you. And you're good for him."

"But you were good for me, too," I say. "And now you're leaving."

She throws her backpack in the backseat of the Plum Mobile and gives me a hug. "Just because I'm going to Carver doesn't mean I won't see you. We don't live in *that* big of a town. Come by the Goats, I'll be starting there next week, too."

"You're leaving Furry O'Malley's?"

She nods. "That passive-aggressive, not-so-subtly racist place can suck my dick."

Plum smiles. "It was my idea. I'm good friends with the Goats' manager, that way we can spend more time together."

They hold hands.

What a perfect relationship—I can picture it now: Julie—excuse me, Juliana—doing her barista thing behind the bar; Plum holding court in her chair, drawing. Yeah, I'm jelly.

"See you, *chica*," Juliana says. "We've gotta go do hot girl shit. Juliana isn't just my name, it's my pronoun!" She climbs into the car. "Go see Truman, Saint Clare—seriously! He's a good guy!"

I wave them away as they drive off in a blur of plum.

Feeling alone. Too alone.

121

"You could have come to the front door."

Truman stares out his open window at me. I'd climbed up the drainpipe to the second floor of his house and tapped on his bedroom window. Yeah, maybe I could have knocked on the front door, possibly saw his mom, and woken up the entire household, but I prefer this method—the more direct approach. It hurt like hell with this stupid knife wound, let me tell you.

"You know me better than that," I say. "At least I'd like to think you do."

He nods. "Yeah."

"Are you going to show a night stalker in, or will she have to lurk out here in the cold?"

"It's almost midnight, I was just about to go to bed."

"It's Friday night—and you're not in bed yet."

He sighs and moves aside, which is a silent invitation for me to enter. There's a rule in old vampire movies that if you let one into your home, you are then powerless against the bloodsucker. Not that I'm a bloodsucker, unless it's a ripe and luscious organic blood orange—then look out! But, yeah, Truman allows a mass murderer inside his domain. He's always been powerless against me, but that's not why I'm here.

His room is warm and cozy, the way I remember it. He has only a bedside lamp on with an amber scarf over it which casts the room in a summery light, and the walls are painted the color of a Tuscan sun. Over his bed, there's a black and white poster of a man with slicked-back black hair with a cigarette pursed between his lips holding a cup. It asks, "Should I kill myself, or have a cup of coffee?" Below that is the author, and presumably the man in the photo, Albert Camus. Truman catches me staring at it.

"Pretty funny in an existential way, huh?"

"Yeah, it's morbid and flippant. Just my taste."

On the ceiling is another poster, Christian Slater from *Pump Up The Volume*, his favorite movie. The tagline reads: *Talk Hard. Steal The Air.*

Yeah, that's what we need to do. Have a hard talk. A hard-to-heart talk, um, I mean a heart-to-heart. I'll probably be the one to talk hard.

"How's your grandmother?" he asks.

"Sleeping like the dead."

"What?"

"She's on a heavy dose of sedatives back at the motel. Her anxiety has been off the scales since...everything."

Truman nods. "Yeah, I get that."

"How about your mom?"

"She's in Lunesta land—*Sharknado* couldn't wake her up either."

I touch the cast on his left arm. "And how are you?"

"Since you stabbed and tried to kill me?" He doesn't move his arm away from my touch, so I guess that's a good sign, right?

"If I'd tried to kill you, we wouldn't be having this conversation. You'd be pushing up daisies like everyone else and waiting to have a park or street named after you."

"Well, that went dark and escalated quickly," Truman says, removing his arm.

I shrug. "You asked."

A beautiful song plays on his turntable, presumably Radiohead. He notices me listening.

"It's Fake Plastic Trees."

"I like the chill vibe."

"Yeah?"

"Remember back at the G-spot? Seems like forever ago. I mentioned I wanted to listen to the 'warm and full sound' on your turntable. Well, here I am."

He bobs his head, and then leans over and takes off the record. "You know, Clare, I thought we broke up. Or that I broke up with you. And now, here you are. What do you want from me?"

"Hey, I made a mistake. With you and Julie, uh, Juliana. With everything. I'm trying to rectify that. Guess when some serial killer from your childhood tracks you down and tries to kill you and all your friends and family, it might make you think about things a little bit. I hate to admit it, but I'm shook. Shook to my fucking core. Now I don't have Gramps, Juliana has Plum, and you're a shadow. Fuck, I don't even have Amity up my ass anymore. I'm feeling a little..."

"Lonely?"

I nod because there's nothing else to say. I've laid it out.

"Now you know how *I* feel."

Yeah, this isn't happening. "You know what, I don't need you to throw all of this back into my face," I say, rising. "I made a mistake coming here. I'll climb out your motherfucking window and you won't see me again, OK? We'll just be a couple of asshole strangers to each other in the halls."

So, I start to make like a baby and head out.

Now it's his turn to put his hand on me. "No," he says. "Don't go."

I turn. "I feel like shit enough. Yeah, I'm sorry I stabbed you to save your life. But my life is shit right now."

He leans in and kisses me. "I want you, Clare. There's nobody like you. But if we do this, I need to know that you care, and you *want* me back."

"So, no more 'Not There Clare?'"

"Yeah, if you can."

The cast on his left wrist gleams in the light. It's a fresh cast.

I'm guessing he got a new one after the other one was probably stained with his blood.

"Nobody has signed your cast."

He glances down at it. "Nope."

"Give me a pen."

He reaches over to his desk and opens a drawer. He pulls out two Sharpies. "Red and black. Take your pick."

Grabbing both, I sign my name in black. Then, under that, with the red marker, I write: PREY ACCORDINGLY. I kiss the plaster. Leaving a perfect kiss mark of vegan-friendly lipstick next to my name.

"Huh. 'Prey Accordingly.' Don't you mean 'pray'?"

I shrug. "Maybe I did. Guess it's one of those Freudian slip faux pas things. I can fix it."

He chuckles. "Don't... It's kinda cool. I've missed your twisted mind, baby."

And I've missed yours, lover boy.

"Pull up your shirt."

"What?"

"Let me see your wound, tough guy."

He does as I tell him, pulling up his gray t-shirt with The Who logo on the front. His wound is still covered by a bandage. He pulls it away. It's stitched up, but the skin is all purple and yellow. It's ghastly and looks like he was put together by Dr. Frankenstein.

"The doc says it will heal up fine but there will be a pretty pronounced scar." He smiles. "Now show me yours, tough girl."

I nod, taking off my black windbreaker and t-shirt that says Vegan Power. All new clothes. This is the first time he's seen me in just a bra, because he only felt it in the car before. I wore my new black one, just in case. He examines my scar under the bandage, which looks similar to his. Yes, I will have a "pretty pronounced scar" too, as the doctor said. My trophy for Wayne Ray Baker's existence in my life. Not only did he kick me in the head when I was little, nearly killing me and causing a traumatic brain injury, but now I have to bear a tattoo of sorts. If that fucker wasn't dead, I'd kill him again. I will definitely take a shit on his grave when I find out where he's buried—a big steaming pile.

"Guess we match," Truman says. "Except you have the extra gunshot scar from last year as a bonus." He cracks a grin. "You'd better put your shirt back on, you'll catch your death of cold."

I also crack a grin. "Keep me warm then."

His expression drops. "Really?"

"Put on some appropriate love music, lover boy."

Truman leans over. He pulls out an album with a purple cover. It's Mazzy Star. He drops the needle onto "Fade Into You." *Nice touch, sir.*

I pull him over to his double bed. Guess Albert Camus and Christian Slater are going to get an eyeful tonight. *Sorry, Grams. After what's happened, I* do *feel older. And I* am *with somebody I truly care about. And there's nary a condom in sight.*

"We don't have to do this," Truman says. "If you're not, you know, ready."

"I think I'm ready as I've ever been." I motion to his cast. "Sure you'll be OK with that thing?"

He smiles. "I'll goddamn manage."

"I love you, Truman James Quirk."

He seems a little shocked that I finally said it, and then smiles. "I love you, too, Clare Marie Bleecker."

And we kiss.

Mazzy Star allows us to fade into each other.

122

"Thanks for coming back on the show, Clare," September Jones tells me on *Top Talk*.

Yep, I'm back, and I'm wearing a smart-looking navy blazer and a gray t-shirt that says *Vegan (noun) 1. A mass murderer of thousands of innocent fruits and vegetables.* Also wearing a new pair of fair-trade designer jeans, which I rarely wear in public, but I'm going for the laid-back look. A new me for a new show.

"Thanks for having me back, September."

"Let's get right into it," my host says. "The world has been wanting to know, Clare. And I'm glad you've agreed to talk only to me. I know you suffered a deeply emotional and traumatic experience."

"Yes," I say. "Reporters on networks nationwide, heck, world-wide, have been hounding me for weeks. And it's time to put all this to rest and move on. Think globally, shop locally, right?"

"Right," September Jones says and grins with her perfectly capped teeth that only serious money can buy. "It's been over three weeks since that event. There's been much written about it, lots of speculation too, but we'd love to hear about your experience in your own words."

"Well," I tell my smiling TV host and the small studio audience that includes Grams, Truman, Juliana, Plum, and even Tracy from Carver High. "Somebody from my past, Wayne Ray Baker, tried to murder me back in Colorado when I was a Firefly Girl. Years later, he tried again. And now I'm glad he's gone because he's responsible for nearly twenty-three deaths. That's how many they are now tallying. He is, uh, was, one of the worst serial killers on record, it seems."

"Indeed, he was," September Jones says. "Netflix recently announced that they're making a documentary about Wayne Ray Baker now that some new evidence has been uncovered."

"Seriously?"

"I read about it on the Deadline app this morning."

"Wonder who they're going to get to play me?"

"Maybe *you* should play you."

"No, I don't wish to be any part of it. Like I said, I want to put this behind me. Just want to finish high school with a decent GPA and do some other things."

"Other things like writing?"

"Yes, I do a little bit of that. It's a cheap form of therapy." This gets some laughs from the audience.

"Speaking of writing, have you heard from your favorite author, Lois J. Cain?"

"She called me a couple of weeks ago. I thanked her and she thanked me. We didn't talk long."

"It's understandable. When I spoke to Lois, she was seeing a therapist as she's been having some post-traumatic stress from the kidnapping."

"Can't say that I blame her."

"But why don't we let her tell us more in her own words," September says. "Lois, can you come on out here?"

Lois J. Cain, my favorite author ever, saunters onto the stage in her trademark ochre suit and paisley scarf. She has a box in one hand—a gift box. The *Top Talk* host gives her a hug, and then Lois and I lock eyes. Her brown eyes are watery, there seem to be more lines in her face than before, and she looks tired. But she still looks like the most wonderful human being on the planet.

I rise, and we give each other a big, long hug. Lois's hot tears trickle on my neck, and her body shudders under me. Wish I could be as emotional as her. Wish I could feel emotion, the way she does right now...to express it. So I act the emotion the best I can, the only way I know how to be "normal." People in the audience rise to their feet and clap. It goes on for what feels like several minutes.

Then my favorite author takes a seat beside me.

"It looks like you have a gift there, Lois," September says.

Lois gazes down at her hands. "Oh, yes, I got so wrapped up in the moment, I forgot." She hands it to me.

It's a flat box wrapped in the same color paper as her suit with a matching bow. It's about four inches wide and ten inches long. It's light. I can only stare at it.

"Open it, sweetie," Lois says.

"Yes," the TV host says with a polite chuckle. "Don't keep us all in suspense!"

I rip open the wrapping. Inside, it's a paisley scarf exactly like the one Lois wears.

"Figured I'd upgrade your wardrobe from all of those old rock T-shirts you wear. Nine Inch Negative or whatever."

"That's Type O Negative," I say with a laugh. "Bloody Kisses specifically." Lifting up the scarf to try it on, there's a white card with the address of a New York publisher as the letterhead. It's from Putter and Sons Books. Lois's publisher. The note reads:

Clare, Lois submitted your manuscript, SHE'S NOT THERE, to me. We love your voice and think it's the most exciting thing we've read from a young author in a long time. How'd you like to publish with us? It's signed Molly Jay Hamilton, who is Lois's editor.

I hold up the card. "Yes, Putter and Sons," I say. "I'd so love to publish with you!"

Lois leans over and gives me another hug, and September Jones smiles. She looks a little envious too, which makes me smile wider.

"Wow, Clare," September says. "Is this not the best day ever despite what happened?"

"It's pretty freakin' cool," I say. "Thank you, Lois. For everything!"

"Aw, you too, sweetie. Since I may retire from novel writing, I'll need someone to take up the literary reins. Try on your scarf."

I do. *Wait, what? Retire? No!* I tell her this.

"Yep," she says. "Gonna spend some time at home. Grow some flowers. Play with my grandkids. Maybe write a memoir, if I can think of anything to say, but I'm done with fiction. Life's proved stranger than fiction. I can't possibly come up with anything more."

Now I feel a brief shudder in my body. Who can replace Lois? Not me, that's for sure, even if I do have a matching scarf.

"There's only one Lois. J. Cain," I say. "And there will only ever *be* one."

"You're damn right, girlie," Lois says with a wink.

The audience laughs and claps. Some people wipe their eyes. It's bittersweet.

Then the *Top Talk* host barges in on the moment. "So, with a possible writing career in your future, your destroyed home in the planning stages for a possible rebuild from what your grandma Arleen has told me, and your family and friends all safe, Clare, do you anticipate any more violence or craziness in your life?"

This will take a moment to calculate. Another loaded question from my TV host. As much as sociopaths love the spotlight, they can hate it equally, especially when they feel singled out. Well, Miss Thing, you're not going to derail me like you did before with your *What's it like to kill?* question you asked me weeks before. Even though you didn't actually ask me that. It was more of my paranoia. *What's it like to kill? What's it like to kill? What's it like to kill?*

So I search out into the audience to find Grams. There she is, smiling at me. She's my center. Wish Gramps was here too. Now it's just her and me. Her eyes are red from crying. She gives me a smile and mouths, "You've got this."

And sitting next to Grams is Mailman Bob. He's waving and smiling at me too. So, I acknowledge him with the briefest of nods. Why does he always show up at the wrong time? Idiot Bob.

What's it like to kill? What's it like to kill? What's it like to kill? Quiet.

"Well," I respond to my host finally. "That's a pretty loaded question, September." This gets the laughs that I hoped it would. And I use this to take another thoughtful pause. "Hopefully...all the violence and craziness...is behind me for good. Over and done with forever." And then I smile to the camera for emphasis—just another healthy, red-blooded American girl in a small town, right? "But we'll see."

ADDENDUM

Since I like you, here are a few more recipes from my book *Killer Smoothies and Other Vegan Recipes to Die For*. Blend responsibly and accordingly!

Blood Lust Smoothie

You'll satiate your blood lust in a kinder and gentler motherfucking way in under five minutes.

> 1/2 cup peeled and chopped raw beet (organic if possible)
> 1/2 ripe banana (fresh or frozen) (organic if possible)
> 1 cup frozen raspberries (organic if possible)
> 2/3 cup of flax or nut milk (organic if possible)
> Pinch of Himalayan or sea salt (optional)

Blend all ingredients until smooth and creamy. Serve.

Sleepy-Time Slayer cookies

> 1/2 cup almond flour 1/3 cup brown rice flour
> 1/4 teaspoon baking soda

1/2 teaspoon ground cinnamon
1/4 teaspoon salt
1/3 cup coconut sugar
3/4 cup old-fashioned rolled oats
1/4 cup unsweetened apple sauce
1/2 cup vegan chocolate-covered espresso beans
1/4 cup olive oil
2 tablespoons water
1/2 tablespoon molasses

Preheat the oven to 375 degrees and line a cookie sheet with parchment paper.

Mix all the dry ingredients in a medium-sized bowl.

Stir in the wet ingredients.

Drop cookies by rounded tablespoons on parchment paper-lined cookie sheet.

Baking time will vary between 8 to 10 minutes.

Death By Chocolate

Show no mercy to your chocolate cravings—indulge healthily. Low carb and high energy, bitches!

1/2 cup full-fat coconut milk
1 cup almond or nut milk
2 tbsp cocoa powder
1 tablespoon coconut oil or MCT oil
Pinch of Himalayan or sea salt
5-10 drops of liquid stevia (optional)
½ teaspoon cinnamon (optional)
Scoop of chocolate vegan protein powder (optional)

Drop all ingredients into a blender and puree until smooth and creamy. Pour into a glass and drink that motherfucker—before somebody else does!

ACKNOWLEDGMENTS

Clare at Seventeen began on August 5, 2017 after initial some movie interest occurred on my *Clare at Sixteen* manuscript. (After I finally had the courage to share it four years later after originally writing it.) *Clare at Seventeen* was written speculatively, and it's unusual to do so when you don't have a publishing agreement in place, but it was an unusual story I had to tell—as it was an important chapter in Clare Marie Bleecker's saga. To help bring this to you, I'd like to thank my team at The Parliament House—owner and operator, Malorie Nilson, editors Hayley Frerichs and Jennia D'Lima, and Jennifer Siddoway in marketing. Also thanks to my early Clare support team—David Chackler, Mark Pavia, Nadia Redler, Marilyn Vance, Bonnie Aarons, attorney Gregory Rose, my family—especially Wilder-Taylor Roff and Molly Ulmen—and to my readers—love you all!

Clare continues to exist because you want to hear her stories, including the new film, *Saint Clare*, out in 2023 starring Bella Thorne, Ryan Phillippe, Rebecca De Mornay, Frank Whaley, Brad Johnson, Joy Rovaris, Dylan Flashner, and Jan Luis Castellanos. Thank you. Slay responsibly and ~~pray~~ prey accordingly. J

ABOUT THE AUTHOR

Photo credit: Molly M. Ulmen

Award-winning author Don Roff has written nearly 20 books, primarily of a scary nature, for children and adults. His bestselling books include *Werewolf Tales, Terrifying Tales, Ghost Hauntings: America's Most Haunted Places* published by Scholastic, as well as *Zombies: A Record of the Year of* Infection published by Chronicle Books/Simon & Schuster UK, and *Snowblind* from Brambleberry Books (currently in pre-production for an adapted film). His book, *Usher House Rising,* a modern series retelling of Edgar Allan Poe's short tale, *The Fall of the House of Usher,* will be available February 14, 2023 from Brambleberry Books. He has won several awards for his screenwriting, including the 2006 PNWA Zola Award for Screenwriting, and has a few original screenplays in film pre-production. He writes a blog for *Save The Cat!* that examines the story structure of popular films, mostly horror. For GoKidGo, he writes a weekly spooky podcast, *R.L. Stine's Story Club: Ivy's Chilling Tales*, which has millions of listeners monthly and is available wherever you get your podcasts. Roff served as a combatant in the 3rd Ranger Battalion in Fort Benning, Georgia. He currently lives in the Pacific Northwest. Visit him on his website, donvroff.com.

CPSIA information can be obtained
at www.ICGtesting.com
Printed in the USA
BVHW032314231022
649781BV00002B/3

9 781956 136029